Queen Hustlaz

Queen Hustlaz

Falicia Love

www.urbanbooks.net

Urban Books, LLC
300 Farmingdale Road, NY-Route 109
Farmingdale, NY 11735

ISBN 13: 978-1-62286-650-2
ISBN 10: 1-62286-650-9

First Mass Market Printing April 2018
First Trade Paperback Printing November 2017
Printed in the United States of America

10 9 8 7 6 5 4 3 2 1

Distributed by Kensington Publishing Corp.
Submit Orders to:
Customer Service
400 Hahn Road
Westminster, MD 21157-4627
Phone: 1-800-733-3000
Fax: 1-800-659-2436

Queen Hustlaz

by

Falicia Love

Chapter One

It was Saturday evening, and the sun was shining brightly. It was early June, and it was already extremely hot. Jeryca and her friends were sitting outside on the stoop in front of Jeryca's apartment, which was their daily hangout spot, unless they were busy with their boos or, in Dana's case, at work. Mostly, they watched the traffic fly by and talked trash to each other.

Jeryca had her radio outside with her, and they were smoking a blunt when "Danger," a song by Mystikal, came blasting from the speakers.

"Oh, shit! Girl, turn that up a li'l bit more!" Farrah shouted as she stood up and started popping her fingers and shaking her ass.

"I know that's right!" Stephanie joined in.

Jeryca turned it up, and she got up and started twirling her hips and shaking her ass to the beat. As she dropped her ass down low, a car that was cruising through slowed down and blew the horn.

"Can I get some of that?" a nigga in the car yelled.

"Hell no! You couldn't afford this ass!" Jeryca yelled as she turned around to give him a full view of her ass and swatted it. He shook his head in awe and drove on down the road.

"I hate a thirsty-ass nigga," Farrah said in disgust.

"Well, don't you think the way y'all are out here dancing you will be approached by thirsty-ass men?" Dana asked, sitting on the stoop and watching her friends display their asses to the whole block. They all had on booty shorts that showed their butt cheeks—all except her.

"Oh, Lord! Listen to Saint Mary! Girl, loosen up and have some fun sometime," Stephanie said.

"Fun don't pay my bills," Dana replied.

"Yeah, but a nigga that you find by having fun will if you put it on him right!" Jeryca said.

"I can pay my own bills, thank you!" Dana said as she rolled her eyes.

"Girl, we are just playing! Damn!" Farrah said as she hugged Dana.

Dana smiled, and the girls enjoyed the remainder of their evening. After the girls left, Jeryca went straight to bed and waited for her man, Thad, to call her.

The following morning, Jeryca woke up feeling a bit disappointed. Thad hadn't called her, and she was horny as hell. She got up, showered, and fixed a bowl of cereal while she peeped out the kitchen window. The night before had been hectic with people arguing, screaming, police sirens, and the constant gunfire that sounded throughout the projects. She didn't mind the fighting that occurred there, 'cause she was a fighter herself. She just couldn't stand it when it happened so late at night. Plus, Thad hadn't called her at all, and they had planned to get a room to relax and spend a few hours together.

As she looked out the door, J-Rock walked by and winked at her.

"Eww." She sighed. She couldn't stand it when the wannabe thugs walked by her door with their pants sagging, looking hungry, and begging for ass or money. She didn't have time for broke niggas that caught the city bus just as much as she did.

Just as she turned from the sink to sit down at the table, her cell phone rang.

"Come outside, girl!" one of her close friends said once she answered.

"Okay, I'm on my way out," Jeryca mumbled with a mouth full of cereal.

As she walked out the door toward the stoop where they always sat watching everything moving, her neighbor Greg yelled out the door.

"Hey, sexy!"

Jeryca rolled her eyes and waved him off. As she approached Dana, she looked up the walkway to see who was out. "What's up? Girl, let me tell you, I ain't had no fucking sleep 'cause these fools want to act like they in the Wild Wild West, shooting up everything, police chasing them all night, and to top it off, I ain't heard from Thad all day. I usually get a good morning call or something. I guess he out chasing that mean green. I swear, I thought Thad would've had me out of these fucking projects by now. We've been dating six months now, and he hasn't once mentioned us moving in together. What more can a bitch do? I tell you what: if he don't hurry up and do something, his ass is history!" Jeryca complained to her best friend, Dana, as they sat on the stoop outside her apartment building.

Jeryca lived on the east side of the Bronx with her mother and 14-year-old sister, Pam. They lived off government funds in subsidized housing. Jeryca was embarrassed by the way they lived, and she dreamed of becoming rich and moving far away from the Bronx.

At nineteen, she didn't have any ambition or drive to work for wealth, but her hopes were that she would find a rich man and he would take care of her. Her mother worked small jobs that barely paid enough to cover one bill in their apartment, much less take care of her and her sister. She didn't have a lot of respect for her mother, 'cause she felt that she could've done more to better their lives. She refused to be stuck in that lifestyle. She had decided two years earlier that with her looks and banging body, she would use what she had to get her a rich man and leave the East Bronx for good.

Jeryca was about five foot nine in height, weighed about 180 pounds, and had light hazel catlike eyes and shoulder-length hair. She was a beautiful young woman. When she started dating Thad, she thought she had struck gold, but he wasn't willing to sacrifice a dime to help her situation, which proved to be a big problem in Jeryca's opinion. Thad was well known in the streets for gaining his wealth and reputation by hustling hard. He could sell the devil firewater if he wanted to, but he chose guns and drugs as his retail. Thad was known to bust anybody's ass that got in the way of making his money, which was why Jeryca had to have him.

"Shit, Jeryca, Thad is a good catch, girl. You need to just fall back and relax. Let things happen like they are. A chick like me wouldn't date a man like Thad, though. I mean, he is rich, sexy, and he demands respect everywhere he goes, but he isn't my type. But he seems to be exactly what you are looking for. Hell, fuck around and someone else will have him as their boo thang. Don't lose that man," Dana said, laughing.

"Whatever, bitch! Being with me and getting this good-good, he ain't gon' want nobody after me," Jeryca said, laughing as she touched her ass and danced in a circle.

"Y'all sluts ain't talking 'bout shit!" Stephanie said as she and Farrah walked up.

"Where the hell y'all coming from?" Jeryca asked.

"We went to the mall to get Travis a pair of shoes," Farrah answered.

"Where is my li'l man at anyway?" Dana asked.

"Girl, he gone with his crazy-ass daddy. He picked him up this morning and gave me a hundred forty dollars to buy him a pair of Nikes," Farrah said.

"Damn! A hundred and forty? That five-year-old boy's shoes cost more than two outfits of mine put together," Dana said in a shocked voice.

Stephanie started laughing as she spoke. "She didn't spend no more than sixty bucks on his shoes, and she spent the rest on a pair of Baby Phat jeans for herself! And if you would get to know Keith, you would be able to buy whatever you want, Dana! You know that man wants you."

Dana shook her head. "If I can't afford it, I don't need it. I refuse to use a man simply for their money. I can make and get my own money."

"Suit yourself, 'cause my man gon' pay to lay, ya feel me?" Each girl, except for Dana, did a high five in the air.

"Oh, before I get sidetracked, have you heard from Thad today, Jeryca?" Farrah asked.

"Not yet, which is weird. Why you ask me that?" Jeryca asked.

"Well, when Larry picked Travis up this morning, he told me that Thad had gotten into an altercation last night with this nigga named Zack, and Thad shot his ass. I don't think Zack died, but Thad is locked up for assault with a deadly weapon inflicting serious injury. Larry didn't say what his bond was, but his brother Toby and cousin Chris are getting an attorney and the bond money together as we speak. They may have gotten him by now, but you might want to call and see," Farrah said.

"Why the fuck didn't you say that from the start? Damn!" Jeryca shouted at Farrah as she jumped up and ran to get her cell phone. "How the fuck can I get my hair and nails done if he in the county?" Jeryca continued to rant.

After Jeryca walked into the house, the girls looked at Farrah, shocked that Jeryca had spoken to her in such a manner.

"Aye, I'ma chalk it up to that THOT being upset, otherwise I would beat her ass when she returned," Farrah said.

"THOT?" Stephanie and Dana asked curiously.

"Yeah, a THOT!" Farrah repeated.

"Farrah, what the hell is a freaking THOT?" Dana asked with laughter in her voice.

Farrah started laughing. "Girl, I heard Larry and Steve saying that shit a few days ago. I asked them what it meant, and they said it mean 'That Ho Over There.' I laughed when they said it, but honestly, it's just another term for whore."

"Okay, so I got a new word," Dana said as she put the word *THOT* in several sentences. "Aye, if you had to classify me as a THOT, what kind of THOT would I be?" Dana asked.

"A stupid THOT! 'cause you got a man with cash flow who wants you, and you won't give him the time of day," Farrah answered as she high-fived Stephanie.

"Yeah, it's all about that money, girl!" Stephanie agreed.

"So, I guess y'all would be ambitious THOTs. 'cause it's all about money, huh?" Dana asked.

"I think the only person who is a THOT with ambition is Jeryca, 'cause her cash cow hasn't paid off yet. Mine has, so I no longer have ambition to hook me a man with cash. I came, I saw, and I conquered!" Farrah said. Again, they all laughed.

Jeryca walked toward them with her cell phone to her ear, and as she approached, she rolled her eyes at Farrah. Farrah looked over at Dana and Stephanie, biting her lip as the crease in her forehead was letting them know she was going to snap if Jeryca didn't chill out.

The four girls had been friends since third grade after their schools combined because of educational funding cuts. They gained respect from their classmates by using scare tactics. They bullied other kids constantly. The other kids had seen the Four Musketeers battle before, and each girl could fight extremely well. To hang around them, to most of the kids, was a blessing, but the four friends never allowed any newbies to join their clique. It was the Four Musketeers only.

They met Thad and his crew about a year and a half prior to graduating from high school. Farrah and Larry hooked up immediately. She became pregnant within months of dating him.

Farrah was a very beautiful woman. She was tall with tan skin and had long, black hair. She was mixed in race, Chinese and black. She had gained a few pounds after giving birth to Travis, yet she was even more dazzling to Larry. He really cared deeply for her.

Stephanie was dating Chris, who was also Thad's cousin. Stephanie was a white girl with shoulder-length hair, and she was also thick. Her ass was heart-shaped, and her smile was perfect.

Keith, Thad's friend, had his sights on Dana, who had a chocolate skin tone. She had long, thick hair, and a body to die for. Unfortunately, she also had no interest in Keith.

Jeryca and Thad had hooked up six months earlier. She played hard to get, 'cause she figured that was the only way to land her a money man. Instead, all she had gotten out of the relationship thus far was a few jewelry pieces, clothes, and a few bucks here and there, which was driving her crazy.

"Okay, so how long do you think it will take y'all to get him out?" Jeryca was saying into the phone. "What! Are you serious?" Jeryca was now yelling into the phone.

Stephanie, Dana, and Farrah looked at one another worriedly, which suddenly changed to curious awe at Jeryca's next comment.

"So you mean to tell me I might not get my money 'cause you don't know how long it's going to take to get Thad out? That's fucked up!" she yelled and hung the phone up.

"Man, I hate that bitch, yo! She didn't ask one time if Thad was okay, or if she should come down. Nothing! All she concerned about is getting her nails and shit done! I don't see what Thad see in her trifling ass!" Thad's brother, Toby, said as he hung up the phone after talking to Jeryca.

"Aye, I got Bruce Jackson on the phone. He says to have Thad make an appointment to come to his office once he is bailed out. In the meantime, he is going to see what he can do to get him a decent bond today so we can go ahead and get him. He knows Judge Kelly, and the judge owes him a few favors. He says he will contact us in thirty minutes or less," Chris announced to Toby.

"Okay, that's what's up. Larry and Keith should be here by then with a few more dollars. When this nigga is released, I'ma let him have it. We got too much going on right now, and he letting his temper get away from him like that. Man, I told that nigga to walk away, but no, he couldn't do it, and now look where he at. We are getting money, easily bringing in seventy-five hundred each day in weed alone, not counting the hundreds of thousands we are getting from the gun play, and he snap like that over a measly hundred dollars? Now look at the money we spending to get his ass out of jail, not counting the attorney fees!" Toby said angrily.

"Yeah, man, but if Thad had let that go, other people would feel that it's cool to fuck us on our money, which would eventually cause us to lose the respect of our peers. What else could Thad do, man?" Chris asked.

"He could've beaten the man senseless and tagged him with a mark to remind him and anybody else that you don't play with our money," Toby replied.

"Well, he did tag Zack technically," Chris said.

Both guys began to laugh and got out of the gray 2014 Navigator they were in. As they walked up to the jail, Keith and Larry pulled up. Toby and Chris waited on the steps of the jail for the other two guys to meet them. As they did, they all gave a quick pound of their fist and a hug.

"My nigga, Thad is okay, ain't he?" Keith asked.

"Yeah, he straight. I talked to him earlier and he good. You know that ho Jeryca called, and all she seemed to be concerned about was money to get her nails and hair done," Toby said.

"Damn, that bitch can be heartless," Keith said.

"Fuck her! Let's go see what's going on in this motherfucker," Larry said as he proceeded up the steps and inside the jail.

Freddy Vanhook, a bondsman that they had used previously, was already waiting on them inside.

"What's up, fellas?" he asked as they all walked in.

"What's going on, Freddy? I'm glad that you could meet us here today. I know you usually don't come out on Sundays," Toby said as he shook Freddy's hand.

"I usually don't, but your family is the exception," he said.

"That's what's up, man. We appreciate the fucking with. Man, we been waiting here all morning, and last we checked they still haven't set a bond for him, but Bruce Jackson is trying to pull a couple strings for us, so hopefully this won't be a wasted trip for either of us," Toby replied.

"Yeah, I just went up there and they were on the phone talking with someone about your brother, so I assume Mr. Jackson has worked his mojo," Freddy said.

"That would be great news for us. Let me go up here and see what I can find out," Toby said as he walked away toward the window to speak to the deputy in charge. After about three minutes, Toby motioned for Freddy to join him. The bond was set at $250,000, and they had to put 15 percent down. It wouldn't have been a problem for the guys to post the entire bond, but they knew that would place a lot of unwanted eyes on them.

After all the paperwork was signed, they sat in the lobby and waited for Thad to come out. Toby took a little time to think about what Chris said, and he wasn't going to give Thad the third degree, but they still had to talk. They had to come up with a different way to handle problems like the one they were now facing. He also wanted to discuss what his plans were pertaining to Jeryca. That girl was bad for Thad, and he was going to tell him just that.

"That's our book, nigga!" one of the inmates yelled out as he stood up and slammed his card on the table.

"Motherfucker, y'all cheating! That jack of spades been played. We taking that pot," another guy yelled. After a few seconds, a fight broke out, and Thad stood watching them, shaking his head.

"These niggas fighting over a three-dollar pot? They crazy, man," he said, laughing.

Thad sat on his bunk, hoping that his brother would come through for him. He had to get out of jail before he snapped.

Thad was in full thought of going straight to Jeryca's house, picking her up, and getting a room. He was in need of some pussy, and at that moment, Jeryca was who he wanted. He liked her, but he knew she wanted more than he could offer her. He wasn't ready for a relationship. He doubted that she would be the woman he would settle down with anyway. She was money hungry and always in need of something. He was well aware of what her and her friends were about. They all were cash hunters, and he wasn't going to let anybody use him. Sure, he provided Jeryca with nice things and gave her a few dollars here and there, but he figured he'd cash out for good pussy. *That's what you do with hoes!* he thought to himself.

"Thad Royster, you're out of here. Get your belongings together, let's go," the guard yelled.

"Hell yeah! I'm out, my niggas. Y'all be easy and hold it down," Thad said as he headed out of cellblock C. After he was processed, he headed toward the lobby.

"What's up, bro? Man, I'm glad to see y'all motherfuckers!" Thad said as he embraced his crew.

"You know we weren't going to leave you up in this bitch," Toby said.

"Man, you good? You all intact?" Chris asked.

"Hell yeah, and what you mean am I intact?" Thad asked.

"You know, you didn't drop the soap, did you?" Chris asked, laughing.

"Man, fuck you, nigga," Thad said, laughing and playfully punching Chris.

"Aye, we need to talk, li'l bro. All jokes aside. We got to figure out a different way to deal with problems. We can't keep wasting money with these crackers," Toby said.

"Okay, man, we can have that talk, but can a brother get laid first? I mean, we can talk tomorrow," Thad said.

"I guess, man. You need to call Bruce Jackson tomorrow too. Don't get sidetracked," Toby said.

"I won't, man. Drop me off at the house so I can get my truck. Damn, let me call Jeryca and see if she can be ready in an hour. I need to fuck something for real," Thad said.

"Man, that chick ain't shit, bro. Why do you fuck with her?" Toby asked, shaking his head. Chris, Larry, and Keith agreed with Toby as they followed them to the truck.

"I know what Jeryca's about, and trust me, I'm not trying to wife that ho," Thad explained.

"That's a THOT for sho," Larry said, laughing.

"Yeah, well, when I fuck that THOT, I wear a condom. Can't make no bitch that thirsty a baby momma 'cause you're stuck with them for life, unlike you, my brother," Thad said to Larry, laughing.

"Yeah, you know all Farrah see is dollar signs, Larry. She cornered her a check for eighteen years," Chris said.

"Whatever," Larry said, rolling his eyes, trying not to laugh. Larry knew he had fucked up, not only by having a kid with Farrah, but also because he was beginning to catch feelings for her. He would never reveal that to Toby and the rest of the guys 'cause they would straight clown him.

"Toby, why did you say that shit though?" Thad asked.

"What shit?" Toby asked.

"Man, don't play. That shit you said 'bout Jeryca," Thad said.

"Man, that ho called me this morning and asked if you were getting out today 'cause she needed to get her hair and nails done," Toby answered.

Thad started laughing. "Oh, word? Well, she got to suck the hell out of my dick! She better swallow and all, my nigga. That's why I say I know what I'm dealing with. Now let me call this trick and see where she at. We gon' catch up with y'all later," Thad said to Keith and Larry as he pulled out his cell phone and dialed Jeryca's number.

Chapter Two

Jeryca was playing Monopoly with her little sister, Pam. She loved her sister and hoped that she would follow in her footsteps. She didn't want her sister to settle for anything less than a rich man. Although they had different fathers, the bond they had was priceless.

"Pam, you see how I just capitalized on Ventnor Avenue? I just turned four small houses into a hotel! That's what you got to do with your life, sis. Always capitalize on every aspect that you can, and use all your assets to gain wealth. You are beautiful, and that ass can get you all that you need," Jeryca said as she placed her red hotel on the board.

"I don't want a man to pay for my love. I want to be a pediatrician when I grow up. You never wanted to go to college, J?" Pam asked, calling her sister by her nickname.

"Yeah, I did, but I didn't have the smarts to follow through with it," Jeryca answered.

"What did you want to be?" Pam asked.

"I always wanted to be a school teacher, but they don't make much loot, so I'm good doing what I do. I spend somebody else's cash on the things I want and need," Jeryca told Pam.

"Well, I just can't see myself using a man like that. Do you care about Thad?" Pam asked.

"I care about him, yes, but I don't love him. In time I'm sure my feelings will grow. Thad—" Jeryca started saying before her phone began to vibrate. She smiled at Pam as she showed her that Thad was calling. "Pure cash," she said as she walked to her room.

"Hey, baby, I see they got you out. I've been so worried about you. I called everywhere trying to make sure my boo was okay. Did Toby tell you I called?" she asked Thad.

"No, he didn't," Thad lied.

"I wonder why not. I was livid when Farrah told me. I went off on her, Dana, and Stephanie earlier, and they got pissed and left. Farrah looked like she wanted to try me, but I know she knows better." Jeryca was talking a mile a minute until Thad told her to shut up.

"Look, do you want to go out for a while and go get a room?" Thad asked.

"You know I do, baby. When will you get here?" she asked him.

"I will be there in about an hour. Is that enough time?" he asked.

"More than enough. I will see you then," she said before she hung up.

Thad pulled up at 2:30, and when he saw how Jeryca looked, he was reminded of why he fucked with her. She always wore an outfit that was sexy, yet refined; and with her beauty and fat ass, he was very attracted to her, but he just couldn't stand her. His plan was to fuck her until he was satisfied and give her over to his boys who ran his prostitution ring. Jeryca would bring in thousands of dollars, and he was going to make it happen in due time.

"Hey, baby," Jeryca said as she got in Thad's truck. As she leaned in to kiss him, he pulled away. She frowned at his movement and asked, "Why did you just do that, bae?"

"I got a question for you: how bad do you want your hair and nails done?"

She frowned with confusion. "Why do you ask that?"

"I was told that you called my brother, and your only concern was if I was going to make it home to give you some money," Thad said.

"Baby, no! That's not how it was at all. I was sick with worry," Jeryca explained as she reached out to rub his arm.

"I got to tell you, Jeryca, he was very believable. Are you saying he lied to me?" Thad asked, looking at her through squinted eyes. Jeryca knew that if she called Toby a liar, it would cause issues, so she decided to own up to what she said to Toby.

"Ok, yes, I inquired as to whether or not I would see you today, and if I was going to get my nails and hair done. But, baby, honestly I was concerned also."

"I'll tell you what: since you showed such a lack of concern for me, I'ma need you to suck my dick right now. Then we are going to the room and you're going to earn the money you want," Thad told her.

"But, baby—" Jeryca started, but was cut off immediately.

"You could do less talking if you fill your mouth up with this dick."

Jeryca felt like a real ho. She had never been handled like that before. As she bent down to undo Thad's pants, she asked herself repeatedly what had made her approach Toby the way that she did.

Thad knew that he made Jeryca feel some kind of way with his request, but he had to put her in her place so she would never get out of pocket again. She was his ho, nothing more, nothing less.

As they rode down the road and Jeryca proceeded in giving Thad a mean head job, a car that seemingly appeared from nowhere blew its horn, alerting Thad that he was about to collide head on into them. As he quickly slammed on the brakes, Jeryca slid forward, falling toward the floor and hitting her head against the steering wheel. As she sat up, stunned and holding her head, the woman who they almost hit shook her head in pure disgust when she realized what had really almost caused their wreck. She pulled off quickly, giving them the finger, and blew her horn one last time. Thad started laughing and pushed Jeryca away.

"You can finish me off when we get to the room. Just so you know, you got a lot of work cut out for you tonight. Once you've satisfied me, then you can get your hair and nails done. I will take you first thing in the morning," Thad told her.

As they pulled into the parking lot of Motel 6, Jeryca couldn't help but notice that throughout their relationship, Thad had never once taken her to his house. It never bothered her until today. She felt lower than dirt at that point, but she needed to do what she had to in order to get back in Thad's good graces. After they got their room and got settled in, Thad's cell phone rang.

"This is Thad. Talk to me," he said as he answered.

"Yes, this is Bruce Jackson. I just got your message and I have one available appointment tomorrow. Can you be at my office in the morning at nine?" he asked.

Thad looked at Jeryca and turned his back to her. "Yes, sir, I can be there. I want to thank you for your attention to my case, Mr. Jackson."

"You are welcome. I will see you tomorrow, Mr. Royster," Bruce said before hanging up.

"Now that we are safely in this room, come over here and get my dick hard," Thad said as he stood in front of Jeryca. She sat on the bed and started stroking his dick slowly without looking at him. Thad wanted to add insult to injury.

"Naw, get on your knees and put it in your mouth, Jeryca," he said as he guided her to the floor.

Jeryca wanted to cry. She had never seen Thad act like that. She put his soft dick in her mouth, and as she sucked and stroked it slowly, she could feel it growing and hardening quickly. The more his shaft grew, the less she could take in her mouth. Thad noticed that she only had half of his dick in her mouth.

"Naw, motherfucker, put it all in there," he said as he grabbed her head and moved the entire length of his manhood into her mouth. Jeryca started gagging and trying to pull back, but Thad laughed and moved his dick quicker and deeper down her throat until he came. He released all his seed in her mouth. She hated how she felt and wondered if it was all worth it.

Thad collapsed on the bed and pulled Jeryca with him. As he lay there, he began to drift off to sleep, but not before he decided that after a few more times with Jeryca, she was going to be his number one hooker. After he visited his attorney the next day, he was going to take Jeryca to his trap house where all his hoes chilled while they waited for their johns to pick them up. They weren't the type of women who stood on the corner tricking. The guys who ran the trap also set up the ladies' jobs. As the thought of all the money he was going to make off her crossed his mind, he smiled and hugged Jeryca as he went to sleep. After fucking her three times that night, he was completely satisfied and informed her that she had earned the money to get her hair and nails done.

"Farrah, where are the Nikes I told you to get Travis?" Larry asked.

"I got him some Nikes, Larry. Don't start questioning me about nothing," Farrah said angrily.

"Look, I will ask what I want. I give you enough money every week so you can get the things you need and want, so when I give you money specifically for Travis, I expect you to get what the fuck I tell your ass to get! Keep this up and you gon' find yourself in the same position as your friend Jeryca!" Larry said in a low, but serious tone.

"Who the fuck—wait a minute, what do you mean 'like Jeryca?'" Farrah asked with a half-frown and confused look on her face.

"Thad is about to teach Jeryca a lesson she won't soon forget. After he learned about her reaction to him being locked up, he came up with a plan to check her ass. And you 'bout to be in the same boat as she is. Keep trying me, Farrah!" Larry said.

"Wow, I kind of figured she was going to play herself one day, acting like she is the queen of Brooklyn," Farrah said.

"Ha! You are one to talk. I promise, you keep it up and I'm going to take my son, and you will be paying me child support," Larry said as he walked away.

"You got to be crazy. Don't ever threaten to take my son again!" she yelled.

"Farrah, that wasn't a threat. That was a promise," Larry said before getting in his car and pulling off.

Farrah stood at the door of her apartment with her mouth gaped wide open. She knew that Larry was serious. She shut the door and went to lie next to Travis. She cuddled with her son all night.

Thad got up and showered. He left Jeryca asleep while he got dressed. At about 7:30, he woke her up and told her to get dressed and to make it quick. He told her he had a few stops to make before he took her to get her hair and nails done.

Jeryca did exactly as she was told. Her body was sore from the abuse Thad had inflicted on her the night before. He put her body in every position he could think of sexually and didn't seem to care that he was hurting her. She moved slowly, and Thad noticed how she was walking, and for a brief moment, he felt sorry for her and what he had done to her, but the feeling vanished quickly.

"Hell, she better get used to the feeling," he muttered to himself. As the bathroom door closed, Thad called Chris. He needed to set his plan in motion now.

After Jeryca finished her shower and dressed, they left the Motel 6 and headed down the Brooklyn-Queens Expressway I-278. Thad had to meet Mr. Jackson first and foremost before he did anything else. He put his Tupac CD in and bobbed his head to the beat of *Better Dayz*. Jeryca watched Thad closely. She wondered what had really changed him. She was almost certain it wasn't just about her reaction to him being in jail. She could only pray that it got better soon. As they veered off the expressway onto Ninety-second Street, Thad turned the music down and looked at Jeryca.

"Listen, I got to go and meet my attorney right quick, and I'm not sure how long it will take. You can go in with me, but I ain't having no shit out of you. Do you understand?"

"Yes, I do. Thad, I'm not a child, you know. I do know how to conduct myself!" she said as she rolled her eyes.

Thad laughed out loud and shook his head at her. He didn't say a word, but his silence and the look he gave her told her to chill out. She turned her head and looked out the window. They finally turned into a parking lot that was surrounded by several corporate buildings.

"Jackson and Associates law firm, here we go right here," Thad whispered to himself.

As they pulled into an empty space, Thad looked at her once again. "Remember what I said."

Jeryca just stared at him for a few seconds and got out of the truck. As they walked into the building, Jeryca looked around and couldn't help but notice how elegant the office was. Everything was laid out in plush Italian leather. The wall trimmings were outlined in gold, and there were beautiful statues that stood in the middle of the room; but what really raised her eyebrow was the handsome Italian man that came out to greet them.

"Mr. Royster, how are you doing?" he asked as he extended his hand.

"I'm ok, assuming I can get out of the mess I find myself in today," Thad answered. Jeryca couldn't help but wonder if he was talking about her or his charges.

"This is my friend, Jeryca," Thad continued as he pointed to her.

"Hi, how are you?" Jeryca said as she shook his hand.

"I'm great. Come into my office so we can see what we are dealing with," Bruce said.

As they walked into the office, he looked at his secretary. "Hold all my calls."

"Yes, sir," she replied.

"Have a seat," he said as they entered the office.

Thad looked at Jeryca and asked her if she could wait in the lobby until they were done. She got up quietly and walked out. While she sat out there, she wondered what was going on with Thad. She couldn't help but feel like she was losing him. *Is it another woman?*

After forty minutes, Thad and Bruce emerged from the office talking and laughing. Jeryca figured that everything had gone okay. As they approached her, Jeryca overheard Thad telling Bruce that his secretary was very beautiful and he complimented his office. "Everything is lovely and elegant in here," Thad said as he smiled at the lady. Jeryca rolled her eyes and walked out of the building.

"We got two more stops to make, and then you can get your hair and nails done," Thad said without looking at her. Jeryca was now infuriated. Not only had Thad disrespected her, but he had also belittled her in several ways.

"That's ok, Thad. I'm good. I will get them done another time. Go take care of what you need to, and I will get someone to pick me up from here. I don't need this shit!" she said as she got out of the truck and walked into the office across from his attorney's office. Thad sat in the truck for a few minutes, and then got out and followed her into the building. When he walked in, Jeryca was on the phone; Thad walked to where she stood.

"Get the fuck off the phone and let's go now!" he said through clenched teeth.

"I told you to go on and do what you got to do, Thad," Jeryca said.

"Get the hell off the phone and let's go. I don't give a damn about your attitude. Don't make me say it again, Jeryca." She realized that Thad was getting angrier by the second, so she did as she was told. When she got into the truck, Thad looked at her.

"Didn't I tell you to fucking behave? You just wasted ten minutes throwing a tantrum. Jeryca, don't keep testing me," he said quietly. Jeryca didn't say a word; she looked out the window as they drove off.

Chris and Keith were at the trap house waiting for Thad to get there. The house was in a low-key suburban neighborhood on the west side of Brooklyn. It was a nice huge brick house, and the prostitutes that worked there were very classy women. They neither dressed nor behaved like regular street women. Thad had the perfect hookers.

"Brenda, we got an easy three hundred dollars for you. Thad needs you to do him a huge favor. Do you want the money?" Chris asked their number one ho.

"Maybe. What's the job?" Brenda asked.

"Well, come in my office and let's chat," Chris said as he motioned her to the back office.

Chris and Brenda had been in the office over ten minutes when Thad and Jeryca walked in. They all exchanged hellos, and Thad ushered Jeryca toward the back as well. Jeryca was amazed at how beautiful Thad's house was. She looked around and noted everything she would've done differently. Just as Thad and Jeryca reached the office door, Brenda and Chris emerged.

"Hey, Thad!" Brenda said, giving him a kiss on the cheek.

"What's up, baby?" Thad asked as he hugged her tightly.

Jeryca shook with anger. She couldn't believe the nerve of Thad taking her somewhere where he had another bitch waiting. Jeryca turned to leave, but Thad held her firm.

"Jeryca, I'd like you to meet my sister Brenda," he lied. Jeryca almost stopped breathing. *His sister*, she thought. *Yeah, they do look alike.* Jeryca smiled as she shook Brenda's hand.

"Nice to meet you."

"Same here, girl," Brenda said with a smile.

They immediately started talking, and went to the kitchen and sat at the table. They seemed to connect instantly, and Chris was amazed at how well Brenda played at being Thad's sister. Thad walked up behind Chris and gave him a nudge to get his attention. When Chris turned around, Thad gave him a smile and a thumbs-up.

"We got a winner, baby!" he whispered.

"You might be right. This plan you devised might be on the money," Chris said, patting Thad on the back as they both turned and walked back down the hall.

Brenda wasn't a stupid ho, either; as a matter of fact, she was quite educated. She finished college with a high GPA, but with all the economy issues that had developed, she found that her current employment was satisfying. She made good money, received benefits, and was respected by all the boss pimps. She wasn't sure what Thad's plans were for Jeryca, but it wasn't any of her business. She was just going to play her part.

"So, how long you been seeing my big brother?" Brenda asked Jeryca.

"About seven months, I'd guess. I'm so happy he brought me to meet you," Jeryca confided.

"Yeah, you must be special if he brought you here," Brenda said as she patted Jeryca's arm.

Jeryca smiled. Just when she was beginning to think Thad was an absolute monster, he proved her wrong.

Chapter Three

Monday afternoon, Stephanie and Chris rode around for hours. He decided to take her on a run that he had to make for Thad. He trusted her enough to have her tag along with him while he handled business. She had counted drug money, gun money, and made a run for him and Thad once before, so he knew it was cool.

"Aye, baby, can we stop for lunch after you take the guns back to the warehouse?" Stephanie asked.

"Yeah, but it's not going to the warehouse, and put your dang seatbelt on, girl. How many times do I have to tell you that when we riding dirty?" he said as he pointed to the seatbelt latch.

Stephanie put the seatbelt on and grabbed a blunt. "Nigga, you don't be saying shit when we smoking and riding dirty. Matter of fact, I'm 'bout to roll up a fatty now."

"My fucking ride-or-die chick!" Chris said as he kissed her.

"You better know it and love it." She laughed.

"I do. Trust that," Chris said. He didn't quite love Stephanie, but he knew she was a down-ass chick, and he respected her for that.

"I love your ass also, babe!" Stephanie said as she lit the blunt up.

Chris was quiet because he really never thought Stephanie would come out and say she loved him. As the thoughts of how he could use her love to his advantage floated across his mind, he smiled and grasped her leg, giving it a squeeze.

"We got this."

As they rode down Foster Avenue, they turned down a side road a pulled up to a church on Flatbush Avenue. Chris pulled the van that he was driving around to the back of the funeral home and parked.

"I'll be right back," he whispered.

Stephanie put the blunt out and cringed at the thought of being at a funeral home. She turned the music all the way down and waited for Chris to come back. About thirty minutes later, Chris emerged with three guys who were wheeling out a box that was the size of a casket. After they placed the box inside the back of the van, they disappeared back inside; a few minutes later, they came out with another box, but this one was a bit smaller. Chris shook the three guys' hands and got back in the van.

"You ready to ride, my lady?" he asked in a playful British accent.

"Yes, I am." She laughed. The two drove away, and as they passed back across Foster Avenue, Stephanie turned the music back up and lit the blunt, sat back against the seat, and relaxed.

Stephanie sat up and looked around as they pulled up to a warehouse that she had never been to before. It was huge, and the parking lot was full of cars. She didn't understand why they would be pulling into the warehouse; they didn't have any room to load any more boxes. Once they stopped and Chris turned off the van, he looked over at her and told her to get out. Stephanie got out of the van, stretched, and looked around. She pulled at her pant leg and followed Chris into an office. Chris had four guys also accompany him into the office. They looked at Stephanie curiously at first, but Chris assured them that they could talk in front of her.

"Look, Devon, I need you and Rick to get the smaller box out the van while Neil and Patrick will get the bigger box out, and then bring them in here. Me and my ride-or-die here will count and log the inventory. Tell Mike to call our connect and schedule a time for the meet up," Chris ordered.

"We got you, boss!" Devon replied.

After both boxes were in the office, Chris opened the smaller box first, which, upon first glance, seemed to be full of straw, but as he dug deeper, he pulled out large plastic freezer bags full of marijuana. He counted twenty-one bags in all; then he lifted a cardboard plate, and under it were twenty-five more bags filled with pure cocaine.

Stephanie had helped him log drugs in before, but not that much at one time. Chris gave her the tablet where they kept count of what came in, and told her to do what she was good at. Chris handed Stephanie a scale, and she set it on the desk. She pulled the blinds down further and started weighing each bag. She wrote down each bag title and the weight. She then grabbed another bigger bag where she would place the logged marijuana and slid it to Chris, who then instructed her to count the cocaine. Once the last bag was weighed and logged, she turned the tablet over and waited for them to open the other box. She informed him that she had logged twenty pounds and one quarter-pound bag of green and twenty-five kilos of white.

Rick and Devon took a wrench and opened the larger crate, and when they opened it, there were several different types of guns. Stephanie saw M60s, Glocks, and AKs. He gave her a second tablet and told her yet again, "Do what you do, miss lady!"

After counting the guns and packing them separately, Stephanie was ready to go. She was amazed at how many guns she saw logged in the book over a period of only four weeks. They placed the logbooks and merchandise in a small room that was down some stairs inside the office.

Stephanie had been there all day working and was ready for her pay. She grabbed Chris's dick as he walked up to her and said, "All work and no play makes me a very bored girl."

"Well, shit, let's go," Chris whispered into her ear before licking it.

Jeryca and her sister were helping her mother cook dinner. Her mother was shocked at how much time she had been spending at home. Jeryca had been there for three days straight, but she knew the weekend was approaching, and Jeryca would be out with either her friends or that boyfriend of hers. She hadn't met Thad, but Jeryca had told her a lot about him, and based on what she had heard from Jeryca and other people around the neighborhood, she didn't have a lot of respect for the boy. If Jeryca meant anything to him, he'd have introduced himself to her.

After the lasagna was placed in the oven, Jeryca pulled the lettuce and other vegetables out for a salad, but before she could cut up the cucumbers, her cell phone rang. She immediately excused herself.

"I'll be right back."

"Hello, baby," she said, smiling.

"What's up? What you doing?" Thad asked.

"Shit, just helping my mother cook dinner. Why, what's up?" she asked.

"Trying to see if you want to come and hang out with me and the crew for a while. Maybe spend the night," Thad replied.

"I'm cool with that. But give me about an hour or so. I want to eat dinner with my family," Jeryca replied.

"Well, Brenda will pick you up, okay? Do you want me to get you a bottle?" he asked.

"Yes, get me some Jose," she replied.

"Okay, I will see you when you get here," he said before hanging up.

"Well, Mom, I'm going out later on, but I'm not going until after dinner," Jeryca said.

"You be careful messing around with that boy, Jeryca. Something isn't right about him," her mother said.

"Mom, don't start that! He is a good guy," Jeryca said, frowning. Her mom noticed that she struck a nerve with Jeryca and decided to fall back.

"Okay, Jeryca. Just remember what I said."

"Yeah, Ma!" Jeryca replied, rolling her eyes.

Twenty minutes after they ate, Brenda was there to pick her up. She ran out to the car and jumped in.

"What's up, sis?" Jeryca asked.

"Nothing, just came to get my bro's sweetheart," Brenda replied. Jeryca waved at her mom and sister as they pulled off. Her mother barely waved as she stood in the doorway, shaking her head.

Jeryca and Brenda laughed and talked the whole way to the upper west side of Brooklyn. They listened to music, and after talking to Jeryca for a little while, Brenda couldn't understand why Thad wanted to fuck her over, but it wasn't any of her business. She was just going to continue to play her part.

When they pulled up, Thad and all the guys were posted up on the porch. He had his two favorite pets outside, slithering around on the ground—his boas. He had a yellow and white snake and a red-tailed Colombian boa. He loved his snakes to death. He had purchased them both for close to $600 when they were young and small. They both now weighed close to two hundred pounds together, and were each twelve feet long.

Jeryca knew he had the snakes, but she had never seen them. She didn't want to get out of the car, but they picked on her until she finally got out. She walked up on the porch, keeping her eyes on the two monsters that lay in the grass. She kissed Thad and sat on his lap. He gave her the bottle of Jose Cuervo, and whispered to Brenda to get Jeryca in the house. Once she was in the house, Thad looked at Chris and Larry.

"Let's get started, boys." Thad gathered his pets and put them back in their cages, and they all disappeared in the house, closing the door behind them.

"Hi! What's going on, mommy?" Stephanie asked as she answered the phone.

"Nothing much. Have you heard from Jeryca?" Farrah asked.

"I haven't seen or heard from her in a while," Stephanie replied.

"Girl, I called her, her mother, and Thad, and her mom said she hasn't seen or talked to Jeryca since she left with Thad two weeks ago.

Thad isn't answering his phone, either. Larry hasn't really been talking to me lately, and I don't know why. I am concerned about J," Farrah said.

"Well, don't get worried yet. She is probably with Thad trying to spend up some of that money," Stephanie said as she rolled her eyes up in the air.

"I wouldn't worry if this was a pattern, but Jeryca would never pass up the opportunity to brag about what Thad was doing for her. You know how Jeryca is," Farrah cried.

Stephanie sighed. "Yeah, you're right. Let me get Chris on the phone and see what he knows. Are you going to be home all day?"

"Yeah, I don't have any money to go anywhere," Farrah announced.

"So Larry really is on the bullshit, huh?" Stephanie inquired.

"Girl, yes. He has been over several times, but he picks up Travis and takes him out to buy him whatever he needs or wants," Farrah replied.

"Chris has been acting kind of weird also. Let me call him, then I will come over and we can try to figure a few things out," Stephanie said.

After the two girls hung up, Stephanie's phone rang again, and it was Dana.

"What's up, slowness?" Stephanie answered.

"I'm just trying to see what you guys are up to," Dana replied quietly. Dana was getting really sick of them calling her everything and anything they wanted. She was the only one out of the group that actually held down a real nine-to-five. She worked as a paralegal at Shaw and Associates law firm in New York City. She drove a little over an hour each day commuting back and forth to work, but it was worth it to her. She enjoyed her job; she had helped defend some of the most dangerous criminals that had graced any courtroom. She was very proud of her accomplishments, no matter how small or trivial they seemed to her friends. Lately, Dana had been feeling that her so-called friends were hating on her, and she couldn't continue to hang around them if all they were going to do was put her down.

"Girl, we can't seem to find Jeryca. No one has heard from her in a couple of weeks. You haven't talked to her, have you?" Stephanie asked.

"No, not since that day we were all over there. I hope she is all right," Dana muttered worriedly.

"Damn, what the hell is going on?" Stephanie whispered.

"I'm going to ride around for a bit to see if I can find her," Dana told her.

"Okay, call me if you find her or hear from her," Stephanie replied.

"Got ya, mommy!" Dana said before hanging up.

Dana rode around every area known to her where Thad and his boys hung out. She saw no sign of them or Jeryca. She was getting more and more concerned. "Where are you, Jeryca?" she whispered aloud. Dana called Stephanie, who was now with Farrah.

"Hey, no sign of her or anyone else. I don't know where she could be. Damn it, I hope she is okay," Dana told Stephanie.

"I'm on my way over to you guys. Don't go anywhere," Dana said.

"We will be here, baby girl," Stephanie said. Dana couldn't imagine what was going on with Jeryca, but she was worried.

Dana pulled up at Farrah's house fifteen minutes after getting off the phone with Stephanie. When she walked through the door, Travis ran up and jumped in her arms.

"Hey, Auntie D," he said as he squeezed her neck.

"Hey, T-man! Give Auntie D a peck on the cheek," she said as she leaned her face over. Travis gave Dana a kiss, jumped down, and ran to his room.

"How you doing, Farrah?" Dana asked as she sat down on the loveseat.

"I'm good, sis. Just trying to find Jeryca's ass." Farrah sighed.

"I looked everywhere I could think of, and I didn't see any sign of her," Dana said.

"I called Chris several times, but he won't answer my calls, period," Stephanie chimed in. Just then, Farrah's phone rang.

"Hey, Larry," she said into the receiver.

"What's up? I see you've called me a few times," he replied.

"We just wanted to know if you knew where Jeryca was. We haven't heard from her in a while, and the last we heard she was with Thad. Thad isn't answering his phone, so I just figured you might know something," Farrah explained.

"I'm sure if Jeryca wanted to get at you she would. I'm not her keeper. But trust me; if she is with Thad, she is in good hands. I will tell her to give you a call if I see her," Larry said, laughing.

"What the fuck is wrong with you, Larry? You been acting funny for a while now, and I don't like it!" Farrah said.

"Bitch, who the hell are you talking to? You are nothing more than my son's mother. Don't get it twisted that you're anything more than that. As a matter of fact, have my son ready in an hour. I'm 'bout to come and take him home with me for a few days. No need to pack him a bag. I will buy him whatever he needs," Larry ordered.

"But—" Farrah started, but was cut off by Larry.

"Do what I said! Ain't no 'but.' You have my son ready, or else," Larry said in a firm tone.

"Fine, he will be ready," Farrah said quietly before hanging up.

"I don't know what the hell his problem is, but he been acting funny for the last week," Farrah said as she slammed her phone down on the table.

"Chris has been acting funny also. He don't come around or call like he used to. Every time I call him, I get the voice mail," Stephanie said.

"Travis, come on and let me get you dressed before your daddy pull up. I don't even want that asshole in my house!" Farrah said angrily.

Dana sat in silence as she watched and listened to Farrah and Stephanie whine about their guy troubles.

"Yeah, I haven't had a decent pedicure in a while, and I don't have any extra money for anything I want or need to do," Stephanie cried.

"I'm going to take Larry to court and get what I'm due. If he wants to play, then I'm game," Farrah said as she walked back into the front room. She opened the front door so that she could see when Larry pulled up. Travis was ready to go spend the day with Larry. That's the one thing Farrah couldn't take from Larry:

he was a damn good father. But Farrah wanted the check and would go to any length to get it. Travis ran into the living room and hopped on his mother's lap.

"When is Daddy coming?" he said, smiling.

"He should be here shortly, T-man," Farrah said, calling him by his nickname.

"Aye, let's hit the club tonight and party," Dana proposed.

"I'm all for it!" Stephanie said.

"Shit, I am too, but I don't have the money," Farrah whined.

"I got you, girl. So are we going or what?" Dana asked.

"Hell yeah!" Stephanie and Farrah answered in unison.

Larry pulled up a few minutes later and blew his horn. Farrah looked at Dana and Stephanie, then at the door.

"I know damn well this nigga didn't just blow the horn. If he wants Travis, he is going to come and get him," she said angrily. After a few seconds, he blew his horn again. Realizing Larry wasn't coming in, Farrah sighed. "Come give Mommy a hug, T-man."

Travis ran and grabbed his mother tightly around the neck. "I love you, Mommy!"

Farrah stood up and walked Travis down the front porch steps, and as she got closer to the car, she saw that Larry wasn't alone. There was another bitch in the car, which caused her to snap instantly.

"Motherfucker, I know you ain't pulled up in front of my house with a fucking THOT in your car!" she screamed.

As she ran up to the car, she snatched the passenger door open, grabbed the woman by the hair, and dragged her out to the ground. Larry jumped out of the car immediately to pull Farrah off of his companion. Farrah had reacted exactly how he expected her to. He just hated that Angela had to endure that beat down. *Farrah is whooping her ass pretty good*, he thought to himself.

"Farrah, get off of her!" he yelled.

Hearing the commotion, Stephanie and Dana ran outside. When they got out there, they saw Farrah pounding on a woman and Larry attempting to pull her off. Stephanie ran down quickly to help. Dana grabbed Travis up, who was crying, and took him back into the house.

"Bitch, why the fuck would you do that in front of our son? You a foolish-ass motherfucker, and you don't deserve to be a mother, trick!" he yelled as he pulled Angela up off the ground.

As Angela got to her feet, Stephanie started laughing.

"Bitch, next time you want to do a ride along, make sure your ass is informed on where you're going and who you're riding to go see, and you won't end up fucked up like you are now! Damn, look at your face!"

"Bring my fucking son back out here! You fucked up, Farrah. You think I'm going to have my son with you and you showing me you can't control your temper? Shit, watch what happens next," Larry said, walking to the steps to get Travis.

Farrah completely lost it at that point and rushed Larry, fists blazing. She struck him repeatedly on his back, head, and arms. Dana ran out, tripping as she hit the bottom step. As her ass bounced off the ground, she jumped up and ran over to pull Farrah off of Larry. Travis was crying and screaming for his mother to stop hitting his daddy. Once Dana finally gained control over Farrah, Larry grabbed a sobbing Travis up in his arms, put him in the backseat, got in the driver's seat, and pulled off with his tires squealing, leaving his son's mother behind, crying and broken, slumped on the ground as her friends held and consoled her.

As he turned the corner riding down Williams Court, he couldn't help but to feel saddened by the orchestrated scene that had just taken place; it really bothered him to see his son crying and being subjected to that violent display.

"It had to happen," he said out loud to himself as he adjusted the rearview. "She would've taken all I got, and without my son, nothing else matters!"

Angela looked over at him curiously from the corners of her blackened, swollen eyes and shook her head slightly. She never imagined that a ride to the store would lead her to receiving an ass-beating like she had just gotten. *I'll take the bus next time!* she thought to herself, rubbing the knot that was now present on her forehead.

Chapter Four

"Girl, you got a fat ass!" Dana said as Farrah walked past her with some tight Cavalli jeans on. Larry had spent close to $1000 on them on their second date, which was the clincher for Farrah. As she danced around the room modeling her jeans, Stephanie rolled up a blunt.

"That California Kush smells loud. Damn, bitch, light that motherfucker up and pass it!" Farrah sang. They were drinking Coronas and sipping on a glass of purple Patrón. After Stephanie lit the blunt, she passed it to Dana.

"Girl, you know I'm not smoking that. You two enjoy it. I'll pass."

"Should've known your bougie ass would say no. What do you do for fun other than hang with us? You are from the ghetto, sweetie. Stop acting like you're from Park Slope, bitch!" Stephanie joked.

"Pass the blunt this way, Steph. I'll hit that bitch, unlike Ms. Crisp," Farrah said, using Dana's last name mockingly.

Dana smiled along with them, but she was angry on the inside. She couldn't stand it when they made fun of her. She wanted to lash out at them and tell them how their comments made her feel, but she always ended up swallowing her outburst and sucking it up.

"Shut the fuck up and let's take a shot of Patrón and get going!" Dana said, smiling.

They took their shots, and Stephanie and Farrah smoked their blunt, teasing and joshing Dana. They were listening to Adina Howard's "Nasty Grind," and Farrah started rolling her hips and slow winding down to the floor with the blunt in her mouth.

"Aye, I'm ready to go. I'm going to get my nasty grind on tonight, guaranteed. My son gone, and my ass need some dick!"

Dana laughed. "Uh oh. Caution: THOT in heat!" Stephanie spit her beer out as she fell down on the couch laughing.

"Fuck you, bitch. But you right, a bitch got needs tonight. Hell, I'm horny and broke, so a nigga got to have cash and a big dick. I'm fucking me a boss player. Nothing less than that matters," Farrah said, still dancing.

"Shit, let's go, y'all. I'm ready," Dana said.

As they walked out of the house, Stephanie checked her appearance in the mirror in the hall. "Looking good!" she muttered.

Once they pulled up and parked at Temptations, a local nightclub on Church Avenue, Farrah noticed there were a lot of ballers, but none of them appeared to be wealthy. She suddenly started wondering about Jeryca. She was worried, but Larry said he had seen her and she was good, and if she was good, then it was fucked up how Jeryca was ignoring them. She started to get angry, because ever since Jeryca had been missing, Chris and Larry had both been acting different. Had Jeryca been telling them shit in an effort to get closer to Thad? It was a question that plagued her, but for tonight, she would keep her suspicions to herself and try to enjoy her night.

"Let's go in, y'all!" she yelled as she got out of the car. All three ladies were looking good, and they each knew it. Farrah was turnt up, and after the day she had experienced, she was determined to have fun. She couldn't help but remember the embarrassment and trouble Larry had started. She would show him, though.

As they walked up to the door, the men were checking them out. Some of the guys shouted vulgar comments at them, and Farrah returned them. She was good at talking shit, and so was Stephanie, who was now standing in line, dancing to the music that spilled out of the club.

"Damn, the DJ doing his thang tonight!" Stephanie shouted.

Once they were inside, they spotted a table toward the back of the club and quickly made their way to it. The waitress walked over and took each of their orders.

"Girl, I'm feeling the vibe in here," Stephanie yelled. The music was banging and weed was in the air.

"Damn, I don't know what kind of weed they smoking, but it smells good!" Farrah shouted, looking around and noticing guys in all parts of the club smoking.

"I'm going to see if I can get in on one of these smoke outs," Farrah said, standing up. As she walked off, she checked out several potential ballers. One guy stood out among the rest. He was about six foot three, dark-skinned, and muscular. He was dressed in dark jeans and a regular T-shirt, but what caught her eye was the glow from his watch. She knew how real diamonds shone, and he had several encrusted inside and around the watch.

"Bingo," she said aloud as she sashayed over to him. "Hello, how are you?" she said once she was in hearing range.

"Hey, I'm great. And you?" he replied.

"I'm great also. I'm Farrah. And you are?" Farrah asked, flipping her hair.

"I'm Bobby! So what brings you out this Saturday night?" he asked.

"I just came with my friends. Our day's been sort of jacked up, so this is our stress reliever," Farrah explained.

"Oh, well, I'm here with my boyfriend Kevin," Bobby announced.

Farrah couldn't believe what she had just been told. Was he telling the truth, or lying because he wasn't interested? Either way, it embarrassed her extremely. Her face grew hot and her fingers tingled. After about three minutes, her question was answered as a tall, slim man walked up and planted a kiss square on Bobby's lips. She turned around quickly and caught Stephanie and Dana looking at her with a shocked, yet humorous expression. She rolled her eyes and excused herself. As she started walking back to her group, she noticed that there was a new body present at their table. *Who in the world is that bitch?* she thought to herself.

Once Farrah reached the table, Dana immediately introduced Farrah to her good friend, Brittany Howell. She had met Brittany a little over a year ago when she first started working at the law firm. Brittany was a partner at Holmes, Howell, and Fuller law firm. She and Brittany hit it off quickly her first day on the job, and their friendship grew. Brittany was known for being a hardcore attorney who won her cases at any cost. She was very good at what she did, but she also was known for dirty strategizing. She was a ruthless player in a dress. She knew the ins and outs of the law so well that she felt invisible in the courtroom. Brittany was 32, and Dana looked up to her like a big sister. She accepted Dana for who and what she was and never made her feel stupid, unlike her childhood friends.

"Hey, nice to meet you," Brittany said.

"Same here," Farrah replied nonchalantly, rolling her eyes and bopping to the music as if she was brushing Brittany off. Brittany gave Dana a side-glance with her mouth set and jaw clenching, which told Dana that Brittany wasn't feeling Farrah.

Dana whispered her apologies as she reached for her hand. Stephanie could feel the tension in the air. She didn't understand why Farrah seemed to have a problem with Brittany because she had just met her and she hadn't said or done anything disrespectful, but she decided to follow Farrah's lead.

Stephanie had seen the looks exchanged between Dana and Brittany, and decided to speak on it. "Why are y'all looking like that?"

Dana looked at Stephanie and quickly spoke up with a frown that couldn't have been mistaken. "What the hell are you talking about, Stephanie?"

"I mean that bitch looking at you like she got an issue with Farrah. Is there a problem or what?" Stephanie asked.

"Hold on. Why are you calling her a bitch and what's with the attitude? Did I miss something?" Dana asked.

"Dana, I'm going to get up with you another time, because I can't afford to go to jail behind irrelevant-ass bullshit with females I don't even know. When you can get out without your 'girls,' call me," Brittany said as she stood to leave.

"No, you don't have to go. I'm sure it's all a misunderstanding," Dana whispered to Brittany.

Farrah started laughing, grabbed Stephanie by the arm, and headed to the dance floor. The two ladies danced together, laughing and singing "Nothing's Free" by Lil Jon, and Farrah made sure it was understood by any man listening that they had to pay to play. Two guys approached them and asked each of them to dance. The two couples danced through four songs straight. When the DJ played "Tonight" by Trick Daddy, the two couples decided to find a table to get to know one another. As they made their way through the crowd, Farrah caught a glimpse of Dana still sitting with Brittany.

"Maybe the ho like pussy!" Farrah whispered to Stephanie, who was walking behind her. Stephanie started laughing at the comment and stumbled backward, bumping into another female and causing her to spill her drink.

"You white bitch! Watch where the fuck you're going!"

"Who the fuck is this tramp talking to?" Stephanie asked loudly. Hearing the commotion, Farrah stopped in her tracks instantly and turned to see what was going on.

"Man, what's up?" the female asked after hearing what Stephanie said.

"Bitch, it's whatever! Don't let the skin color fool you. I'll beat your ass and leave you wishing you'd never fucked with me," Stephanie said, stepping closer to the girl.

As the girl moved forward, Stephanie swung, punching the chick in her face. Farrah ran up to help as the crowd formed a circle around the women. Dana, who was engrossed in conversation with Brittany, looked up when she heard the loud noise of yelling and glass breaking and realized that her friends were nowhere in sight. Dana jumped up and ran to crowd, and just as she thought, Farrah and Stephanie were fighting.

Stephanie had one chick's head, banging it into the floor, while Farrah had another chick in a chokehold. Both girls began to throw punches, and after three minutes, Brittany and Dana pulled Farrah and Stephanie away, leaving the girls that they were fighting laid out on the floor.

"What the hell is going on?" Dana asked as she pulled Stephanie out of the club.

"I accidentally bumped into that ho, and they decided that they wanted to fight, so I gave them what they wanted!" Stephanie yelled.

"Dana, they did what they had to do. Got to respect that," Brittany said as she held on to Farrah, laughing.

Farrah couldn't even flex; Brittany was strong as shit. She hadn't broken a sweat grabbing her up and toting her out the club.

"Brittany, I'm going to drop my girls off, and I will talk to you Monday at work," Dana said.

"Okay, sweetie. Call me tomorrow, though, and let's finish our conversation," Brittany replied.

"Okay, I will," Dana said as she walked toward her car with Farrah and Stephanie in tow.

Once they were in the car, Farrah looked at Stephanie.

"Damn, I didn't even get that nigga name!"

"What nigga?" Stephanie asked.

"The dude I was dancing with. Damn. You can't be that slow. I thought you were on the same level I was, but it seems like you on the level with Dana, slow as fuck." Farrah laughed.

Dana wanted to put her ass out at that point. She had realized that she was going to have to separate herself from the group, and the quicker she did that, the better she would be.

"Has anyone seen Jeryca?" Thad asked as he walked through the house.

"I haven't seen her since yesterday, Thad," Brenda replied.

"I told y'all not to let her out of your sight. Go find her now. Look everywhere, damn it," Thad ordered everyone.

"Thad, I told you this may be a bad move for you," Toby said, shaking his head.

"Man, I don't want to hear that. I just need to find her before she does something crazy!" Thad yelled.

"You should've known that this could happen. I told you from day one to leave that bitch alone, but no, you wouldn't listen to me. Then, to make matters worse, you turn around and make her your—" Before Toby could finish, Thad cut him off.

"Damn, man, I don't need to hear this shit right now," Thad shouted sarcastically. "What the fuck you want me to say, that you were right? That's not going to solve shit, but hey, if it soothes your soul, you were right, Toby!"

Toby looked at his brother for a second, shaking his head. He couldn't believe that his brother was this gone over a THOT that wasn't 'bout shit. Toby walked away after muttering, "Man, you need to get yourself together. You put this game together; now fix it."

Thad picked up his glass of Paul Masson, took a sip, and then threw the glass against a mirror, causing the glass and mirror to shatter.

Chris, Toby, and Keith ran into the room after hearing the loud sound of the glass breaking, and once in the room, they saw Thad seething and about to explode. Each one of the guys knew that when Thad got to that point, there was no calming him, so they all turned around immediately and walked away, not wanting to be a target of Thad's rage.

"Girl, I can't believe how shit played out last night. I know those are your friends, but Dana, you have to use your head. You can't put yourself in worthless situations like that. I understand that they were defending themselves, but the way they came at me foul for no reason says a lot about their characters," Brittany said.

"We've been friends for a long time, but like I told you last night, they always make fun of me for not being money-thirsty like they are. I mean, I like money, but I don't need a man to give it to me," Dana replied.

"Well, shit, Dana, you know what you got to do. Get your money how you need to. I'm behind you and will help you any way I can," Brittany stated.

"Thank you, sis. I appreciate it so much, but a sister hungry as hell," Dana said, rubbing her stomach.

"I know a nice Chinese spot. It's in the hood, but the food there is great, and their establishment is clean and cozy," Brittany informed Dana.

"Any place is good for me," Dana responded.

"Golden Dragon it is," Brittany stated, merging into the left lane to exit off the expressway. This was the fourth time Dana had hung out with Brittany, and she really enjoyed it. She wasn't belittled for being who she was, and it felt great.

As they turned left onto the avenue, Dana's attention was immediately drawn to the corner store. There, posted up looking like a woman of the night, was Jeryca!

"Oh my God! Pull over! Pull over please!" she shouted as she pointed to where Jeryca was standing. As Brittany slowed down to stop the car, Dana was already opening the door to jump out.

"Jeryca!" Dana yelled. Jeryca turned, and once she realized who Dana was, she attempted to run, but Dana stopped her in her tracks.

"Jeryca, if you move one inch, I will call your mother and tell her where I saw you and what it looked like you were doing!"

Jeryca stopped and stared at Dana. "I don't give a damn who you call. If you want to talk to me, it's going to be fifty dollars for one hour."

"Jeryca, what are you doing to yourself? This isn't you, sweetie. Have you seen what you look like?" Dana asked as she stepped a little bit closer with each word spoken.

"Dana, I just need one quick hit. Please, just let me hold fifty dollars real quick, and then we can discuss anything. I will eat your pussy if you want me to," Jeryca replied.

"Jeryca, when the hell did you start using drugs? You're acting crazy, and you look awful. What do you think your mother would say or do if she saw you like this?" Dana asked. A small crowd was starting to form, listening to Dana talk with her friend. Some people were offering their input on the situation as well.

"Girl, listen to your friend," one woman yelled.

"I'll pay one hundred dollars to watch you eat her pussy," a man yelled.

"Hell, I'll pay seventy-five dollars if the ho suck my dick," another man snickered.

"Y'all should be ashamed of yourselves. Girl, go with your friend and get off these streets," another person said.

"I don't give a fuck about what my momma think. She should've been out here doing exactly what I'm doing, and maybe my life would be different," Jeryca cried.

"You know what, Jeryca? Pam deserves to have her big sister with her, 'cause what you're doing could leave you dead. Get the fuck in the car now before I beat your ass. I'm done trying to coax you like you're a child," Dana said between clenched teeth and with her fist balled up at her side.

Jeryca could see the anger building up in Dana, and just the mention of her sister's name set her emotions off. Jeryca started crying and started backing up to the wall of the store, and once there, she began to slide to the sidewalk. Brittany and Dana ran forward to grab her.

"Let's get her in the car," Brittany said as she grabbed Jeryca. Dana ran to the car and opened the door. Brittany placed Jeryca in the back seat and looked at Dana. "Girl, this can't be the friend you were telling me about."

"The one and only!" Dana said quietly as she got into the passenger seat. Once Brittany was seated back in the car, she put the car in drive and pulled away.

"We can take her to my place and figure out what to do next. It's evident that she is on something," Dana said. Brittany turned the car around and headed back to the expressway en route to Dana's house.

"Aye, man, Tonia just called and said that she saw Jeryca, looking rough standing on the side of the corner store. She said that she left in a gray car," Chris informed Thad.

"Man, damn. I hope she isn't out selling her ass on that corner. I know Brenda explained to that stupid-ass junkie that tricks are done by telephone request only," Thad said as he paced the floor of the dining room.

"Well, man, you got her hooked on drugs, and besides, I don't think she is on the clock. Tonia said she left with two females in a gray Honda. From the description she gave me, it sounded like it could've been Dana," Chris said.

"Fuck. All the work I put in on that bitch. I guess that money train has left the building." Thad sighed as he leaned up against the edge of the doorway that led to the kitchen.

"What are we going to do now?" Chris asked.

"Shit, ain't much we can do, is it? We will just move without her. We were just fine before Jeryca," Thad said.

"No, that's not what I meant. Do you think Jeryca will talk about our little operation here? If that was Dana, you know we might have a small issue. Those girls don't play when it comes to one of them getting hurt or mistreated. I told you how Stephanie and Farrah went off the other day with Larry," Chris said.

"Man, ain't nobody worried about them bitches. It's business as usual," Thad sneered.

"Thad, never underestimate those girls. This could be a real problem," Chris replied.

Thad didn't say a word as he turned and walked away, leaving Chris nervous and confused.

Chapter Five

"Jeryca! Look at me!" Dana yelled.

Jeryca had been sitting quietly, fidgeting in the same spot for ten minutes. Her skin was moist with sweat, and she was clicking her tongue constantly. She rubbed and scratched at her skin nonstop, and to top it off, she stank. Jeryca kept asking Dana to get her a fix.

"Come on, girl, just one more time, please."

Dana turned to Brittany with tears in her eyes. "What should I do? I can't keep her here, 'cause I have to work, but I can't send her back out there."

"What about your other friends? Maybe they will do it. You should ask them and see what they say," Brittany told her.

"It's worth a try, I guess," Dana replied as she grabbed her cell phone.

"Watch her for a second, okay?" Dana asked Brittany.

"I got you, sis. Go handle your business," Brittany replied, shutting the door behind Dana as she walked out of the room.

Dana sat on the couch and picked up her phone. She called Jeryca's mother first. The phone rang four times before she picked up.

"Hello, Ms. Mebane, this is Dana. I'm calling to let you know that Jeryca is here with me. We picked her up from Thad's today."

"Thank you, Lord! I've been so worried about her! I got to call Detective Rogers to let him know she is okay," Sheila Mebane cried. She was in tears as she spoke.

"Detective Rogers?" Dana asked curiously.

"Yes, after the third day of not hearing from Jeryca, I filed a missing persons report. I've been worried sick and so has Pam. That was my only recourse," Sheila explained.

"Wow, okay. Well, I just wanted to let you know that she is here and she's just fine. She is in the bedroom asleep right now," Dana said.

"Okay, have her call me when she gets up. And thank you for calling me," Sheila said before hanging up.

Dana rubbed her head vigorously before calling Farrah.

"What the hell do you mean you're going for custody of Travis? Nigga, you try it and I will tell the judge everything about how you make your money. Just because I acted out one time, that ain't shit to the life you lead. So do what you do!" Farrah yelled into the phone.

"Bitch, you ain't talking 'bout shit! I will drag your ass. My son needs to be where he will be safe!" Larry yelled.

"Safe? Nigga, you sell drugs, prostitute women, and sell guns, and you think he will be safe with you? Like I said, do what you got to do. I'm hanging up now, and I'm going to call an attorney to see what my options are. Bet you won't get my son, you bastard!" Farrah said before she ended her call.

Farrah sat in her wingback chair, staring off in space and trying to figure out what happened to make Larry turn on her like he did. Ever since Jeryca had gone missing, all the guys had been acting real funny, and she was going to find out why. If Jeryca had anything to do with it, she was going to regret it. Just as Farrah started plotting on Jeryca, her phone rang.

"Yeah, what's up?" she answered.

"Farrah, it's Dana. We have a situation here, and I need you to come over ASAP."

"What's the problem? 'Cause I'm kind of dealing with my own issues here," Farrah replied.

"It's Jeryca. We found her today, and girl, she is fucked up. I need y'all to help. Please," Dana pleaded.

"What do you mean 'fucked up?' Dana, I got a lot I'm dealing with right now that I can't figure out, so I'm not going to be any good to y'all."

"Farrah, I don't want to call Sheila 'cause you know she will have her placed in a treatment center, and I can't leave her to the streets 'cause she won't survive. I just need a little help," Dana cried.

Brittany shook her head at the way Dana had to beg Farrah to help their so-called best friend.

Farrah sighed. "Okay, I'll come, but how am I going to get there?"

"I'll send my homegirl Brittany to pick you up. I'm going to call Stephanie and see if she can come as well," Dana informed Farrah.

"That's what's up. I'll be here," Farrah replied.

After Farah and Dana hung up, Dana couldn't help but wonder what kind of mess Jeryca had gotten herself into. Brittany looked at her.

"I'm going to go get her, but you know if she say anything out of tact, her ass is mine!"

"She won't say anything to you. If she does, I'll handle it, big sis. I sure do appreciate you," Dana said softly.

"I'm here for you. Let me go get this trick for you," Brittany said, laughing.

"Damn, baby, give me that dick. Fuck me faster. Oh shit, harder, deeper! You feel how wet my pussy is, huh?" Stephanie moaned.

"Just throw that ass back and shut the fuck up," Chris growled as he grabbed a handful of her hair. Stephanie bucked back harder and harder until she came. Chris moaned and pulled his dick out and lay on his back.

"Get on top of me and ride this dick."

As Stephanie did as she was told, her phone rang. She looked over at it and ignored it as she proceeded to sit on her man's dick. She slid down on it and rode him fast and hard. He grabbed her hips and guided her ass down on his dick how he wanted to. Stephanie enjoyed the way Chris fucked her, and she figured she had a long night ahead of her.

Thirty minutes later, Stephanie had come once more, and Chris had as well. He jumped up immediately and went into the bathroom. Stephanie watched as he walked by her, naked, and admired his muscular back and thighs. He was a handsome man with long braids and thick eyebrows. His eyes were light brown, and his lips were full. She knew she had a great catch.

When Chris came out of the bathroom, he was fully dressed, and he walked to the chair where his jacket was and put it on without looking at her.

"Wait a minute! Where are you going?" she asked.

"What? Girl, I know you didn't just ask me that. I don't have to answer to you. Remember that shit," Chris snarled nastily.

Before Stephanie could speak, Chris was walking out the door. Stephanie sat on her bed with her legs tucked beneath her, looking at the door in disbelief. She couldn't believe that she had allowed Chris to use her like he just did. After a few seconds, her cell phone began to ring. Thinking it was Chris, she quickly grabbed for it, only to see that it was Dana.

"What the heck does she want?" she whispered to herself. "Hello," Stephanie mumbled into the phone.

"Hey, it's me. We found Jeryca, and she is in bad shape. I need you to come over and help me with her," Dana explained. Stephanie immediately agreed to help.

"Yes, I'll be there, but I can't come until my mother gets here so she can bring me."

"I got that covered already. My friend Brittany will pick you up after she picks Farrah up," Dana informed her.

"Okay, cool beans."

After Dana sent Brittany to get her two friends, she checked on Jeryca. When she unlocked the door to where Jeryca was, she walked in and saw her sitting in the corner of the bed, with her knees to her chest. The smell of rotten ass filled the air, and Dana had to blink several times to keep her eyes from tearing up. She walked over and asked Jeryca if she wanted to get in the tub.

"Dana, just help me find me a hit, please! I'm dying and you don't care!" Jeryca yelled.

"Are you hungry?" Dana asked, ignoring Jeryca's outburst.

"No, I'm not hungry! I need a fix now! If you're not going to get it for me, I'll go get it myself!" Jeryca yelled as she attempted to stand and push past Dana.

"You aren't going anywhere!" Dana shouted as she pushed Jeryca back down on the bed.

"Bitch, don't put your hands on me! I'll kill your ass!" Jeryca yelled, jumping back up swinging her frail arms wildly. She hit Dana repeatedly, but Dana grabbed at her arms, used her body to force Jeryca back on the bed, and sat on her, pinning her arms up over her head.

"Let me go, damn you!" Jeryca yelled as she fought to free her arms. Dana couldn't believe how strung out Jeryca was. Whatever had happened in the last few weeks had affected Jeryca extremely.

Ignoring Jeryca's pleas and tightening her grip on Jeryca's arms, Dana wondered if she was going to be able to carry through with helping Jeryca.

After a few minutes, Jeryca appeared to be calm, and Dana released her grip on her, but as she proceeded to move off of her, Jeryca pushed her way off the bed and made a dash for the door. Dana fell to the floor, jumped up quickly, and raced after her. As Jeryca reached the front door and opened it, she came face to face with Brittany, Farrah, and Stephanie.

"Hurry up and grab her! Don't let her out!" Dana yelled. Brittany grabbed Jeryca and slung her back in the house on the couch. Stephanie and Farrah immediately jumped to Jeryca's defense.

"Leave her the fuck alone, bitch! Dana, how the hell are you cool with this motherfucker handling Jeryca like that?" Farrah asked angrily.

"Number one, Brittany ain't a bitch, and you need to apologize. Number two, we found Jeryca trying to sell her ass for a fucking fix. Brittany helped me get Jeryca here," Dana snarled. Silence fell in the living room as Stephanie and Farrah looked at Jeryca, realizing for the first time that Jeryca looked and smelled awful.

Over the course of six days, the girls had their hands full with Jeryca. She fought them, begged them to get her a fix, tried to leave several times, and vomited repeatedly any and everywhere. Stephanie and Farrah had their own issues to deal with, but they set them aside for Jeryca. They didn't want to seem uncaring to Jeryca's needs. Farrah was disturbed by the fact that Dana insisted that they help her with Jeryca, even though Dana had Brittany to assist her with her current issue. With Larry and the possible custody fight, Farrah still felt that Dana could've handled Jeryca without their help. Farrah envied and hated the fact that Dana had everything going for herself, and didn't understand why she couldn't take a few days and deal with Jeryca on her own. Farrah decided that, before it was over with, she was going to give Dana a piece of her mind.

***

Monday Morning

Dana left Farrah and Stephanie at her house with Jeryca while she went to work. Brittany had allowed her to sit in on a case that she was working on, and it was very important that she be present.

Jeryca awoke and walked into the living room, where Farrah and Stephanie were.

"Hey, babes." She sighed as she plopped down on the sofa.

"Hey, how are you feeling today, sweetie?" Stephanie asked.

"I feel somewhat better. You guys don't know what I've been through," Jeryca said, shaking her head and then running her fingers through her hair. She held her head down as she spoke.

"I couldn't even imagine, Jeryca," Farrah admitted.

"Has anyone talked to my mom?" Jeryca inquired.

"We've talked to her daily. She doesn't know the full extent of what's been going on, but she knows you've been sick. She has been very worried though," Farrah explained.

"Think it will be okay if I called her?" Jeryca asked.

"I don't see a problem with that," Stephanie said, looking at Farrah, who nodded her approval before handing Jeryca her cell phone.

Thad called Chris into the shipment area at the warehouse they had bought in New York three years earlier. Thad figured if he purchased the building in the big city, he could haul and house his shipment of illegal guns there without scrutiny. The saucing company that he and his brother started, which was very profitable, was mainly a front for their illegal activities. They manufactured barbecue sauce, hot wing sauce, and packaged various seasonings.

"Chris, what time did Orlando say his guys would get here? It's too early in the morning for him to be playing with me. I have to be in court at one this afternoon, so he needs to get his dudes here. Call him and see what's up," Thad ordered.

"I'm on it," Chris replied.

While Chris was on the phone with Orlando, Thad motioned for his brother, Toby, to join him in the office. He wanted to update him on the issue with Orlando, and how they needed to handle it if Orlando and his goons tried to play them on their shipment.

"Look, big brother," Thad began, "it is ten o'clock already, and Orlando was supposed to been here two hours ago. If the nigga ain't dead or laying somewhere hurt, I think we should bust they ass when we see them," Thad said.

"See, Thad, there you go. You are making decisions based off your emotions and not your brain. We don't need the extra heat, man. It's more than one way to deal with them other than violence," Toby pointed out.

"Oh yeah, well enlighten me as to how. They could pull up on the bullshit, trying to rob us or setting us up with the cops. Name a time when they have ever been this late. You can't do it. Like I said, we need to deal with these niggas like we do everybody else that jeopardizes our business. We can't afford to go soft now," Thad argued.

Toby sighed as he looked down, rubbing his head, and then he looked up. "You right, man, but we can't allow any of the heat from what we do to reflect back on us at all."

"True dat. So what's the plan?" Thad asked as he shut the door to the office.

"You tell me. We can't do shit here, so we got to work this—" Before he could finish his statement, Thad's phone rang.

"Hello."

"Hey, baby, it's me, Jeryca. I can't talk long, but I need you to come and get me. Farrah and them got me held up in this damn house and won't let me go. I miss you. I got to go, but I will call you later," Jeryca whispered.

Thad didn't get a chance to respond 'cause she hung up quickly. As he began putting his phone back on his hip, he looked up at Toby with a puzzled look.

"Man, that's another loose end we need to tie up."

"What?" Toby questioned.

"Jeryca and her crew of hoes," Thad muttered.

"Well, right now we got more important fish to fry," Toby replied.

"You right. Well, let's work it out 'cause I got to be in court by one," Thad reminded Toby.

As the two put their heads together to devise their attack on Orlando and his goons, Thad still had Jeryca on his mind. He needed her back on his payroll, but could he really trust her to do the right thing this time? He knew that he was responsible for her getting strung out on heroin, but she should've been stronger mentally. She had made him thousands of dollars in the two weeks she was with him, and she owed him way more than that. Once he found out where she was, he was going to get her and move her where no one could find her.

Thad and his brother discussed several ways to get rid of Orlando but didn't plan anything out. Thad left at twelve and headed for court.

As the Kings County Supreme Court filled, Dana watched the attorneys talk and discuss different cases. Brittany was there representing one Zack Brown, who was shot during a brawl at The Foxy Gentleman's Club by one Thad Royster. Even Though Zack was the victim, he had warrants for assault himself, so he was appearing before Judge Evelyn Smith both as a victim and a defendant. When Brittany informed Dana that she was representing the man that Thad had shot, Dana was thrilled and begged Brittany to allow her to assist her in the case. She didn't know why she felt the need to be involved, but she did.

Zack had been locked up since he was released from the hospital and hadn't had time to talk to anyone just yet. Brittany was going to ask the judge to lower the $250,000 bond that her client was hit with.

As Zack was brought out, Dana noticed that he was limping and he looked tired. His face hadn't been shaved, and his hair was nappy. He had a muscular build under his county uniform, and although he wasn't groomed, she could tell he was a good-looking guy. As she inspected Zack for a few moments more, her attention was drawn to the door as she saw Brittany nod her head in that direction. As Dana's gaze found the door, she locked eyes with Thad.

As Thad sauntered into the courtroom, he regarded Dana for a minute, but soon focused his eyes on Zack. Zack gave Thad an evil smile and a nod. Thad glared at him emotionless, which caused Zack to turn his head. Dana watched the two men's interaction intently, and again, her eyes met Thad's. Somehow, she knew that Thad knew they had Jeryca, and she didn't give a fuck. She wanted him to try something so she could fuck him up. The way he kept staring at her had her wondering what he was thinking.

As Judge Smith walked in, the bailiff said, "Hear ye, hear ye, all rise for the honorable Judge Evelyn Smith. Turn your cell phones off and do not talk while court is in session. You may all be seated."

As everyone took their seats, the judge's assistant called the docket. Dana broke her gaze with Thad and rolled her eyes. She listened, and as each name was called, someone would enter their plea of guilty or not guilty. When they got to Thad, a handsome foreign man stood up and answered for him.

"Not guilty, Your Honor."

Dana looked back in shock at Thad, who was smiling from ear to ear. As she swung back around, she glanced at Brittany, who was also smiling. Dana sat back, confused by everyone's demeanor. She stole a quick glance at Zack, who didn't seem bothered one way or another, and she wondered if they had somehow gotten to Zack to take back his statement that Thad had shot him. Whatever the case, she was going to find out what all those looks were about.

As the remainder of the docket was called out, Dana pondered what was going to happen. She knew that Thad had something to do with Jeryca's current condition, and she wanted him to pay one way or another. If he got off scot-free for shooting Zack, she didn't know how she could protect her friend from him. She had to come up with a plan.

"Court is now in recess. We will adjourn in fifteen minutes," the bailiff announced.

As everyone shuffled about and formed small groups, Dana walked to the front to meet Brittany as she moved out from the bench. Thad walked up on her quickly.

"Hey, Dana."

"Thad, how are you?" she asked.

"I'm great. How is Jeryca?" he sneered.

"You tell me. I haven't seen her," Dana lied.

"Oh, really. Well, I got a call from her that says otherwise. You know it's against the law to hold someone against their will, don't you?" Thad smirked.

"I don't know what you're talking about. Now if you will excuse me, I have to go," Dana replied. Before she could move completely away, Thad blocked her path, leaned close to her ear, and whispered, "I'm coming for my top ho." Thad laughed and walked away to talk with his attorney.

Dana couldn't believe what Thad had just divulged to her. Jeryca a ho? That couldn't be true. . . . But as she thought back to where they found her, what she was saying, and how she smelled, she knew that it was in fact true. She also believed that Jeryca had called Thad as he stated, and once she got back home, she was going to talk to Farrah and Stephanie and tell them everything that she found out and go ham on whoever let Jeryca use the phone. How could they help her if they couldn't stick to their task?

"What the fuck did he say to you that got you looking so bewildered?" Brittany asked as she approached Dana, who was lost in thought.

Dana shook her head as she snapped back into reality. "A bunch of nonsense, but what's going on here? Is Zack Brown not testifying against him?"

"Well, my client won't testify because of his belief that snitching is against a man's code, but the District Attorney has several witnesses who will testify, so Thad will not walk away from this untouched," Brittany explained.

"I just wanted to know. I was shocked when he pled not guilty with Zack in the courtroom," Dana said.

Before Brittany could respond, two men approached her and pulled her to the side. They nodded in Zack's direction, and Brittany started smiling. Dana didn't know what was going on, but she felt like something was about to go down, and when Brittany returned and whispered in her ear, "Once court is over we need to leave immediately," Dana knew for sure that her feelings were correct.

She didn't know what was going on, but she smiled, realizing that Brittany was as crooked as she always thought she was, and that it would be a great benefit for her and her friends.

Dana followed Brittany outside the court-room, where they stayed until court was back in session. As Dana looked around at the different people who were in groups talking, her eyes found Thad's, who hadn't seen her due to the fact that he was hugged up with a young, beautiful, light-skinned female. She shook her head, but quickly pulled out her cell phone and took several pictures of the two together. If Jeryca had called Thad, she was going to get a great eye opener when she returned home.

After the docket was called, Brittany approached the court with her plea to have Zack's bond reduced, which was granted. It went from $250,000 to $75,000. Brittany walked back to the bench; she had two more clients to represent before she could leave.

At five o'clock, as the courtroom was cleared out for the day, Brittany gestured for Dana to move quickly outside away from the courthouse. Once they were across the street, Dana turned back to the courthouse as she heard several male voices shouting. When she spotted the source of the noise, she saw the two guys who had approached Brittany earlier pushing and arguing with Thad. They were causing a scene, which immediately drew a huge crowd. Dana couldn't see much as the crowd grew bigger. A few seconds later, the police were separating

the group of people, and Thad, along with the
two guys who started the altercation, hurried off
in different directions.

Brittany looked at Dana, smiling. "Thad won't
get away with anything."

Dana smiled and gave Brittany a high-five,
understanding completely what she was insinu-
ating. She got into her car and drove off. As she
looked in her rearview mirror, she saw Thad's
truck pull up behind her. She immediately
reached for the revolver that she kept in her
dashboard.

As they pulled up to the stoplight, Thad pulled
up on the side of her and rolled his window
down, smiling and giving her a quick nod of
his head. Dana returned his smile but waved
at him with her gun in her hand. Thad's smile
disappeared for a quick second, but as they
pulled off, he smiled one last time and flew down
the road past her.

Dana couldn't believe that she once thought
he was her type. Honestly speaking, he hadn't
done anything directly to her, but seeing how
he and his friends were treating her friends, she
had lost respect for them. To top it off, he had
gotten Jeryca involved in drugs and prostitution, and he thought it was funny. There wasn't
anything funny about ruining someone else's

life, especially someone she considered family. As she drove home, she couldn't wait to show Jeryca the pictures and help her come to grips with the fact that Thad meant her no good.

Chapter Six

"Orlando, I've been trying to reach you all day, bro," Chris snapped.

"Uh, I'm sorry, dude, but something came up, and I had to handle it first and foremost. You feel me? It was a family issue. Tell Thad and Toby I apologize and maybe we can meet Wednesday," Orlando said.

"Well, I will get with them and then let you know what the move will be," Chris responded.

Okay, man. Again, I do apologize for everything," Orlando said, sounding a bit nervous, which was weird to Chris.

After Chris hung up, he called Toby and informed him of his conversation with Orlando. He told Toby that Orlando didn't answer his call until 5:30 p.m., and when he did, he sounded nervous and was stuttering here and there. Toby told Chris to wait on his or Thad's phone call before calling Orlando back. After Toby hung up from talking to Chris, he called Thad.

"Aye, man, where you at? How did it go in court?" he asked once Thad picked up.

"It went okay. Had a run-in with Zack's boys, but it wasn't no big deal. I also saw Dana there at the courthouse," Thad explained.

"Oh, word. That's one of the finest bitches on Jeryca's squad, boy!" Toby said, smiling.

"Man, can you believe that bitch waved a gun at me?" Thad snorted.

"What? You mean to tell me that Dana is smart, sexy, and thuggish? Shit, I need a bitch like that on my team!" Toby laughed.

"Oh, yeah? Well, I wonder what your wife Tiffany would think about that," Thad said, laughing.

"Li'l brother, don't go there. Besides, we got a situation we need to work on that's more important than talking about Dana. Chris just called me and said that he is just now getting in touch with Orlando, and that he seemed kind of shaky. You were right; we need to handle that issue ASAP," Toby informed him.

"Nice way to dodge that Dana bullet, bro. But I'm almost at your house, so talk to you in a few," Thad said, laughing as he hung up the phone. Five minutes later, he was pulling into Toby's driveway. Thad got out of his truck and locked the doors. He walked into Toby's house without knocking, but yelled to announce his entrance.

"Aye, nigga, where the fuck you at?"

"Shit, I'm right here," Toby said as he walked up on Thad and slapped the back of his head, playfully putting him in a headlock. "Now what was that shit you was saying about Dana and Tiffany? Huh, negro?" Toby said as he started rubbing his knuckles into Thad's head.

"Okay, okay, man, you got me!" Thad yelled.

"All right, remember that next time you want to be slick at the mouth," Toby joked, walking away like he had won a wrestling match with his arms up. Thad walked behind him, rubbing his head.

"So what's the deal with Orlando?"

"I don't know, but they didn't bring us our product, and we've paid for half of the shipment as agreed upon, so if they don't have our guns, money, or if they trying to set us up, we will kill them. We need to prepare now for anything. I think you should call the guys for an emergency meeting tonight. Tell Chris to get Neal and his crew. Larry needs to get at Junior and Rick and let them know what's up, and Keith needs to call Fresh and his crew, and we need to meet at the Oasis," Toby replied.

"I'm on it. What time do I need to tell them to be there, bro?" Thad asked.

"About ten," he answered.

"Cool," Thad replied.

While Thad was on the phone coordinating the meet up, Toby was rolling a blunt and singing, "I'm Gonna Git You Sucka," smiling at the thought of blasting on Orlando and his crew. Toby was usually against any violence that could reflect back on them, but he knew that Thad had a point. In their particular business, they had to set boundaries and examples for anyone who felt like they could get one over on them and play with their money.

"Come and hit this blunt, nig," Toby said after taking a few pulls off it.

"Naw, man, I'm good. I'm trying to figure out how we are going to handle these motherfucking clowns and hoes that feel they can play around with me," Thad said, remembering how Dana waved her gun at him. He knew that if he went after one, he was going to have to hit them all where it hurt them the most.

"Well, hitting this blunt will stimulate your mind and help you relax and focus on how you need to go about getting all of them, but let me fuck Dana before you make any moves on them," Toby said, waving the blunt at Thad.

"Man, give me that shit! Dana ain't trying to fuck with you, nigga. She ain't that type of chick. But the bitch may be a problem for me, so I'm getting all of them out my hair ASAP." Thad laughed as he took the blunt and pulled on it.

"Shit, do what you do, man. I'm behind you one hundred percent," Toby announced.

"That's what's up," Thad said, shocked by how Toby was acting and involving himself in something that he always preached against: violence.

"Aye, what do you think about us starting a record label? We can call it T&T Music. Our first single we write can be called 'Death to Our Haters.'" Toby laughed as he handed the blunt back to Toby.

"Man, you don't need to smoke no more of this shit. You tripping, Toby," Thad said, walking to the bar to pour himself a shot of vodka.

"Naw, I'm straight, but for real, let's think about doing another venture," Toby said as he lay back on the couch, taking a draw from the blunt.

"Sounds good, but first it's death to our haters," Thad sang as he began to plot his next move on Orlando and his crew, as well as Jeryca and her friends, especially Dana. She was going to learn that you don't wave a gun at a man like him. She was going to regret it.

***

While Dana was driving home, she received a phone call from Jeryca's mother.

"Hi, Ms. Mebane. How are you?" she asked.

I'm good, Dana, but I was wondering why Jeryca hasn't been home yet. If you found her, then where the hell is she? If I don't see her soon, I'm calling the police. I haven't heard from her like you said I would, so either you produce her or else," Sheila yelled.

"Hold on, Ms. Mebane; let me pull over real quick," Dana said, placing her cell phone on the passenger seat as she pulled over. Once she parked, she grabbed her phone.

"Ms. Mebane, there are things going on that we felt that you shouldn't know, but we could've been wrong."

"You damn right you were wrong! Pam is missing her sister and can't even function in school. What the hell is going on, Dana?"

"We found Jeryca, but she was in bad shape. She was on the corner, high off heroin and stinking. She had been selling herself for money, and we believe that her boyfriend at the time was responsible for that. I figured if I hid her at my house away from him, and help her clean her system, that would be a better solution for her," Dana explained.

There was a moment of silence, but then, "I don't believe you. Jeryca would never do that!" Sheila cried.

"I will give you my address, and you can come see her for yourself, and if you still feel that there is nothing wrong with Jeryca, then you can take her home. Ms. Mebane, Jeryca and Pam are like sisters to me, so I hope you know I wouldn't do anything to hurt either of them," Dana cried.

"Fine, give me your address, and I will be there first thing tomorrow morning," Sheila replied.

Dana gave her the address and hung up. She was starting to second-guess her decision to help Jeryca, because it seemed to be causing her more headaches than she could handle. As she proceeded to get back on the road, she turned her radio up and hummed to the sound of Jill Scott. It soothed her, despite all the drama with Jeryca.

Her relaxation was short-lived as she pulled into her driveway and saw her front door ajar, with smoke spilling out, and a sobbing Stephanie sitting on the porch. Dana jumped out of her car and ran to the house.

"What happened?" she screamed.

"I was cooking some chicken, and Chris called, accusing me of being laid up with another man.

He said that I was a slut, and he never wanted to see me again!" Stephanie cried.

"Where is all the smoke coming from?" Dana asked.

"I got distracted, Dana. The food burned," Stephanie sniffled.

"You let that no-account nigga get to you so bad that you almost burned my fucking house down? That's pathetic," Dana stormed.

"That's all you concerned about? I'm stressing and going through some things, all because I'm here helping you!" Stephanie yelled.

"Helping me? You are here for Jeryca, and if you don't want to be here, then take your trifling ass home. I got this," Dana said angrily.

Dana walked into the house to see if any damage was done to her house, only to find Farrah sitting on the couch, staring at her like she was the devil.

"Dana, why did you just say that to her? That was uncalled for!"

"A lot of things are uncalled for, but I'm going to see if anything is smoke-damaged, and then check on Jeryca. I need to tell you and Stephanie something in a few."

"Whatever," Farrah replied, looking at Dana hard.

Dana stood watching Farrah for a few seconds, shook her head, and proceeded to inspect her house. Once she saw there was no damage, she looked in on Jeryca, who appeared to be sleeping.

"Can you ask Stephanie to come in for a second, please?" Dana asked.

Farrah looked at Dana as if she had spoken a foreign language.

"Steph, come here," Farrah yelled.

Dana started laughing, amused by how her two friends were acting. When Stephanie came in, she sat next to Farrah and dropped her head, still crying.

"Look, I saw Thad at the courthouse, and he told me that he was responsible for Jeryca being out on the streets hooking. He said she was his top ho, and that he was coming for her. He said that she called him earlier today. Now I know this isn't true, especially after I told y'all to monitor her phone calls," Dana said curiously.

"Dana, Jeryca is a grown fucking woman, and she can do whatever it is that she wants. Who are we to tell her who she can call and can't call? I don't even know why we are here going through this! I got my own troubles that I got to deal with, damn it! I'm not going to hold Jeryca's hand like she is a child. She needs professional treatment, not you trying to live her life for her," Farrah raged.

"So it don't matter to either of you that Thad is ruining Jeryca's life?" Dana asked.

"Look, Ms. Goody-Two-Shoes, Jeryca didn't care if he ruined her life, so why should we? My son is my main focus, not Jeryca, so with that being said, I'm leaving. Whatever you and Stephanie decide to do with her is on y'all, but I got more important shit to do with my time!" Farrah shouted.

"I'm leaving too. I can't put my life on hold any longer. I just lost my man due to this, and regardless of what you or anybody else think or feel, he was my heart. Shit, Jeryca can't feel like her life is ruined that much. If you believe what Thad told you about her calling him, then she got to be okay with being a ho!" Stephanie exclaimed.

"You bitches are fucked up. Farrah, I understand that you are worried about Travis, but Brittany told you that she would assist you with keeping custody of him. He is with his father, and will be until Friday, so I figured you wouldn't mind helping me out, but it is what it is. Get the fuck on," Dana whispered in a low growl.

"Bitch, I ain't asked you to talk to Brittany 'bout shit dealing with my case. I don't like that slut anyway. She seems phony, just like you have been acting lately," Farrah said as she stood up and walked up on Dana.

"Bitch, don't walk over here and get your world shook. I ain't the one to try, and you already know that. You don't know shit about Brittany, period. If y'all had more going for yourselves, none of what is going on concerning those fuck-ass niggas would be a problem for either of you. You'd have common sense on how to deal with them and come out on top. I tell you what: get the fuck up out of here, and when you come to your senses, call me and I will show y'all how to win!" Dana snapped.

As Farrah stood in front of Dana, she pointed her finger close to her face. "Shake my world! I've wanted you to try me for days now. You think your life is so perfect, bitch, but I will fuck you up today!"

Just then, Farrah poked Dana in the face with her fingernail, and they started scuffling. Dana punched Farrah in the face, causing her to fall across the coffee table and knocking over her statuettes that she had on there. Stephanie jumped up and grabbed Dana by the hair and pulled her down on the couch.

"Bitch, we are going to teach your ass today!" she said.

Farrah got up and dove on Dana, and she and Stephanie punched and scratched Dana in her face. Once they were finished, they gathered their belongings and walked out, leaving a bleeding Dana sprawled out on the couch.

After a few minutes passed, Dana got up and washed her face and cleaned the scratches. Her lip was busted, and she had a black eye. She walked back into the living room and found Jeryca standing there.

"I heard some of the things you were saying to Farrah and Stephanie, and really, you got some nerve trying to dictate my life."

"Jeryca, listen," Dana started but was cut off.

"No, you listen: I love Thad, and whatever we go through is our business. You acting like you did this to help me; you really did this to try to run me. Well, it's over with!" Jeryca said, looking like a wild woman.

"Jeryca, look at this!" Dana said as she pulled up the picture of Thad hugging on another woman.

After Jeryca looked at the picture, she looked up with hatred in her eyes. "Bitch, you will do anything to get your way! Just stop it, Dana.

Your lonely ass just don't want to see me happy. I'm going back to Thad, and you keep your distance!"

At that point, Dana was tired of trying to help her. Maybe they were right. She had to let them find out on their own about Thad and his crew. She just hoped it wouldn't be a lesson learned too late. She waited until Jeryca left and lay across her bed. She was hurt, not only physically, but also emotionally. All she had done was try to help those girls and be a good friend. She fell asleep for a few hours, but was awakened by her cell phone ringing.

"Hello," she answered weakly.

"Hey, what's up?" Brittany asked. At the sound of the voice of her only friend at the time, Dana began to cry.

"Dana, what's wrong?" Brittany asked. Dana didn't respond, so Brittany asked yet again, "What's wrong, man?" Seeing that Dana was completely gone, Brittany said, "Listen, I'm on my way over."

"It's just that Jeryca and my other so-called friends have totally turned against me. Farrah and Steph jumped on me in my own fucking house. It took the two of them to get me down, though. Then Jeryca stormed out, saying I was trying to run her life. Brit, all I've tried to do was help them, but it's unappreciated," Dana cried into the phone.

"Listen to me, honey. I told you that those girls meant you no good and you needed to leave their asses alone. I'm on my way over, okay?" Brittany announced.

"No, you got to go to work in the morning. I'm okay, really," Dana protested.

"I'm on the way," Brit said firmly before hanging up.

Thad and his crew had been at the Oasis strip club for over an hour. They had discussed the matter and decided to handle the Orlando situation next Saturday night. They were going to meet him and his boys on the north side of New York, where Orlando's tattoo shop was located. They wanted him to feel comfortable and safe enough to agree to meeting with them. They were going to send two of their new recruits to the shop to get tattooed up, and while they were there, they were going to familiarize themselves with the shop's layout and take pictures. They were also going to shadow Orlando and get a feel for his day-to-day routine. The day of the meeting, they were going to be well-prepared for whatever.

As Chris placed the call to Orlando, updating him on the new meeting arrangements, Thad was sitting back smoking a King of Denmark cigar that he had gotten personalized with his name on it. He had paid $4,000 apiece for his cigars. As he smoked it, he was getting a lap dance from a beautiful chocolate sister with a fat ass. He watched as she bounced her ass up and down on his lap. He was enjoying every second of it. As the dancer known as Juicy finished giving Thad his dance, he motioned for her to bend down.

"You want to make some extra money?"

Juicy nodded, knowing what she had to do. Thad stood up and told Toby he would be right back. He walked toward the back room where private dances were allowed. Before they reached the room, he bumped into Larry, who was talking to Steve, one of their new recruits.

"Juicy, go ahead to the room. I will pay the bill when I get there." Juicy did as she was told, and walked on to the back while Thad spoke with Larry.

"Aye, what's going on with you and Farrah?"

"Man, that bitch tripping. I told her I was going to seek custody of Travis if she didn't straighten her ass up," Larry explained.

"Man, I think you should go through with it. Those hoes think everything is a game. We got to show them it's not. Li'l man would be much better with you, anyway. Think about it, bro," Thad said as he patted him on the shoulder and proceeded to the back.

Once Thad paid the doorman, he received a ticket for room three, where Juicy was waiting for him.

"Shit, let's get it, sweetie."

Juicy looked at him and started swaying her hips, but Thad shook his head.

"Naw, baby, you know I ain't talking about dancing. Bring that ass over here and sit on this dick, but wait one second." Thad pulled out a magnum and told Juicy to put the condom on his dick with her mouth.

Juicy did as she was instructed, and once the condom was on, she straddled Thad and rode him for a second or two before he told her to turn around. He stood up with his pants around his ankles and fucked her from the back until he came. After he cleaned himself up and fixed his clothing, he gave her a tip and walked back out to where Toby was sitting.

"Man, that wasn't thrilling at all. She could make us some money on the street, but man, that pussy was dry as hell. All that ass and jiggling she was doing, and she was a lazy-ass fuck." Thad started laughing as Toby shook his head.

"Man, you will fuck anything!" Toby said.

Thad laughed. "I got to test the pussy out before I put it out there, man!"

"Your dick gonna fall off one day, nigga," Toby said, shaking his head.

"Some of these hoes been checking you out too, bro. You need to get you a li'l head or something, man," Thad joked.

"I'm good. I ain't hard up for no pussy, dog. I got some at home I can get. If I wanted something strange, you already know who I'd fuck," Toby said, smiling at the thought of Dana.

"You know Keith got his sights on her, man." Thad laughed.

Toby looked at Thad sideways. "Keith ain't ready for a chick like her. She needs a man that will take control of her ass."

"Dana doesn't want a thug, street nigga. She don't do guys of our breed," Thad continued.

"Shit, she would be happy to have a man of my caliber and breed approach her," Toby replied with confidence.

"Damn, you sure do sound full of yourself, bro," Thad laughed.

"No, sir, I'm not full of myself, just sure of myself." Toby purred jokingly.

Toby was a nice-looking man. He was six foot three and two hundred forty pounds, all of which was muscle. He had long dreads past his shoulders, his abs were toned and cut, and he was light-brown-skinned with gray eyes. He was a ladies' man for sure, but he only desired women with intelligence and class.

Thad shook his head and gave Toby a pound. "My nigga." Just then, Thad's phone began to ring, and when he looked at it, he didn't recognize the number.

"Hello?"

"Hey, baby, it's Jeryca. Are you busy?"

"I'm kinda in the middle of something. Why, what's up?" he asked.

"I need you to come and get me, please," Jeryca begged.

Thad looked at Toby, who was checking another model out.

"Aye, man, this is Jeryca. I'ma go get her and see what's up. I will get at y'all later," Thad announced.

Toby shook his head again and looked Thad in the eye. "You got to let that trick go."

Thad didn't say a word; he just got up and walked out of the club. He knew what Toby was saying was true, but he couldn't let go just yet. He had a point to make and some money to get back from Jeryca, one way or another.

Chapter Seven

Jeryca stood at the corner of Brooklyn Avenue and St. Marks Avenue, where the museum was located, and she thought about the things that Dana had said to her. She was angry at the thought of Thad being publicly hugged up with that woman, and she wanted to know who she was. After all she had done for Thad, she thought that he at least owed her an explanation, but she had to confront him at the right time in the right manner.

After staying with Dana for the amount of time that she did, she had gotten the chance to get her bearings together a little more than they had been. She couldn't believe that she had been tricked into selling herself and vowed to never do it again. Thad had said that he loved her, and now was the time to prove it.

After about twenty minutes of waiting, she saw Thad's truck rounding the corner. When Jeryca saw him, a feeling that she had never felt before toward Thad washed over her: pure sickness. She walked slowly to his truck and got in.

"Hey, baby, how are you?"

"Jeryca, where are you going?" Thad asked, emotionless.

"With you, baby, of course. I missed you," she answered.

"I don't have time for your games. You caused me a lot of despair when you left. Do you know that we lost money because you couldn't control your habit?" he asked, looking at her sideways. Thad knew he was the cause of her breakdown on heroin, but he refused to let her know that. He was going to make her bear the burden all on her own. His plan was to belittle her and play on her emotions until she broke, and force her to trick for him willingly.

"How am I responsible for that?" Jeryca asked quickly.

"You lost control, Jeryca. You allowed your so-called friends to take you away, and that bitch Dana cracked on me, and when I turned down her advance, the bitch pulled a gun out on me. These are the type of friends you keep around you. I can't trust you, Jeryca," Thad said softly.

The tone of voice he used hit Jeryca near the heart, and even though she knew he was lying, she gave in to his charm once again.

"Baby, I won't talk to any of them again. Just take me with you," she begged.

Thad looked at her for a long moment and agreed to take her. He pulled off and took Jeryca back to his trap spot. Once they arrived, he held her hand as they walked through the door. "Home sweet home," he said, smiling.

Dana had sat up well past midnight talking with Brittany. Brittany helped her face a lot of truths that she hadn't paid attention to before, and although those she thought were her true friends had mistreated her, she would still be there for them if they needed her. Dana called out of work to get herself together. Her face was bruised and swollen. Her body ached along with her pride and heart. After she cooked breakfast and groomed, she lay back on her bed, grabbed her *People* magazine, and flipped through the pages.

A few pages in, she heard a loud knock at the door.

"Fuck, who the hell is that?" she whispered. As she tiptoed to the hallway, she wasn't quite sure if she should answer. No one knew that she was off work but her employers and Brittany.

"Who is it?" she yelled.

"It's Sheila Mebane! I'm looking for Dana Crisp."

Damn, I forgot she was coming.

"Hold on, give me a second!" Dana yelled as she searched her room for her jeans. After getting dressed, she opened the door to find Sheila and Pam standing and talking.

"Hi, come in," Dana said.

The duo walked in and looked around, impressed by Dana's apartment.

"What happened to your face?" Pam asked.

"I got into an altercation last night," Dana answered.

Sheila looked at Dana through squinted eyes. "With who?"

"It's not important," Dana replied.

"Where is Jeryca?" Sheila asked as she walked around the apartment.

"She left last night. She wouldn't listen to reason when I asked her to stay. I can't help someone who doesn't want my help," Dana explained.

Sheila stood in the middle of the room, staring at Dana, then spoke in a low tone through gritted teeth. "Was she even here? Did she do that to your face? What the fuck is going on?"

"I told you what happened, and if you choose to not believe me, cool. Get the fuck out my house!" Dana said.

"I know you're not speaking to my mother like that!" Pam shouted as she walked up in Dana face.

"Sheila, you need to get your daughter and leave before shit gets out of hand."

"It's already out of hand!" Sheila said, and at that moment, Pam slapped Dana in the face. Before Dana realized it, she slapped Pam back and sent her sprawling to the floor.

"Man, get the hell out my house right now," Dana yelled. Pam rolled over and got up to her feet. She walked to the door with her mother behind her.

"You will be getting a visit from the police, 'cause I know you got something to do with Jeryca's disappearance."

"Send them! Just brace yourself for the moment when you learn that your junkie-ass daughter is where she wants to be: with a no-count nigga 'cause she want to get away from you," Dana informed her angrily.

"That's a damn lie. You should be ashamed of yourself for saying that bullshit!" Sheila cried.

Tired of the whole topic, Dana spoke. "Just get out!"

The two of them walked out, but not before Sheila told Dana again that they were calling the cops. Dana shut the door and leaned back against it.

"Man, it's too early in the morning for this shit!"

Larry took Travis out to McDonald's for breakfast. He wanted some one-on-one time with his son.

"You been having fun this week?" he asked Travis.

"Uh huh! But I miss Mommy," Travis answered.

"I know you do, son, but how would you feel living with me and visiting your mom here and there?" he continued to question.

"I don't know, Daddy," Travis said sadly.

Larry changed the subject when he realized that Travis wasn't happy with the questions he was asking.

"What do you want to do today?" he asked Travis.

"Can we go to the park and ride the rides?" Travis asked, perking up once again.

"We can do whatever you want, son, but Daddy has a quick stop to make before we go, so eat up. I'll be right back, okay? I'm not going far. I'll be over there by that window, okay?" Larry said as he pulled a small piece of paper out of his pocket.

"Okay, Daddy," Travis replied.

Larry dialed the number on the paper as he walked toward the window. "Hello, may I speak with Debra Fuller, please?"

"May I ask who's calling?" the lady on the other end asked.

Larry didn't respond immediately. He was trapped in thought about Farrah. He actually cared for her, but he couldn't let the guys know that a ghetto chick had stolen his heart. They clowned him enough about her, and he had gained his respect by being heartless and ruthless.

"Hello, sir? Are you there?" the woman spoke again.

"Uh, yes, I'm Larry Bigelow," he answered.

"One moment, please," she said as she placed him on hold.

Larry decided to do as Thad had suggested. He was going to go for custody of Travis. He wouldn't let his feelings for Farrah distract his mission in life, which was being respected in the dope boy lifestyle. He wasn't soft and wasn't going to lie down now.

***

Jeryca and Thad hung out most of the day. It was Tuesday, and Thad didn't have any plans. He had to try to figure out a way to gain a little of Jeryca's trust back. Since he had picked her up, she seemed stronger mentally and wasn't being manipulated by his accusations of losing money because of her. He didn't know what it was about her that had him fucked up. He felt she owed him, and he wasn't going to be satisfied until he got every ounce of her dignity.

Jeryca, on the other hand, was determined to make Thad give her what she wanted and treat her how she deserved to be treated. Yeah, she had been fucked up for a moment, but now she was in control, and Thad was going to treat her like a queen.

"Thad, can you please get me a bottle of water?" she asked seductively.

"Yeah, I can do that," he said.

"Unopened, if you don't mind," she stated, letting him know she didn't trust him.

Thad started to tell her to get her ass out of his fucking house. She had called him to pick her up, and he wasn't going to continue to take her attitude. The look he gave her let her know that she was going too far.

"If you don't trust me, Jeryca, why be here?" he asked solemnly.

"I-I didn't mean anything by it," Jeryca stammered.

"I hope not, 'cause I can take you back where I picked you up at," he snorted.

Jeryca didn't say a word. She dropped her head and lay back on the bed. Thad walked out of the room and got her the water, and ran into Toby and Chris on his way back to the room.

"You really bought her back here?" Toby asked.

"Yeah, where else was I going to take her?" Thad whispered as he ushered the two into the office from the hall.

"Man, you know you are crazy, don't you? She is going to bring real heat down on us. I feel it," Toby murmured.

"I got this under control. Damn. Trust me, okay?" Thad replied.

"Wasn't it you who told me and Larry to get rid of our problems. But you're holding on to yours, man," Chris said.

"Look," Thad started, "this is different."

"How so?" Chris asked.

"I ain't got time to explain, but I know what I'm doing. Now excuse me," Thad said as he walked out of the room and back to where Jeryca was.

"I see trouble brewing," Toby whispered to Chris.

"Yeah, me too," Chris said, shaking his head.

Wednesday morning, Dana walked into work feeling lost and confused. She was tired and hurting, but she couldn't let that stop her. After she got to her desk, one of her bosses, John Dresher, walked in.

"Dana, I need you to pull up the Galveston case file and do some research on two separate case laws. I need two good ones where the case law will show that, without a doubt, our client should get every bit of the five hundred thousand dollars we are suing for."

"Okay, I'm on it, Mr. Dresher," Dana replied.

At that moment, Mr. Dresher looked at Dana and asked, "What's wrong? Look up at me please, Ms. Crisp."

Dana looked up slowly, trying to tilt her head at an angle, hoping he would miss the dark black-and-blue circle around her eye.

"I'm okay, sir! I will get right to it," she answered quickly.

"You aren't all right, Dana. What's wrong with your face?" he asked as he advanced on her to get a closer look.

"Well, sir, it's kind of a long story, and I just really don't want to get into it right now. I mean no disrespect at all, sir, and I do appreciate your concern," she said with a weak smile that also reflected a busted lip.

"I'll let it slide, but you know if you need to talk, you can come to my office," he said.

"Thank you, sir. I'll remember that," Dana replied as she stood to go to the cabinet to pull the case file.

After John left, Dana threw herself into her work until lunchtime. When she shut down her computer, she walked out of the office to grab a bite of lunch. When she walked into the lobby area, she noticed the three main partners looking at her strangely.

"Damn, Mr. Dresher can't hold water," she whispered to herself.

Dana went to Luigi's, an Italian restaurant that was within walking distance of her job. She needed the exercise and the fresh air to clear her mind. She thought about everything that had occurred over the last few days and still couldn't understand why or how things went so haywire. Dana was seated for about ten minutes when her cell began to ring.

"What's up, Brit?" Dana ate and talked to Brittany through her entire break. She had proven to be a great friend.

An hour later, Dana walked back into the office and was greeted by two police officers.

"Dana Crisp?" The first officer asked.

"Yes, I'm Dana," she answered, looking around, embarrassed by the scene that was taking place.

"I'm Detective Rone, and this is my partner, Detective Harris, and we need to talk with you about one Ms. Jeryca Mebane. We were told that you had information on her disappearance."

"Follow me into my office, please," she replied.

As they walked to the office, Dana noticed the disapproving stares she was getting, and she understood why. This should never have taken place at her job.

Once they were inside, Dana sat down and started without offering either man a seat. "Listen, I don't appreciate you coming here to my job, and like I told Ms. Mebane, Thad Royster is who you all need to be talking to. Jeryca made the decision to go back to that drug-dealing loser, not me. Now please leave!"

"Ma'am, we do apologize for showing up here, but we were told that you wouldn't be returning to your residence, and we'd be able to get you here," Detective Rone explained.

"Is that right? Well, I've answered all your questions, so again, I ask that you kindly leave, sir," Dana retorted.

"Have a good day, ma'am," both detectives said before leaving the office.

"What a fucking week!" Dana said as she rubbed her forehead.

Dana finished her day without any other distractions. After she clocked out for the day, she headed home to again try to get some under-standing of her week.

Thad was heading out of the house early Thursday morning to go meet with Toby and Chris. He was going to drop Jeryca off at the hair salon while he handled his business. As he walked to his truck, a black car swooped up behind it, blocking him in. He immediately grabbed at his side for his gun, but as the two men who were in the car got out, they were holding badges.

"Mr. Thad Royster?" one of the men asked.

"Yes, I'm Mr. Royster, and who are you?" Thad asked, frowning.

"I'm Detective Rone, and this is my partner, Detective Harris. We are looking for a Jeryca Mebane. A Dana Crisp told us that you may know something about her disappearance," he explained.

"Is that right?" Thad asked.

"Yes, sir, anything that you can tell us will be greatly appreciated." As the officer was talking, he was looking around and inspecting Thad's house and vehicle, which didn't go unnoticed by Thad.

"Well, you can ask Jeryca where she been yourself. She will be out here in a few seconds," Thad replied.

"Oh, really? Well, that would be great. We can close this case and move on if she is here," Detective Rone said.

While they waited, Detective Harris asked, "What do you do for a living? With this nice truck and lovely home here, you got to be making big bucks."

Thad didn't respond right away. He knew that they were prying, and Dana was probably the cause of it. Thad was going to nip that in the bud as soon as he possibly could.

"Well, I own a saucing company. We make barbecue sauce, hot wing sauce, chili, and seasonings."

"Sounds interesting," Detective Harris replied. Before he could inquire further, Jeryca walked out of the house toward the three men.

"Ms. Jeryca Mebane?" Detective Rone asked.

"Yes, I'm Jeryca," she answered.

"May we have a word with you, please? Just step over here, behind the car," he instructed as he pointed to the back of their car.

"Yes, what do you want?" Jeryca asked, but not before she glanced at Thad, causing Detective Harris to also look over at him.

"Is there something wrong, Ms. Mebane? Would you like to go somewhere else?" he asked her as he looked back at her.

"Oh, no, I'm good. Again, what do you want?" she asked.

"Well, your mother reported you missing, and we were placed on the case," Detective Pone replied.

"Well, as you can see, I'm perfectly fine," she stated.

"Yes we can see that, but do you have any identification?" Detective Harris asked.

As Jeryca pulled her ID out and presented it to the detectives, Thad walked over to his truck and got in. He sat in the driver's seat, angry at the fact that Dana had just messed up his and Toby's plans, 'cause he was sure he would be seeing those detectives again.

After Jeryca finished talking to the detectives, they called her mother to inform her that they had found Jeryca, and that she was fine. She asked to speak to Jeryca, but Jeryca declined.

She got into the truck with Thad and waited for the detectives to pull off so they could leave.

"Jeryca, I can't believe that bitch sent twelve to my crib. That ho knows what the fuck I do. Y'all some trifling heffas, I swear!" he yelled as he dialed Toby's number.

Jeryca looked over at him, frowning. Why the fuck was he yelling at her, and who the fuck was he calling a heffa?

"Aye, man, listen: call Chris and tell him to call Orlando and tell him we might have to reschedule the pickup for the guns and weed 'cause Dana done sent the fucking police to my house looking for this bitch," Thad yelled into the phone. As he continued to explain to Toby what happened, Jeryca listened very intently to what was being said as she looked out the window. She wasn't going to let Thad run her off until she got a cut from the plan she had just learned that he was putting together. As they pulled up to Min's Hair Salon, Jeryca waited as Thad pulled out a hundred dollar bill from his wallet.

"Brenda will pick you up and take you back to the house when you're finished," he said, not looking at her. Jeryca was about to get out of the truck when Thad's cell phone rang, and a familiar picture of a female popped up on his phone. After she got out, she walked slowly into the salon.

"What the fuck was Stephanie calling Thad for, and why did he hide it from me, and where did he get that picture of her from?" she wondered aloud.

Chapter Eight

Jeryca couldn't get over the thought of Stephanie calling Thad and Thad hiding it from her. How did she get his number anyway? If it were innocent, Thad would've talked to Stephanie in front of her. Jeryca had gotten her hair done in an up-style bob, which took only an hour to finish. After she called Brenda, she sat outside on a bench and watched a handsome man get out of a red Dodge Challenger.

As he walked past her, his eyes lingered on her a few seconds longer than usual, which told Jeryca that he was interested. She gave him one of her most dazzling smiles and said hello. He stopped, complimented her hair, and they talked for a few moments. Jeryca got his phone number and planned on calling him. As soon as he walked into Kinfolk clothing store, Brenda pulled up seconds later. They drove toward the house, and Jeryca was once again wondering what was going on between Thad and Stephanie.

"Brenda, have you seen Thad with any other women while I was gone?"

Brenda liked Jeryca and wanted to tell her the truth, but she knew who paid her salary. "No, I haven't, but you know I don't sit around here too often. Why you ask, sissy?" she replied.

"I've just been hearing shit from different people. Girl, I know he playing me, but I'm going to win when all this is said and done," Jeryca muttered. Brenda looked over at Jeryca and saw a determined woman sitting next to her. She was certain that Thad had a problem brewing on his hands.

Larry got the call from Chris that their meeting with Orlando might have to be rescheduled, and he was okay with that. He got Travis dressed and called Keith to see if he wanted to ride with him. Keith was his number one partner, and they hadn't really hung out much lately. When he pulled up to Keith's apartment, he was already outside waiting.

"Trav, my man!" Keith said as he got in the car, giving Travis a small pound.

"Hey, Uncle Keith," Travis said excitedly.

"Where your father taking us early this morning?" Keith asked.

"I don't know, Uncle Kevin. He won't tell me."

"Well, I guess we 'bout to see, li'l man." Keith laughed.

They drove about ten minutes and then pulled into a large parking lot. Keith frowned and looked at Larry when he realized where they were.

"Dude, are you really going to see an attorney?" he asked.

"What's an attorney?" Travis asked.

"Uh, it's nothing for you to ask about, son," Larry said, giving Keith a wicked side eye. As they got out of the car, Larry looked at a still frowning Keith.

"Man, I will explain everything later."

"I just hope you don't regret what you doing," Keith whispered.

"I'm just going to talk to them, man," Larry explained.

"I hear you!" Keith sighed, shaking his head. They walked into the building and a tall, older woman approached them.

"May I help you, gentlemen?"

Larry walked forward. "Yes, I'm here to see Debra Fuller."

"And do you have an appointment, sir?" she asked.

"Yes, ma'am, I do. My name is Larry Bigelow."

As the woman picked up the phone on her desk to let Debra know her eleven o'clock appointment was there, Larry's cell phone began to ring.

"Oh my God. It's damn Farrah. She would call at this fucking time," he muttered to Keith.

"Hello," he whispered into the phone.

"Hey, Larry, can I speak to my li'l man, please?" Farrah asked.

"I'm kind of in the middle of something and he isn't—" he started, about to tell her that Travis wasn't with him, but before he could say anything, Travis ran up to him.

"Daddy! Daddy! Uncle Keith said that Mommy is on the phone. Can I talk to her?"

Larry looked at Keith with a serious frown, but he gave in to his son's request.

"Here, talk to her while I'm handling my business."

"Hey, Mommy!" Travis said as he walked to the chair next to Keith.

"Hey, baby, how are you doing? Mommy miss you," she said quietly.

A crease formed in Travis's forehead, which didn't go unnoticed by Keith.

"Mommy, why you sound so sad?" he asked her.

"No reason really, baby. I just miss you. Are you having a good time with your father?" she asked.

"Yes, we been so many places, Mommy. We at a torneys office now," he replied.

"You're where?" Farrah asked to make sure she understood him.

"At a torneys office," he repeated.

"I thought that was what you said. Where is your father now?" she asked.

"He is in the office with the lady, Mommy," he answered.

"Tell him to call me when he comes out. Okay, baby?"

"Okay, Mommy," he replied.

"I love you, son," Farrah said.

"I love you too."

Farrah slammed the phone down after talking with Travis. Was Larry really going to seek custody? She didn't have any money to get an attorney, and the one person that had offered to help her was the same person that she and Stephanie had jumped on and really shitted on. Farrah didn't know what she was going to do, but she wasn't going to lose her son, and she wasn't going to wait on Larry to tell her he was seeking custody. She needed time to figure shit out, and she knew in her heart that she didn't have long to work it out.

Larry couldn't keep his eyes off Debra. She was intelligent, beautiful, and employed. When he walked into her office, he couldn't help but watch her hips sway from side to side. His ears tingled when she spoke. He, in fact, told her she had an angelic voice. She smiled, but she continued with business. He took in her beauty as she read her disclosure to him. As she attempted to hand Larry some forms that he needed to sign, she caught him staring at her, smiling.

"Mr. Bigelow, is something wrong? Are you having second thoughts?"

Larry started to make a bogus excuse, but decided to tell her the truth. "Honestly, Ms. Lady, I'm just admiring your beauty. Are you single and would you ever consider dating a client?"

"No, I wouldn't. I'm all about business, and to answer your other question, yes, I am very much single," she said, smiling. "Now, I must tell you, once we sign these papers, I go hard for a win, so if you have any feelings left for Farrah Walker, you may want to think about this move you're making."

"I'm ready. My son is my main concern," Larry said, giving his approval to continue.

"I'll be right back. Let me go speak with my partner," Debra said.

As she got up and walked away, Larry's eyes followed her and landed on her ass. He had to give her props; she was fine. When she returned, she was accompanied by another woman.

"This is my partner, Brittany Howell. She will be helping me with building your case."

"Damn, you're fine as well. I love to see sexy black women thrive in business. It's not often that I get a chance to blend my energy with sistas like you who are smart and successful. I mean, after this bit of business, I would love to see if we can do some sort of business together. I'm sure my guys would be very interested," he said.

"Well, we are good at the moment, Mr. Bigelow. Let me take a look at your file so we can get this case started," Brittany said as she picked up his paperwork. As she flipped through it, several names popped up at her. She placed the file back on the desk and asked, "Okay, have you two discussed payment?"

"Yes, we have, Ms. Howell," Debra answered.

"Okay, well, I look forward to working with you. Debra, when you are finished here, I'd like a word with you. Take care, Mr. Bigelow." Brittany walked out of Debra's office and into her own. She sat back and smiled at the irony of the whole situation. She couldn't wait to talk to Dana.

Dana had been at work a little over four hours, and at about twelve o'clock, the head attorney, Mr. Gregson, came to her office.

"Dana, we need to have a word with you."

"Yes, sir. May I ask what it's concerning?" she asked.

"Well, as you know, we pride ourselves on being professional at all times, and there have been a few things that have been brought to our attention. We received a few calls yesterday that weren't too favorable toward you, and then we had those two detectives show up to question you. Now, we don't know what's going on, but we cannot tolerate such things, so we have decided to let you go. You can work until the end of this pay period if you want to," he informed her.

Dana wondered who had been calling, but quickly realized there were only a few people who could've called.

"It's on!" she cried after he left her office. She sat stone-faced for a few minutes, but then she started laughing uncontrollably.

"Them bitches done got me fucked up. I just lost my job behind some hoes that's sour 'cause they life jacked up."

Dana decided to call Brittany. "Brit, I just got fired! Can you believe that shit?"

"What? Why did they let you go?" Brittany asked.

"They said they had gotten phone calls, and then those detectives came. It was too much for the partners," Dana explained.

"Wow, are you serious? Dana, listen, I can find a spot for you here if you want me to. I need help with a few cases, one I think you will be very interested in."

"Are you serious? When could I start?" Dana asked.

"Shit, girl, you can start tomorrow if you want," Brittany replied.

"Well, they told me I could stay until the end of my pay period," Dana whispered as she noticed a few of the big wigs walking past her office.

"Listen, get out now. Meet me after work and we will go over the hiring process," Brittany replied.

As the two ladies discussed where they were going to meet, Dana had started packing up her personal belongings. She decided that she needed to take Brittany's advice and make it her last day. As quitting time approached, Dana walked out of her office with her belongings in a box, and a smile spread across her face. She informed her formal employers that she wouldn't be returning.

When she reached her car, she let out a sigh of relief. She was so glad that she had Brittany to help her. She was a real friend.

As she headed down Morgan Street, she noticed that she was being followed. She knew the car but couldn't remember how. As the car got closer, she saw Thad on the passenger side and Toby driving. Thad smirked at her and pointed his finger at her as if it were a gun, and acted as if he had pulled the trigger. No cars were around, and Dana became instantly frightened. Toby swerved his car in her lane, causing her to run off the road. As she moved back into her lane, she sped up, but they were quickly on her tail. Toby rammed her from the back, causing her to lose control of her car once again, and she had to brake fast. Once she did, a car rolled past her slowly. Dana jumped out of her car and ran into the path of the approaching car, flagging them down.

As the car stopped, Toby and Thad sped off. Dana's heart was beating hard and fast. A man and woman stopped to assist her. She didn't tell them what had happened, but she did ask if they could follow her to her destination. She offered to pay them if they could. They agreed, but refused the money.

Once Dana made it to Sharkey's Bar & Grill, she waved the couple off and ran inside. She didn't know what to do, but she knew she wasn't going to let any of them win.

She was going to wait for Brittany to arrive and get some real advice from a real friend. She was glad that this was her last day at the firm. Thad and Toby had to have been waiting on her to leave in order for them to have been around to attack her. She sat down at a table where she could see everything around the parking lot.

An hour later, when she saw Brittany's car pull up, she relaxed. When Brittany walked through the door, she spotted Dana immediately, and as she walked toward the table, the smile she had on her face changed.

"What's wrong, li'l sis?"

Dana told her about how Toby and Thad had followed her and damn near made her crash. She told her that if that nice couple hadn't stopped, she didn't know what Thad and Toby would've done.

"You know what, Dana? That's it! I'm sick of hearing about those motherfuckers. You need to move on and just stop dealing with them bitches and niggas. It's getting too serious, and you don't deserve this bullshit. I mean it too. Stay away from them," Brittany growled.

"But how do I do that when they are bothering me?" Dana asked.

"I'm going to tell you how," Brittany said.

As the two women talked and ate dinner, Dana gained insight into Brittany's day, and was glad that she had chosen to join her team. She was going to use the information she had just received to her advantage somehow. Dana felt some comfort in the fact that it appeared that she had found a real friend in Brittany, yet she also felt angered at how her so-called best friends and their sidekicks had been treating her.

Toby and Thad walked into the trap house where Jeryca was at, rambling through his office. She was determined to find out what Thad had been up to. Since he didn't want to tell her the truth about shit, she was going to find out on her own. She smiled as she flipped through his notebook. She tore out a single page full of numbers on it and placed it in her pocket. She continued snooping, and about five minutes later, Jeryca stood and found herself face-to-face with Thad.

"What are you doing in here?" he asked as he advanced on her.

"Nothing, Thad. I was just looking for a book," she lied.

"Bitch, I don't believe you and either you— never mind that. I'ma show yo' ass that you don't steal from me." As he talked, he grabbed Jeryca by the throat and tossed her back against the wall. As she slid to the floor, he kicked her in the stomach repeatedly, causing her to grunt with each blow. He grabbed her by the legs and pulled her to the middle of the floor, kneeled down, and grasped her cheeks roughly.

"You were going to try to steal from me?"- Jeryca shook her head no, but Thad didn't pay her any mind. He pulled her up by her hair and head-butted her. She screamed and begged him to believe her.

"Bitch, you ain't shit! You're a nasty whore, and I'd never make you my lady. I got a real lady, and I can't believe I wasted my time with your ho ass!" he yelled as he slapped her in the face, splitting her bottom lip.

Jeryca fell down. Thad kicked her in the back and walked out of the room, and told Brenda to tend to her.

Thad and Toby left as Chris pulled up. They didn't get the opportunity to explain what had just happened, so when Chris walked in, he was thrown by the sight he saw. Brenda was crying as she wiped the blood from Jeryca's mouth. Chris ran forward and asked what had happened. Brenda explained the situation, and Chris helped Jeryca up as she begged him to take her away. Chris felt sorry for her and did as she asked. He helped her into the car, and she was very much bruised and bleeding.

As they pulled off, Jeryca sat up a little bit and reached over to him, and as he looked over at her, the look in her eyes told him she wasn't ready to go home. He pulled over and parked at an empty condemned apartment building close to her house. They sat silently in the car, and Jeryca began to rub Chris's thighs. He rested his head back against the headrest. He hadn't fucked anyone in weeks. He knew that Thad wouldn't give a damn if he fucked Jeryca, and he was going to do just that. Chris pulled his pants down to his knees and Jeryca began to massage his dick.

"Damn, Chris, you got a monster dick. I see why Steph was in love. Shit."

"Man, just shut up and put it in your mouth," Chris moaned.

Jeryca licked the pre cum off his dick head and then slipped his whole dick into her mouth.

Chris guided her head up and down. Although her mouth was hurting, she enjoyed what she was doing. She moved faster and faster, and he pulled back before he came. He took a condom out of his glove compartment and put it on.

"Come on and sit on this dick."

Jeryca climbed over and rode him until he and she came. She was breathing hard, and he was too. After they put their clothes on, Chris pulled off only to come to a quick halt, realizing that his tires were flat. Upon inspecting them, he saw that his tires had been slit. He didn't know when it could've happened or who would've done it, but if he found out, someone was going to pay.

Stephanie couldn't believe what she had just seen. She had walked close enough to Chris's car to positively identify Jeryca as the bitch who was there. They were so engrossed in each other that they didn't even see her approach the car. Chris was a sorry-ass nigga, and Jeryca was a trifling-ass bitch who wasn't worth the spit she coughed up. Fuck both of them. She couldn't believe the two of them. If she had a gun at that moment, she would've killed both of them on the spot.

Stephanie was livid and needed to vent, but she knew Farrah was going through her own problems, plus she would probably find a way to side with Jeryca. Hell, there was only one person she could think of to call, and she probably didn't want to talk to her. Stephanie decided to call her anyway and see if she could come over.

Chapter Nine

Dana awoke with a new outlook on life. She had several missed calls from Jeryca and Stephanie, but she wasn't the least bit interested in what they wanted. Just as she got up to take a shower, her phone buzzed. She looked at it and it was Jeryca calling again. Dana sighed and walked into the bathroom. She was going to go look at a house on her lunch break. She had to relocate immediately.

After she took her shower, got dressed, and fixed a cup of orange juice, she heard a faint knock at her door. When she opened it, a bruised and beaten Jeryca stood there.

"I know you are mad, but I need you, Dana. Please don't make me leave," Jeryca cried. Dana shook her head no, but after a few seconds, she let Jeryca in.

"He jumped on me, Dana," Jeryca blurted out and began to cry. Dana wanted to reach out to her, but Jeryca had burned her, and she wasn't going to get burned again.

"Who jumped on you, and why did they do it?" Dana asked.

"Thad jumped on me! I thought he was going to kill me," she yelled.

Dana dropped her head. "Why did he do it, Jeryca?"

"He said I was trying to steal from him. After he did what he did to me, Chris came in and took me to my mother's," Jeryca explained.

"Why would he think that you were trying to steal from him?"

"Well, after I saw the pictures of him with that woman, and then I saw Stephanie of all people calling him—"she started before Dana jumped in.

"Wait, how you know Steph was calling Thad?"

"Because her picture popped up. How would Thad get a picture of her, and how do they got each other's phone number? It doesn't add up to me," Jeryca said with tears in her eyes.

"Damn. Well, maybe it wasn't what you thought it was, but I got to go to work. If you want to chill here 'til I get off, you can, but I'm not trying to have your momma call the cops on me again," Dana replied.

"She knows where I am, and it's not going to be a problem at all. I just need to get my head together," she responded.

"All right, well, I will see you later on," Dana said as she grabbed her purse and keys.

"Thanks, girl," Jeryca said as she got up and hugged Dana.

Dana left and decided to see what Stephanie wanted. She dialed her number.

"Hey, Dana. Listen, I need to talk with you. First, I'm sorry for how things played out the other day between all of us. I know it's no excuse, but I was in a bad place. Dealing with Chris and trying to help with Jeryca was too much for me," Stephanie started off top.

"You're right, there is no excuse! Then I know y'all called my job and got me fired. That was some real bullshit, but it's cool, 'cause that didn't break me," Dana yelled.

Stephanie started crying. "You are right, Dana, but I really need a friend to talk to. I saw Jeryca and Chris yesterday, and they were having sex in the car!"

"What?" Dana said as she slammed on the brakes, causing a few cars behind her to do the same. As she pulled over to the side, a few cars sped past her, blowing their horns, and a few dirty gestures were thrown her way.

"Tell me you are lying. Stephanie, I got to get to work, but meet me at my house around six thirty this evening."

"Okay, I will. Thanks, Dana, and again, I'm sorry for being an ass to you."

"I hear you, but I got to go, okay," Dana said and hung up.

When she got to work, Brittany was waiting on her.

"Dana, come on into my office and let's sign some papers," Brittany said. After they signed all the documents, Dana was officially an employee of Holmes, Howell, and Fuller law firm.

"Come and take a look at this custody case against Ms. Farrah Walker," Brittany said with an evil smirk on her face.

"I'm ready," Dana replied. As they walked into the second office, Dana was introduced to Debra Fuller.

"Hey, this is our new legal secretary, Dana Crisp. She will be assisting us with our caseloads. She is very good at what she does," Brittany explained.

"Nice to have you join us. We needed another diva on our team," Debra replied.

"I'm happy to be a part of it. So what do you need for me to do for you?" Dana asked.

"Oh, shit, our new diva is ready, huh? Shit, let's get down to it." Debra laughed.

As they handed Dana Larry Bigelow's file, Brittany gave her a funny look. "Here you go, Dana."

Dana knew why she looked at her like she had, but she wasn't sure what she wanted to do with it.

Dana worked nonstop until lunch. Around 12:20 p.m., her cell phone rang, and to her surprise, it was Farrah.

"What the fuck is really going on? Why are they all calling me? I know it's a setup, but I'ma be ready for they ass this time. They want to play. Well, game on!" she whispered to herself. She didn't call Farrah back until it was close to the time for her to return to work.

"Yeah, you called me?" she asked as Farrah answered. Dana could tell that Farrah had been crying. Her voice was raspy and dry.

"Dana, I need you. I know we've been through a lot, but Larry has been talking to an attorney. Please, Travis is my life, and if I lose him, I have nothing. Please help me!"

Dana was shocked. How did Farrah know so quick that Larry had started the custody process? She knew Debra hadn't said anything, because the case wasn't even drawn up. Dana decided not to say a word to Farrah about the case.

"How do you know he has done that?"

"Travis told me yesterday that they were at an attorney's office, and Larry told me that he was going to do it. Travis is supposed to come home tomorrow. I need to talk to you," Farrah pleaded.

"Okay, Farrah, listen, call me later and I will see what I can do to help."

"Okay, thanks a lot."

Dana walked into the office and went straight to Brittany's office. She told her about her day's events and asked her what she thought.

"Girl, you know what I told you; I think that they are all snakes and you should keep your distance, but then again," Brittany said as she leaned forward, "keep them bitches close and find out what their motives are. Just stay aware of their sneaky asses."

"Exactly what I was thinking," Dana said with a smile.

"Aye, y'all niggas come on and let's get this car moved to the paint room," Austin yelled.

Austin was the owner of Precision Auto Painting & Detailing. He had a huge shop on Atlantic Avenue. He was the only white boy in the hood that could use the word *nigga* around the brothers in the neighborhood. They looked at Austin as if he were black. He was tall, muscular, and sexy. He had blue eyes, long black hair, and his skin was tanned year round. He and Toby had been best friends since grade school.

Toby was getting Tiffany's car painted and detailed from the inside out. It was a birthday gift from him to her. He bought her a '79 Monte Carlo and was getting it painted amaranth, which was a rose-red color. He had seven-inch television monitors installed in the headrest facing the backseat. He was having 24-inch tires with Bristol Star Silver Rims and a Pioneer Pro radio system installed too. He was going all out for her.

While they worked on the car, Thad and the crew had set up in the back, outside the shop.

"Man, I swear I was being followed yesterday! That bitch better not have called the cops on me, or the next time I won't be so easy on her," Thad growled.

"Man, you weren't easy on her at all this time. What the fuck are you saying?" Chris interjected.

"I tried to be, but anyway, what are we going to do about Orlando and his crew? The meet-up is next Saturday, and we need to formulate our plan. We have had to put this off once, so it needs to go down as scheduled. Has anybody heard from Blaze and Lonny? We sent them to check out Orlando's shop, and I haven't gotten an update from them at all. Have they checked in with you yet?" Thad asked Chris.

"No, I haven't heard from them at all. Matter of fact, I will call them now. Give me a few minutes," Chris said as he walked off to call Blaze. Thad leaned back on his truck and pulled out a blunt.

"Let's stimulate our minds, gentlemen."

Everyone who smoked surrounded Thad, and they each matched his blunt. As they smoked, Chris was talking to Blaze.

"Aye, man, we have been waiting on you guys to contact us. What's going on?"

"Oh, shit, bro, we been waiting on you to call us. I guess we had a misunderstanding. But check it: ol' boy setup is sweet. He got a few guys that sit outside his shop daily. I don't know if they are with him or if they are the police, but dude got to be aware that they are there. He smooth with his hustle, though. We followed him to a warehouse on the outskirts of Harlem. We figured that's where he is hiding his merchandise. We followed him twice in the last few days," Blaze replied.

"Okay, so while you were following him, who was following you?" Chris asked.

"Shit, bro, we weren't followed at all. We made sure of that. Once we reached the warehouse in Harlem, we circled around twice and parked about a three-car distance from it. I doubt

Orlando was followed. He left in a big rig that was parked out back of his tattoo shop. That's how I know he knows he's being watched. But his movements, in my opinion, are legit. If he knows he is being watched, he probably didn't feel safe coming to meet y'all with the merchandise. I could be wrong, but my instincts are usually right," Blaze replied.

"That's what's up, bro. Just keep us updated," Chris instructed.

"All right, we got you!" Blaze replied.

After they hung up, Chris walked over to where Thad and everyone else stood. "Oh, hell naw. Y'all done started the smoke fest without me? That's beat up!"

"Nigga, stop your fucking whining and come hit this fatty." Thad laughed.

Chris walked over and told Thad what Blaze had told him. Thad dapped him up.

"My nigga, you are the real deal."

Keith stood back watching them and wished he had a bond like that with Thad. They treated him like an outcast at times, but he rode with them regardless. He was the quiet one out the bunch, but he was the mastermind behind a lot of their plays. He just didn't get credit for it like he felt he should.

Toby and Austin joined them a while later with some Grey Goose and Patron. They sat around and got fucked up all night. Thad decided to push his worries to the back of his mind. That night was about having fun; he would figure out what to do about Dana and Jeryca another time.

Dana, Farrah, Stephanie, and Jeryca woke up Friday morning with one thing in common: they each had serious issues with Thad and his crew. The previous night, Stephanie and Farrah had called Dana, and she invited them both over. She told them that Jeryca was already there, and they all needed to put their differences aside and discuss their common threat. Stephanie didn't say anything to Jeryca, and Jeryca didn't say anything to Stephanie. Farrah was so upset about the custody issue that she didn't notice that the two girls weren't speaking. Neither Jeryca nor Stephanie knew why the other person wasn't speaking, but they didn't care.

Dana had been up all night listening to everything, and when Jeryca shared the information that she had learned about Thad's upcoming hustle, Dana came up with an idea that each lady was more than happy to go along with.

They were going to rob Thad and his crew. They had enough information between Jeryca and Stephanie to plan and execute the robbery successfully. Dana just had to get Debra and Brittany to agree to hold off on the custody case.

"Farrah, Travis comes back today, right?" Dana asked.

"Yeah, he does. I'm not sure what time, though," Dana replied.

"When he gets here, you and Stephanie take him shopping," Dana instructed.

"Shopping?" Farrah asked.

"Yes, take him to a costume shop. Pick out wigs, masks, and bulky shape outfits for each of us. We will also need gloves, which I will get, but also take Travis to the toy store and buy four of these masks I googled this morning. They will change our voice up. They're called Star Wars Rebel voice changers," Dana said as she showed them the picture on her phone. Dana gave them $300 to get the costumes.

"Jeryca, draw a map of how the house you were at is laid out, and we will go over it and memorize it. Farrah, call me around 12:30 p.m. so I can get off work. We got a week to get this shit together," Dana said.

Everybody had their tasks, and Dana drove Farrah and Stephanie back to Farrah's house to wait on Travis. Jeryca stayed at Dana's house and began drawing out the layout of Thad's house.

After Dana dropped Stephanie and Farrah off, she headed straight to work. She knew Brittany would get Debra to hold off on preparing Larry's case against Farrah, but she didn't know how she was going to explain why she was going to help them out of their problem.

When she walked into the office, Debra was sitting in the office on the phone. Whoever she was talking to had her smiling hard. Dana whispered, "Is she in?" and pointed to Brittany's office. Debra nodded and motioned for her to go on in. Dana knocked lightly and entered.

"What's up, boss lady?"

"Shit, working on this damn case. It's been working my nerves. What's on your mind? You look like you're up to no good," Brittany said as she leaned back in her chair.

"Well, I was confronted with a situation yesterday, and I devised a plan to deal with it," Dana explained.

"Well, spit it out then," Brittany said, smiling.

Dana told Brittany everything that had occurred, and when she finished talking, she looked at Brittany, who wasn't smiling at all.

"Dana, why are you even still interacting with them? They have fucked you over several times, and here you are still dealing with them." Brittany got quiet for a minute then began speaking again. "On second thought, I'm going help you take Thad and whoever else with him for all they're worth, just on the strength of how they tried you. But be clear, those bitches ain't got shit to do with why I'm helping you. At lunch we will talk," Brittany replied.

"Okay, I'm all for that." Dana walked out of Brittany's office and into her own, but it was hard for her to work with everything on her mind. She couldn't wait to get back at Thad. He had tried to run her off the road, which could've possibly killed her.

Farrah and Stephanie waited for Larry to pull up with Travis. He had been with his father for over two weeks, and she missed him like crazy. She couldn't wait to hug him and smell him. He was all she had, and she wasn't going to lose him to Larry. Around eleven o'clock, Larry finally pulled up. He had Keith with him, and this time he got out and brought Travis in.

"Hello, Farrah, Stephanie," he said as he walked in.

Keith came in seconds later and spoke to both ladies as well. Farrah didn't want to cause a scene in front of Travis, so she spoke back quietly. She couldn't look at Larry, though, 'cause she really wanted to slam his ass, but she kept her cool.

"Can we go in the other room and talk for a minute?" Larry asked.

"Whatever you got to say, you can say it right here. I will send Travis to his room, and I'm sure Steph and Keith won't mind leaving us in here for a second," she responded.

Larry looked at her, shocked that she said no. What the hell was that all about? "You know what? Never mind. Here, take this money and make sure there's food in here for my son. I've paid the rent up for the month, and your bills are caught up, so you shouldn't need anything else," he said in a menacing tone.

Farrah felt more like a charity case than a parent. She looked at Larry hard for a second, then glanced at the money. She knew if she took it she would always be dependent on him, and she could no longer give him that power over her.

"Keep it. We are good. I got plenty of food in there, and anything else I need I can get on my own. Thank you anyway, though. Y'all take care, okay?" she stated as she turned her back on Larry and started playing with Travis.

"Fine. That's cool with me. But you better not have my son in here hungry, Farrah!" Larry shouted.

Travis looked at his father and began to cry. Farrah hugged him, completely ignoring Larry's outburst. Larry stormed out of the house with Keith in tow.

Farrah looked at Stephanie and started smiling, "One for me!"

After Dana, Brittany, and Debra met for lunch, she had a newfound respect for both ladies. Dana texted Jeryca, Stephanie, and Farrah, and told them they should meet and go over a new, revised plan. She wasn't going to tell them who had given her the ideas, because she knew they wouldn't respect it, but she was going to let Brittany explain her part in the robbery after it was over. They needed to know who was really behind their successful siege. Dana usually wasn't with all the drama, but after all the problems she had recently endured, she felt what she was about to do was warranted. She was going to take all she could from Thad and Toby, and she felt good about it.

Dana and the ladies had created a monster plan. Stephanie and Farrah had bought four chrome faceless masks with pull-over padded sweaters and pants. They also bought the voice disguisers. Over the course of two days, they scoped out the trap house and noted who came and left regularly.

"Shit, look at all those boss niggas walking in and out of there," Farrah said.

"The money that is made in there is ridiculous. They don't move the money until the third Tuesday of each month. I know where the safe is, but the only other person who has the combination to the safe other than Thad and Toby is Keith. We need to get to him," Jeryca said, looking at Dana and smiling.

"Oh, hell naw! It's got to be another way," Dana groaned, understanding what the smile meant.

"Dana, we all are making some sort of sacrifice, so you got to do the same. You know Keith likes you, and we only have a few days to get the code," Stephanie replied.

"Yeah, Dana, stop acting like a goody two-shoes." Farrah laughed. Dana rolled her eyes and bit back her comment.

"Listen, you don't have to sleep with him, but just act like you're interested enough to where he will want to spend Saturday with you, and we will handle the rest," Jeryca commented.

"How can we get him involved in what we're doing Saturday without him knowing who we are? That doesn't make sense to me. We need to come up with another way to get the code."

"Dana, there is no other way!" Stephanie yelled.

Dana dropped her head and thought about what they said to her, and other than Farrah's snide remark, it did make sense.

"Okay, I will do it," she conceded. "Stephanie, while I make my move on Keith, you need to be planning out how you are going to get to Chris. He is the only one with a key to the locked room at the warehouse. That's going to be our biggest hit, so we definitely need that damn key."

"I got this. I doubt he will pass on this good pussy! He has been texting me like crazy, so I will get back at him tonight, and I will arrange to meet him tomorrow afternoon. But I need to text Justin, this guy I met a few days ago, 'cause he is going to give me some Rohypnol, which will put Chris's ass to damn sleep, 'cause ain't no freaking way I'ma sleep with his nasty ass. But damn it, Justin may want me to give him some head for the med. The shit I do for the money!" Stephanie said, glancing at Jeryca.

No one noticed the look but Dana, who instantly frowned and shook her head, looking at her through the rearview mirror. "You didn't tell him what you needed it for, did you?" Dana asked curiously.

"Hell naw, girl! I ain't new to this. I told him I been having trouble sleeping, and he said he was going to look out for me. Damn, I told you I got this!" Stephanie rapped.

Everyone laughed.

"Look at who we have here. It's Thad with his new lady. She is gorgeous, isn't she?" Stephanie snickered as she glanced again at Jeryca. The look on Jeryca's face was priceless to Stephanie. Farrah looked at Stephanie frowning, still unaware that Jeryca and Stephanie had unresolved issues.

"Steph, what was that about?" Farrah whispered.

"Oh, nothing, girl. I was just pointing out how much of a slimeball Thad is. He deserves what we are about to do to him," she lied.

"We all know he deserves this, and so do the rest of them. This lick will affect all of them, and I can't wait to do this!" Farrah said, thinking about Larry.

They knew that all the guys would take a loss from the robbery. They weren't just going after money; they were going to break them down to the core.

Jeryca remained quiet as she stared long and hard at the woman with Thad, who resembled Stephanie to the max. It was at that moment that she realized that it was that ho, and not Stephanie, whose picture had popped up on his phone that day in the truck. She instantly felt sick to her stomach about everything she did to get even with Stephanie, and it turned out she was innocent.

They watched as Thad and the lady walked into the house. A few moments later, Toby, Chris, and Keith pulled up. Dana suggested that they leave and handle a few other things so the guys didn't see them. They had staked out that place for two days and gotten enough insight on everyone's movement around the area. They also knew who wasn't going to be there Saturday. Thad and his guys had business to handle, and so did Dana and her entourage.

They had decided to rob them at the last minute, but they had everything they needed, and it was as if everything else was falling in place on its own. They were amazed by how much information they had gained in so little time.

Chapter Ten

Sunday evening, Jeryca walked into the living room and found Dana looking through the newspaper.

"What's up, D? What's new in the world?" she asked as she tapped the newspaper.

"Nothing new at all. Just looking to see who got arrested over the weekend," Dana replied, closing the paper and setting it down on the end table.

"Nosy ass," Jeryca said, laughing.

"Yeah, that's me," Dana said as she shifted in her chair to face Jeryca.

"Listen, we need to get a few more people on board so we can do a double lick," Jeryca replied.

"I'm listening," Dana said. She had already made preparations for a few more arms to be available, but why not give the impression that it was somebody else's idea?

"Well, I think we can handle getting the loot from the house, but the warehouse is something else. We are women, and may need—no, let me rephrase that—*will* need a few strong arms.

So, do you think we can work that out?"Jeryca asked.

"Let me see what I can work out," Dana said, loving how things were playing out.

Sunday night, like clockwork, Chris texted Stephanie:

Girl, why are you ignoring me? he texted.

Just had a lot on my mind, she replied.

Damn I need to see your ass! You ain't been home for days, he wrote.

I know, but I will be back tomorrow. You want to meet somewhere? she asked.

Hell yeah I do! Where? he texted.

After Stephanie and Chris finished texting each other, Stephanie called her newfound friend, Justin, and asked if he wanted to get up, and just like she thought, he said yes.

"I love it when a plan comes together." She laughed.

Monday morning, Dana waited outside Keith's house for him to come out. Keith wasn't an ugly man, but she found him goofy. He didn't have any style. He wore thick glasses that made his eyes appear bigger than they actually were.

He was five foot six with a thin build. He had no muscle tone at all. He was just average. On the plus side, he lived alone and carried himself in a clean-cut manner. She knew he was very smart, because they went to school and college together. He was a wizard with numbers, which, in Dana's opinion, was the only reason Thad kept him around.

When Keith finally emerged, Dana shook her head. She couldn't believe she was about to do. Dana blew the horn and then waved Keith over.

"Hey, how are you doing?" she asked once he was standing at her car window.

"I'm good. Um, what are you doing here?" he asked.

"Well, I've been waiting on you, to be honest. You've been on my mind lately. Everyone is going through their own situations, and I've been lonely. I thought we could get up and go out later."

Keith took a step back and looked at Dana, frowning. "Are you serious?"

This threw Dana off a bit. "Are you seeing someone?"

"No, I'm not, but I'm shocked that you're asking me out, considering how much I chased you." He laughed as he shifted from foot to foot.

"I'm just tired of being alone. I hadn't seen or heard from you in a while, and I guess it bothered me," Dana explained as a feeling of sickness washed over her.

"Is that right? Damn, if I had known that me falling back would have you wanting me, I would've stopped a long time ago," he said, laughing.

"Well, what's up? Do you want to get up later or not?" Dana asked after swallowing the real reply she wanted to give him.

"Hell yeah! Where and what time do you want to meet?" he asked.

"We can meet at Tisha's Lounge over on Kingston Avenue. It's closer to my job," Dana replied.

"That's what's up. Here. Take my number and call me when you are on your way there," he said.

After they exchanged numbers, Dana pulled off with Keith cheesing.

Keith walked into T&T Sauces, grinning from ear to ear. When he walked into the office, Thad and Toby were sitting with their heads together, looking over their truck logbook.

"What's going on, fellas?" Keith asked as he sat down across from them.

"Shit, just trying to make sure all of our products were logged in correctly. We could use your input, though," Toby replied.

"That's what I'm here for, but I'm out of here around five," Keith informed them.

"Oh, yeah? What you got going on?" Thad asked.

"Shit, my nigga, I finally got Dana to go out with me." Keith laughed.

Toby looked up. "You lying!"

"Nope! As a matter of fact, she asked me out," Keith admitted.

"Really? That's hard to believe. Dana don't seem like the type of woman to do that. Man, you don't think she doing that because—" Toby stopped talking after he remembered that they hadn't told anybody what happened the other day.

"Because what, man?" Keith asked curiously.

"Because of the shit that's been going on with her friends," Toby said, changing his story.

"I don't have anything to do with all that. That's between y'all. Why would she come at me?" Keith questioned Toby.

"You know what? I'm just tripping, I guess. I'm glad you finally broke her down. Let's get this paperwork done so you can get on out of here," Toby answered.

After they balanced the logbook, Keith told them he was going to leave so he could get ready for his date. Thad and Toby dapped him up, and he left.

"Man, something ain't sitting right with me about Dana and Keith," Toby admitted to Thad.

"Me either. We need to find out what's going on with her," Thad said.

Thad picked up the phone and called Jeryca. He hadn't tried to contact her since the day he beat her ass, but she was going to tell him what he wanted to know. After several rings, Thad hung up.

"That bitch just ignored my damn call."

Toby laughed. "You aren't as irresistible as you thought you were."

"Fuck you, nigga," Thad said irritably.

Stephanie and Chris arrived at the Holiday Inn at 1:30 p.m. They got their key to the room, and once they were in it, Chris immediately began undressing Stephanie.

"Whoa, buddy, can a sista get a drink first? Did you bring the Ciroc?" she asked.

"You know I did. Pour me a drink while you at it," Chris ordered.

"Yes, sir!" Stephanie laughed.

Stephanie poured the first drink and opened up two Heinekens. While Chris drank his, she stood by the sink and poured hers out. She took out a blunt and sat on his lap.

"Let me give you a gun, baby?"

"Blow, baby, blow," he said.

As she blew the smoke in his mouth, her lips touched his, and for a brief second, she almost gave in to temptation, but the memory of him and Jeryca fucking in his car woke her up. She sat up and tried to stand up.

"Hold on, baby. Take those jeans off," Chris instructed.

Stephanie stood up and slowly began taking off her clothes. "Shit, one more drink for the road?" she asked as she seductively began touching herself.

"I'm all for it," he replied as he stood up and walked over to the bed. Stephanie waited for him to lie back before she poured their last drink. As she slipped the liquid Rohypnol in his drink, it fizzled, and she sloshed it around to mix it. She walked back over to the bed and sat on top of him. She drank her drink and watched him as he guzzled the shot down.

"Now give me that tongue, baby," he whispered.

Stephanie started kissing his neck instead and began rubbing his nipples lightly. He turned her over so that she was on her back and stuck his finger inside her pussy. She began slowly rotating her hips with the beat of his finger. He started moving it faster and faster until he felt her body jerk, and he knew she had come.

Stephanie was now in the mood, and she moved Chris up so that he could slide his dick inside her. *Shit, I was going to get me a second nut and a third*, she thought as she completely forgot why she was there, until she felt Chris go limp on top of her.

"Fuck," she yelled as she wrestled to move him off of her. She sat on the edge of the bed for a few minutes to clear her head. She stood up, put her clothes back on, went through Chris's pockets, and pulled out his keys. She automatically knew which three keys she needed, because they were the biggest keys on his ring that had the letters *WS* engraved on it.

She slipped the office key and his car key off the ring, and then put the other ones back in his pocket. She grabbed the room key off the night table, checked Chris out to make sure he was still asleep, and walked out of the hotel room.

As she got into her car, she called Dana and left her voice message, letting her know that she was on her way to the CVS pharmacy to make a copy of the key.

As she walked into CVS, she looked around to see where she had to go to get the copy of the key made. She found the station easily and walked over. She glanced at her watch to check her time. She had been gone about ten minutes. *I'm making good time*, she thought to herself. As the attendant walked over to her, she noticed that the young girl was very beautiful. She looked like an African princess. Her skin tone was dark, she had curly hair, and her eyes were very lovely. There wasn't anything special about them, but they held a gleam in them that did something to her.

"If I was into women, I'd definitely get at you," Stephanie said, smiling.

"Well, I guess it's your loss," the girl replied, obviously flirting back.

"Shit, might not be. I'm Stephanie, and you are?"

"I'm Robin. Nice to meet you."

"Likewise. Listen, I need to get a copy made of these three keys, and after that, I'm going to need your phone number," Stephanie replied.

"Yes and yes," Robin replied as she took the keys from Stephanie.

"It will take just a few minutes," she informed Stephanie.

"That's what's up," Stephanie replied.

When Robin walked away, Stephanie glanced down at her ass and was turned on. She had never been attracted to a woman before and didn't know the first thing about being with a woman, but she was sure willing to try it.

Robin returned and handed Stephanie the three keys and a slip of paper. "Anything else I can do for you?"

"Maybe later," Stephanie purred as she paid for the duplicate keys.

"We will see," Robin said as she walked away to help another customer.

"Damn," Stephanie whispered.

Stephanie walked slowly to the car and got in. She sat there for a second before she cranked up the car and pulled off. When she got back to the room, Chris was still asleep. She quickly undressed, placed his keys back on his key ring, and lay next to him.

Chris slept for a few hours, and when he woke up, Stephanie was next to him. He grabbed her by the waist and pulled her back against him. He started massaging her breasts and slowly moved his hand down to her clit. Stephanie could feel his dick hardening and pressing against her ass.

One for the road! she thought shamelessly.

***

At around 5:15 p.m. and with no call, Keith was beginning to think Dana had stood him up. But then, she called.

"Hey, I'm on my way to Tisha's lounge."

"Okay, boo. See you soon," he said softly.

"Okay, see you in a few," she said. After she hung up, she shuddered at how he had referred to her as *boo*.

Once she arrived at the lounge, she noticed a few guys checking her out. She knew she was looking good, and she smiled at the few admirers who were around. As she sat down at a booth by the window and glanced down at the menu, a waitress approached her.

"Hello. That gentleman over by the bar asked me to bring you this vodka tonic."

Dana looked in the direction the waitress pointed and saw a familiar face. She smiled and nodded her head. A few seconds later, she was accompanied by Keith.

"I see you started without me," he said as he slid into the booth.

"Yeah, I did. But they just brought it," she explained.

"Okay, cool."

The same waitress returned. "May I take your order, sir?"

"I will have a glass of water for now," he answered.

Keith and Dana talked, danced, and ate dinner. Dana really enjoyed herself with Keith. She also noticed that the man who bought her that first drink was watching her intently. She wondered what he was doing there and why the apparent interest in her.

At eight o'clock, she had talked Keith into meeting her the following day for lunch. Keith was happy that he was getting the opportunity to blend his energy with Dana. Dana, on the other hand, hated that she had to play with Keith's feelings like she was. He was clearly a nice guy.

Keith walked Dana to her car, and she allowed him to kiss her on the jaw. She acted like she was calling someone while he walked to his car. Once he pulled off, she got back out of her car and walked back into the lounge. As she walked over to the bar, she smiled.

"What's going on, Zack?"

"Nothing, sexy. I'm just checking on my hot girl," he replied.

"How did you know I was going to be here? Never mind," she said, realizing that there was only one person who could've said anything: "Brittany," she answered, laughing.

"And you are correct," he said, smiling. "But come on and have a seat. Let's chit-chat!"

"Man, you are a mess," Dana said as she sat down next to him.

"I'm game. I know you talked to Brittany, so what's up? Are you in or out?" Dana asked.

"Shit, I want to be in and out if you will let me," Zack whispered in her ear.

Dana smiled at his remark. Just then, Gerald Levert's "Can You Handle It" began to play.

"Come on, let's dance, sweet thang," Zack said as he grabbed her by the hand and pulled her to the floor.

While they were dancing, Zack began to sing in Dana's ear. "Got a lot of love to give, and I wanna give it to you, but all I wanna know is, can you handle it, baby?"

Dana lifted her head off his shoulder and smiled. "Definitely!"

Chapter Eleven

Tuesday morning, Farrah got a phone call from Larry.

"Hello?" she answered.

"What's going on?" he asked.

"Nothing much, just watching Dr. Phil," she replied.

"Oh, okay. Where is my bad-ass son?" he asked.

"He's with my mother. He stayed with her last night," she replied.

"So what did you get into?" he asked.

"Larry, what do you want? This isn't twenty questions. Stop all the small talk and get to the point," she stated, agitated.

"Damn, Farrah, why does it have to be like that? I called 'cause I wanted to know if you would meet me at the corner store," he replied.

"For what?" she asked.

"I just think we need to sit down and discuss our issues and try to come to some resolution, for Travis's sake," he stated.

"This was your doing from the start," she said.

"Farrah, it doesn't matter who started what. I just want to try to fix this. We can grab us a sub or something," he explained.

Farrah agreed to meet with Larry at twelve. She wondered why he wanted to meet at the corner store and not her house. She figured it was due to all the threats fired back and forth between the two of them. Whatever the reason, she was more than happy to discuss their issues.

By the time 12:00 p.m. approached, Farrah had bathed and was looking fresh. She walked out of the house, ready to meet with Larry. She got to Jim's Market ten minutes later. As she walked in, she immediately saw Larry sitting at a table. The quick grill was crowded, so she bypassed it and joined Larry.

"You look nice," he said as she sat down.

"Thank you. So let's talk," she replied.

"Well, wait one minute," he said as he looked toward the quick grill. Farrah frowned as she followed his gaze. What, or rather *who*, were they waiting on?

After a few minutes, her questions were answered as a middle-aged beautiful woman approached.

"Farrah, this is my attorney, Debra," Larry introduced.

"Hi, how are you today?" Debra asked.

"Bitch, get your hand away from me. You bastard, this is why you called me here? To railroad me with your lawyer?" Farrah yelled.

"Farrah, calm down. We wouldn't want you to cause a public scene," Larry whispered, smiling.

"Fuck you and this bitch. I don't give a damn about none of these people seeing me act out!" Farrah shouted even louder. Farrah turned the table upward, causing the drinks and food that Debra had set down to slide to the floor. She grabbed Larry by the face, digging her nails into his skin.

"You dirty, bitch-ass nigga!" she shouted as she began to punch him in the head.

Larry ducked and tried to cover up as best as he could, and Debra ran behind a soda rack. Farrah felt a pair of hands grab her up, and when she whirled around, she was looking into the eyes of two police officers. It finally dawned on her that she had been set up.

"Miss, what seems to be the problem?" the first officer asked. Farrah dropped her head and shook it. The officer pulled her to the side and explained that she was under arrest for assault and for being a public nuisance. She refrained from saying anything. She looked over at Larry and noticed that he was agreeing to press charges against her, but the weird thing was that his so-called attorney was massaging his shoulders in a manner that didn't seem appropriate for an attorney/client relationship.

After Farrah was placed in the backseat of the police car, Larry walked out and glanced in her direction. She turned her head and didn't look back up until they arrived at the precinct. After she was booked, she sat in a holding cell for two hours, and then was taken to see the magistrate. Her bond was set at $1,000 cash bond. She asked to make her one phone call.

"I really enjoyed hanging out with you yesterday. You are a very cool guy," Dana whispered seductively into the phone. Just as Keith began to speak, Dana's phone beeped.

"Hold on, bae," she said. "Hello?" she answered.

"You have a one-time free call from Farrah, an inmate at the Brooklyn Detention Center. To accept the call, press one." Dana immediately pressed one.

When the call connected, she shouted, "What the hell are you doing in jail?"

"Dana, that bitch-ass nigga Larry set me up," she cried.

"Set you up how? Farrah, what's your bond?" Dana asked.

"They got me under a thousand dollars. What am I going to do?" Farrah asked as she sniffled.

"You have two minutes left." The recorded warning interrupted them for a second.

"Farrah, we will try to get you out today. Give me a couple of hours."

"Okay. Thanks, Dana. I knew I was calling the right person," Farrah replied.

"Yeah, I got you," Dana said before hanging up.

Her phone rang back immediately. "Damn, I forgot he was even on the phone."

"I'm sorry 'bout that, Keith, but I've got to go handle something for a client. I will call you back later," she explained.

"All right, sexy. Talk to you then," he replied.

Dana got off the phone, walked out of her office, and headed toward Brittany's office. As she walked in, Debra looked up and smiled.

"Hey, ladies, I know it's almost quitting time, but may I have a word with you for a moment?" Dana asked as she sat down across from her.

"Yes, you can. What's up?" Brittany asked.

"How about Farrah done let Larry play her into a situation where she has landed in jail?" Dana said calmly.

"What the fuck! We need Farrah, Dana," Brittany said as she sat up straight in her chair.

"I know. That's why I need to leave early so I can go get her out," Dana replied.

"Shit, go on and handle that. Call me later on after you get her," Brittany said.

"Okay, I will. Talk to y'all later," Dana said as she stood up to leave.

Debra hardly looked at Dana as she walked by her.

"Man, I hope this shit play out like it's supposed to, Brittany, 'cause I ain't trying to get caught down bad," Debra whispered.

"I'm going to make sure it does," Brittany replied, looking at the door.

Dana walked into the Brooklyn Detention Center and approached the officer on duty.

"I'm here to get Farrah Walker."

"Hold on for a moment," the officer replied as she typed in Farrah's name. "Okay. Assault and a public nuisance charge. One thousand dollars is her bond."

"I will need a bondsman. Can you recommend one?" Dana asked.

"No, ma'am, I can't, but there is a list over to the right of the double doors you came through," the officer answered.

"Okay, thanks," Dana replied.

Dana walked over to the list and called four of the names on the list before she found one. Bondsman Tammy King agreed to do Farrah's bond at a 15 percent fee that was due when she got there. Dana accepted the terms and walked to the waiting area to wait for Tammy. Fifteen minutes and two magazines later, Dana heard a familiar male voice echo through the room.

As she looked up, she saw the same two officers that had come to her job looking for Jeryca. Dana turned her head in the opposite direction of the officers, but Detective Rone saw her. He tapped Detective Harris, and the two headed in her direction.

"How are you doing, um, miss? Do you need help with anything?" Detective Rone asked.

"It's Dana, and no, I'm good," Dana replied flatly.

"That's good. We just wanted to make sure you had been taken care of," Detective Rone replied with a half-smile.

"Yeah, I bet," she muttered under her breath.

Detective Harris heard the comment and looked at her. "Listen, we were just doing our job when we came to your office. And the lead you gave us was right on point. We found Ms. Mebane and closed our case."

"Well, that's great for you, but y'all's little visit got me fired!" she exclaimed.

Both detectives stood silent for a moment.

"That wasn't our intention, but we did have a job to do. I apologize for getting you fired, and if there is anything I can do for you, let me know. Take care."

Dana rolled her eyes and watched the two officers walk away. A few seconds later, a thought entered her head, and she ran after them. "Wait!" she yelled.

The two stopped and walked back to meet her. "Yes ma'am?"

"I'm here to get someone out of jail, and right now I'm waiting for the bondsman, but if I may have a word with you before I leave, I can guarantee you it will be worth your time to speak with me," she explained.

Detective Rone gave Dana directions to his office and told her to come see him after she dealt with the bondsman. He told her that they would have plenty of time to talk, because it was going to take them a while to process her friend out. Dana agreed, and thirty minutes later, she was walking into Detective Rone's office. As she shut the door, she prayed that she wasn't making a mistake.

***

Wednesday

Thad was sitting in his office, going over the monthly report for the amount of wing sauce units sold. He was pleased by the progress that his company was making. He was confident that when it was time to let all his illegal activities go, he was going to still win. He was going over the last report when Larry tapped on the door.

"You busy, boss man?"

"Shit, just going over a few reports. What's up, Larry?" he asked.

"You know I had Farrah locked up yesterday. That bitch attacked me and Debra yesterday at Jim's Market."

"Was it a coincidence that you were all there at the same time?" Thad asked.

"I may have asked her to meet me there, but she acted out like she did on her own," Larry admitted, smiling.

"Whatever, man. So where is Travis?" Thad asked.

"He is with his grandmother, but I think Farrah is out now. But I doubt any court will allow her to have custody of a child with a temper like hers," Larry replied.

"You're going to hell for that." Thad laughed.

"I was already going to hell for all the things I've done with and for you, so what you saying?" Larry joked.

Thad laughed as he stood up and patted Larry on the shoulder. "Come on. Let's go get us a drink and light this loud."

"I'm all for that," Larry said.

As they walked out of the office, Thad looked at Larry with a puzzled expression. "You and Ms. Debra have become chummy real quick."

"Well, she and I have found that we have a lot in common. She is a lady that I'm very interested in," Larry replied.

"She seems like a good girl. You gonna try to make her your main lady?" Thad asked.

"I don't know. I'm just enjoying what we got going on now," Larry answered, smiling.

"That's what's up. Pour your own troubles," Thad said as they walked into the bar room.

As they poured their drinks, Thad looked at him. "Hey, let's toast to parenthood. I think that was one of the best moves you made yesterday, boy."

"Zack, how many Glocks do we have versus the nines?" Brittany asked after Zack handed her two bags of guns.

"It's four Glocks and five nines, two of which has silencers. I also brought three Tasers," he replied.

"Tasers? Nigga, we ain't going in to arrest anybody. It's a fucking robbery!" Brittany laughed.

"Shut the fuck up, Brit! They may come in handy. What else do we need? I got duct tape, rope, and plastic bags." Zack paused when he saw Brittany's eyebrows lift. "Just in case," he finished.

"I'm not even gonna ask, Zack. Anyway, have you spoken to Dana today? I told her last night that I was taking the day off to handle this, so I haven't talked to her today," Brittany said.

"I called her and said good morning. That was it. I'm going to get up with her after work for dinner, then we are meeting you all to go over the plans for Saturday," he responded.

"I can't tell y'all what to do, but I don't think it's a good idea to get involved until this robbery is over. Debra will meet us here later, but I'm starting to think having her ride out with us would be a mistake," Brittany told him.

"Why you say that?" Zack asked.

"She just don't act like she is really wanting to be involved in this," Brittany replied.

"Shit, Brit, you know her better than we do, so it's your call. Either way, I'm in it to win it, damn it," Zack sang.

"Zack, has anybody told you that you're corny as hell? Lord have mercy. Got to love your ass." Brittany laughed.

"Girl, stop—you know I'm an original don. I'm sophisticated and original. Ain't none like me," he said in a high, playful voice.

"Shit, that's what I'm saying, corny ass," she replied.

"Damn you," he said, throwing a bean bag at her. They laughed and put all the guns together and in separate boxes. Once they were finished, they went to the pool hall to meet Zack's people.

Wednesday evening, Jeryca, Stephanie, and Farrah were going to meet Dana, Brittany, and a few others at the pool hall. Farrah decided that she wasn't going to go at the last minute. She wanted to spend some time with Travis. She didn't know what the outcome was going to be once the weekend was over. Everyone respected her decision, and Dana pretty much expected it.

Once she got off work, Dana picked Stephanie and Jeryca up. When they arrived, Brittany was already there, sitting with four guys. Jeryca immediately began flirting with Zack, but he dismissed her intentions quickly by grabbing Dana and pulling her to the bar.

"You got a fan," Dana said, laughing.

"Aye, you see where I'm at. Don't play. You know I'm at you," Zack said, smiling.

"Is that right? I'd like to know more about that. But to be honest, I can't focus on that right now. Let's wait 'til after Saturday and see what happens."

"Brit said the same thing earlier today," Zack replied.

"So you two have been discussing me on the low, huh?" Dana asked, smiling.

"Just a little bit. Don't get no big head, though. You ain't all that." Zack laughed.

"Oh, yeah?" Dana asked as she pinched his side.

"You better watch that, girl. You trying to start something you can't finish." He laughed as he grabbed her by the hands.

"Anything I start, I can finish. Trust that," Dana whispered in a low tone close to his ear.

They walked back to the table, and Jeryca glanced up at them but returned her attention to Pete, who she now was flirting with.

Dana whispered to Zack, "Looks like you've been replaced."

"Yes, hold me," Zack whined playfully as he laid his head on Dana's shoulder.

Brittany looked at them and smiled. "Looks like you guys are getting along."

"Who, us?" Dana said, pointing to her and Zack. "Girl, I can't stand him." She laughed, playfully pushing him away.

"She loves me already, Brit," Zack said, also laughing.

"Whatever!" Dana said, rolling her eyes.

"You two are too much. Let's talk business, and then turn up in this bitch!" Brittany laughed.

After they laid the plans out and discussed who would carry out each task, they partied until the wee hours of the morning. Zack and Dana danced the whole night, and so did Pete and Jeryca, who seemingly hit it off immediately.

Chapter Twelve

Thursday

Stephanie called Robin to see if she was going to be available for lunch. Since meeting her at CVS, she couldn't stop thinking about her. She had never been attracted to a woman and couldn't believe that she was contemplating being with one.

Robin told her to meet her at the Olive Garden over by her job at twelve. Stephanie was going to have to catch the bus over to that side, but she felt Robin would be worth the long ride.

While Stephanie was getting ready for her lunch date, Farrah called.

"What's up, Steph?"

"Nothing much. Just getting ready to head out for a while," Stephanie replied.

"Oh, that's what's up." Farrah sighed.

"What's wrong, jailbird?" Stephanie joked.

"Fuck you, Steph! Anyway, I'm just kind of nervous about Saturday. Did you guys meet up with whoever Brittany and Dana found to help us?" Farrah inquired.

"Yeah, we ended up partying all night. They were some cool guys. Debra, the other chick, didn't show up, though, so we didn't get a chance to meet her," Stephanie replied.

"Is that right?" Farrah asked.

"Yeah, but all in all, we got shit arranged, and I think Dana is going to get at you about a few things as well. But I really got to go right now. I will call you when I get back," Stephanie told Farrah before hanging up.

Stephanie arrived at Olive Garden thirty minutes earlier than she was supposed to, so she took that time to analyze what she was venturing into with Robin. She had been in two relationships since the age of sixteen, and she was still young. She figured it wouldn't hurt to experiment, and considering how sexy and intriguing Robin was, she was going to do a lot of experimenting.

When Robin finally walked in, Stephanie couldn't take her eyes off of her. As Robin sat down at the table Stephanie had chosen, she smiled at her.

"What's up, sexy?"

"Just sitting here waiting and thinking 'bout yo' fine ass," Stephanie replied as she looked Robin over once more.

"So what shall we order?" Robin asked.

"Hell, I'm good with a side of you and a short glass of red wine," Stephanie said as she flicked her tongue at Robin.

The two ladies ate lunch and talked about almost everything that they enjoyed. It was the first time in a long time that Stephanie felt at ease. She didn't know what it was that had drawn her to Robin, but she was so happy that she'd taken the chance to do something different.

After they ate, Stephanie walked her to her car.

"I enjoyed myself with you."

"I did too. Would it be asking too much if I asked for a kiss?" Robin asked.

"Hell naw! I have wanted to taste those lips," Stephanie replied.

Robin leaned into Stephanie and kissed her lightly on the lips, and before she could pull away, Stephanie pulled her in even more and slid her tongue in her mouth. Robin wrapped her arms around Stephanie's neck, and the two kissed for two minutes.

Robin pulled away and thanked Stephanie for lunch. She had a huge smile on her face as she got into her car and pulled off. Stephanie was stuck in place for a few seconds as she watched Robin pull off. Once she got herself together, she headed to the bus stop. When she sat down on the bench, her phone rang.

"Yes?"

"I miss you already. I just wanted to say that I can't wait to see you again," Robin replied.

"Same here. I will call you when you get off work, okay?" Stephanie said.

"That's what's up," Robin replied.

Stephanie hung up the phone, and when the bus pulled up, she decided to go home and reevaluate her life. After the lick on Saturday, Stephanie decided it was time to do things the right way. Dana seemed like the right person to call on.

At home, she dialed Dana's number and asked if she would assist her with applying for college courses. Dana asked her what she was looking to major in and when she wanted to enroll. Stephanie explained that she didn't have all of that decided, but she knew it was time for a positive transition in her life. Dana expressed how happy she was that she had made that decision. They both agreed that, after the weekend, they would start the process. After they got off the phone, Stephanie lay across her bed and fell asleep with Robin on her mind.

"Damn, man, you've seen Dana every night this week, haven't you?" Toby asked Keith.

"Not every night, but we talk all the time. She really is a wonderful woman. Matter of fact, we got another date tomorrow," Keith replied proudly.

"I'm glad you and her are finally getting the chance to get to know one another, but keep our business out of y'all conversations. We don't need any of those messy-ass bitches in our business. If we find out you told her anything, you will be dealt with," Thad warned Keith.

"Man, I'm not stupid. I know not to do that. My loyalty stands with y'all," Keith replied.

"That's what I needed to hear," Thad said as he patted him on the back. "Now let's head over to the warehouse and count some money."

Friday night, after Dana and Keith left the club, she invited him over to her house. She had to get him there to persuade him to give her the code to the safe at the trap house, or she would have to get it the hard way. Zack and the other girls were waiting on her to get there. Dana was nervous but ready for the play of her life. This was something that Jeryca and the other girls would do, not her. Hell, it was Dana's plan, so she couldn't be as bougie as they thought.

Keith agreed to go back to her house as Dana expected. The smile on his face told Dana that she had him. Keith got into his car and followed Dana to what he presumed was her home. Once inside, Dana turned on the charm immediately. She was kissing him and tugging at his clothes. As she grabbed him by the collar, she pulled him into the bedroom. Before Keith knew it, someone grabbed him around his throat.

"Damn, you are a cutie," Brittany murmured.

"What the hell is going on, Dana?" he shouted.

"No, Keith, we will be asking the questions, and we better get the answers we want, or else," Dana replied through clenched teeth.

After they handcuffed Keith and laid him down on the bed, Brittany walked around to face him. She was holding a 9 mm in her hand. When she sat down, she placed a silencer on the end, never taking her eyes off of Keith. He watched her intently. He didn't know what to expect. He couldn't believe that Dana had played him. He thought she really liked him.

After Brittany got into position, Dana walked out of the bedroom. As the sound of the front door opened and shut, Brittany looked at Keith with a puzzled expression, then began smirking. As she lifted her eyebrows, taunting Keith, the bedroom door opened, and Dana walked back in with Zack trailing her.

"I know you're wondering what this is about, and I will be more than happy to tell you. You see, your boys tried to kill me a while ago, and they been playing my girls like shit. Now, I don't really get into anyone's personal business, but what y'all are doing to us is wrong. What we are going to do is take the one thing that we know y'all love, and that's money," Dana said, smiling.

"Dana, I didn't know anything about them trying to kill you. I swear it," Keith cried.

"That might be true, but I'm after what you do know. And don't try to lie your way out of it, because I know for a fact that you got what I need. So what I'm going to do is let you decide on whether or not you are going to give me what I want willingly, or if we got to get it the hard way. It's really all up to you. Oh, this is Zack. I'm sure you've heard of him. He is the guy that Thad shot." Dana laughed after seeing the expression on Keith's face. "Yeah, I see by the look on your face that you've heard of him. Well, he is going to keep you company while you think things over."

As Brittany and Dana walked out the door, Dana paused before shutting the door and looked at Zack.

"Remember, we need him conscious and able to speak."

"Dana, I got this!" he replied.

"I bet you do," she joked.

"I can show you better than I can tell you, sweet cheeks," he grunted.

"We will see, but you heard what I said, man," Dana mumbled.

As Dana shut the door, she heard Keith yell, "Dana, wait a minute!"

She ignored his cries and walked into the kitchen where Brittany was and grabbed a Natural Light. "I can't wait 'til this is over. You and Debra got y'all stuff ready?"

"Yeah, we got everything we need. What time are we going to get the others?" Brittany asked.

"When we get what we need from Keith. I can't deal with them being here while this is going on," Dana replied as she took a huge gulp of her beer.

"I feel you on that. Damn, what the hell is Zack doing to ol' boy?" Brittany said with a concerned look on her face.

"Hell, I don't know, but I'm going to find out," Dana growled. As she ran to the bedroom door, she heard a loud thud. She busted through the door and found Zack slamming a handcuffed and almost unconscious Keith up against the closet door.

"Zack! What the fuck did I tell you? Damn it!"

"Man, he okay," Zack shouted as he let Keith go.

Keith slid to the floor and could barely open his eyes. Dana ran to his side and ordered Zack to help her get him on the bed. Zack immediately did as Dana asked.

"Keith, I really don't want to leave you in here with that crazy-ass muthafucka again, but I will, so all I need you to do is give me the code to the safe at the ho house y'all got, and give me the key to the office where the safe is located. Now, before you say no, let me ask you: are the contents of that safe worth dying for?" Dana asked as she kneeled down, rubbing his hair.

Keith jerked his head back away from Dana's touch. "I'll give you what you want, bitch, but trust me when I tell you that Thad will get you for this."

"I'm waiting on that," Zack said as he stood next to Dana.

Keith gave Dana the code to the safe and told her where the key was located. Brittany got Keith's house keys out of his pocket, and she and Dana went to his house to get the other key and discuss what they were going to do with him after the robbery. Zack stayed behind with Keith.

After Brittany and Dana left Keith's house, they headed over to the east side to pick up

Jeryca and the rest of the girls. It was a little after twelve in the morning, and they had to finalize the last few details of the robbery.

Dana figured that Farrah could stay with Keith while they went to collect their "dues." Zack and his two cousins, along with Brittany's nephew, had volunteered to help them.

Zack, Brittany, Dana, and Minx, one of Zack's cousins, were going to hit the warehouse, while Jeryca, Stephanie, Brittany's nephew Deondre, and Zack's other cousin, Pete, were going to hit the trap house. Brittany and Dana also decided that Debra shouldn't be involved in the robbery, because she was nervous from the first mention of robbing the guys. They didn't have any time to hold her hand if she got spooked. They wanted to get in and out as quickly as possible.

They pulled up on Farrah first. They wanted to explain a few changes in the plan that affected her.

When Farrah got into the car that they had rented two days before, she spoke to both ladies.

"What's up, chick?"Dana said.

"Shit, girl, just getting myself pumped," she replied.

"That's what's up. Listen, I wanted to run something by you. It's a minor change in our plans," Dana said as they pulled off, heading to pick up Jeryca.

"Speak." Farrah laughed.

"Well, we were thinking that you might be better off staying with Keith while we go on our spree," Dana explained.

Farrah immediately got defensive. "Why should I stay with Keith? I'm just as capable, if not more, as any of you to help with the robbery."

"Farrah, that's not why I wanted you to stay behind," Dana started.

"Then tell me why the hell I should stay behind," Farrah asked, interrupting Dana.

Brittany answered instead, annoyed that Farrah even questioned their reasoning. "Farrah, I know we don't get along, but this decision was made solely for your sake. You have a son that depends on you, and we all know that there are risks that we are taking. If we get caught down bad, at least you will be out of harm's way. It's all for the best."

Farrah sat in the backseat quiet for a while, then finally agreed to stay with Keith.

After they picked up Jeryca and Stephanie, they headed back to Dana's house. When they walked in, Stephanie and Jeryca headed straight for the kitchen to get a drink, while Farrah followed Dana and Brittany into the bedroom to help load the guns.

Stephanie looked at Jeryca and turned her head. She couldn't stand being around her, but she was going to deal with her until after the robbery. Before Stephanie could open up the Corona she had grabbed from the refrigerator, she heard a low scream. She dropped the beer and took off running with Jeryca on her ass.

When they got to the living room, they saw Farrah standing with her hand over her mouth. Stephanie looked in the direction Farrah was staring at and immediately took a step backward.

"What the fuck!" she cried.

Dana ran outside to see if she could find Zack. She should've known he would do something crazy to Keith. Hell, she hadn't thought shit out all the way through, which was why she saw the logic in Zack killing Keith. But why did he have to do it there and in the manner that he did it? Never in her wildest dreams did she think she would come home and find Keith hanging from her closet rod. How were they going to get rid of the body, the smell, and the memory of death from her home? She had seen dead bodies before, but not that close up.

When she rounded the corner to where his car was parked, she saw Zack pulling plastic from his trunk.

"What the fuck, man?" she growled angrily.

"Dana, we both know that it had to be done, so I did it while you were handling other things. I didn't want you to concern yourself with it. It's cool. He didn't put up much fight," Zack said as he continued pulling things out of his trunk.

At that moment, Dana fell to the ground and vomited. When she looked up, Zack was standing next to her, rubbing her hair.

"It's okay. You got to be strong. Now ain't the time to fold, sweet cheeks."

Dana knew he was right, so she collected herself and helped him take the supplies he had gathered out of the trunk inside the house. When she walked in, she looked around at everyone.

"If anyone has a problem with what you are seeing, please go into a different area. But we do need some help if someone is willing to help."

Brittany, Stephanie and Farrah all assisted Dana and Zack with getting Keith out of the closet and wrapped up in the plastic. Zack told Dana to clean up the room while he and Brittany went to dispose of the body. Dana did as she was told.

Jeryca, who stood back watching, felt somewhat disgusted by Dana's demeanor. Over the course of a week or so, Dana had become rude, abusive, bossy, and hard. That wasn't Dana's character, and she was curious as to why the sudden change. Jeryca was all for the robbery, but killing people wasn't her thing, and she wasn't going to have any part with cleaning up somebody's blood.

The girls finally dozed off to sleep. They had a long day ahead of them, and they needed to be well rested. Zack called Dana and left her a message saying that he had gotten rid of Keith's body and would see her later. Dana felt horrible about Keith, but she couldn't stress about him at that moment. She had other things to plan out.

The Day

After the girls woke up, got dressed, and ate breakfast, they headed over to a rest stop, where Deondre and Zack's cousins were meeting them with a big rig that one of Zack's cousins drove. They were going to use it as a tool to gain entrance to the warehouse.

Minx, who had been driving trucks for years, was the driver. He started out delivering furniture for Colfax Furnishings and graduated to delivering drugs up and down the East Coast for a few bigwigs in the street game. Minx was ready and more than willing to help Zack get even with Thad. It was a smart move on Zack's part, because he was getting even with Thad in a way that wouldn't land him in jail, unless shit went south and someone got killed, which was a risk everyone took daily. What really amazed Minx was the fact that chicks were organizing everything. It was a rare event.

When everyone got to the rest area, they all spoke and separated into their groups. Dana looked at everyone before they got into their vehicles.

"Yo, ain't no turning back now. If anyone is having second thoughts, now is the time to say so. I ain't got time to babysit somebody else's nerves."

"Damn, when did she get so hard? She got to be talking to one of y'all, 'cause I'm a grown woman, and if I didn't want to be here, I know how to leave," Jeryca whispered to Stephanie.

Stephanie looked at her, rolled her eyes, and walked over to Dana. "I'm ready to do this," she said as she dapped Dana.

"That's what I'm talking 'bout," Dana said, smiling.

"So are we ready?" Brittany asked.

"Hell yes!" Zack yelled as he walked up behind Dana and nudged her.

"Stop playing, negro!" Dana laughed, playfully punching Zack.

"Okay, you two, you can pass love licks later. Let's do this," Brittany said.

As everybody got into their designated cars and trucks, Jeryca couldn't help but see how Stephanie had been treating her as of late, and she was going to find out why. She just hoped that Chris hadn't told her what happened between them.

Chapter Thirteen

It was ten o'clock, and Thad and his crew were heading out to meet Orlando. They were three cars deep with six men in each. They were tailing three empty U-Haul trucks.

As they traveled down the highway, Thad and Toby discussed their plans to take the drug and gun game to the next level. They had gained a well-established and well-deserved reputation as being ruthless yet trustworthy businessmen, so much so that they had caught the attention of some very important men in the drug world. This particular shipment they were picking up was the first of many trades they were going to oversee.

With the money that they had already gotten and the money that they still had to collect, the result of this play was going to be extraordinarily huge. Thad felt relaxed; excited as well as powerful. If the play went off without a hitch, Thad was going to make more money than he could ever imagine having—not to mention he would then become the number one man on the East Coast.

They pulled up to the warehouse building owned by Orlando, who was waiting with three of his men at the gate for Thad and his boys. As they all rolled into the gates, two of the warehouse docks doors raised up slowly. There were several guys standing, preparing to load all three hundred crates onto the three U-Hauls that Thad and Toby had purchased.

"What's up, Orlando?" Chris said as he got out of the first truck.

"Shit, nothin'. Y'all ready to get started?" Orlando asked, looking from Chris to Thad, and then to Toby.

"Yeah, let's get going. Time is money," Toby replied.

As they began loading the truck, Thad, Toby, and Chris stood on the empty dock talking to Orlando. A movement toward the back caught Chris's eye.

"Man, I thought the building was going to be cleared for this pickup," he said.

"What are you talking 'bout? It is. There is no one here but your men and mine," he answered.

"Then who the hell is that back there?" Chris asked.

As all the men turned, police officers jumped out from everywhere.

"Everyone freeze! DEA!" a few of the officers screamed with their rifles drawn.

Everyone scrambled to get out of the building. Thad ran behind Toby. He wasn't concerned about anyone else. As long as he and his brother got out of there, he was good.

As they hit the fence, Thad yelled for Toby to follow him into the woods across the street. The DEA had the area locked, and once Thad and Toby had run far enough down in the woods to take a quick breather, Thad looked at Toby.

"Man, what the fuck!" he asked breathlessly.

"Man, it was a setup. Either Orlando played us, or someone on our squad has turned on us. Either way, somebody gon' answer for this, man."

Before Toby could say another word, they heard rustling behind them. They both pulled their guns out and moved slowly and close to the ground. When they saw Orlando run by, they looked at one another and gave chase behind him. Toby caught up to him first and dove on him, knocking him to the ground. Orlando's head missed hitting a log by mere inches.

"Damn, man! You scared me," Orlando panted.

A few seconds later, Tim, Orlando's right hand man, was running through. Thad tripped him, and when he hit the ground, Thad turned him over, placed his hand over his mouth, and put the barrel of his gun to Tim's head.

"How many other muthafuckas came this way?" Tim mumbled with fear in his eyes as Thad slowly removed his hand from Tim's mouth.

"I don't know who all ran this way, but man, there are feds and DEA agents all in the warehouse," Tim sputtered.

As the two men got to their feet, Thad kept his gun on him and looked over at Toby, who was holding Orlando. "Man, let's go before someone else come through. We need to figure out a spot to go, 'cause home ain't it right now," Thad said.

"Yeah, I know. Let's get safely out these woods first. I know where we can lay low until we know exactly what's going on," Toby said.

The four guys made their way through the woods safely. Once they made it to the street, Toby called the only person he knew who could hide them.

Zack, Brittany, Stephanie, and Minx arrived at Thad's warehouse and began to back the truck up to the dock. Stephanie got out and used the key she had copied to gain entrance to the building. Once inside, she raised the door of the dock so that Minx could back the truck up to the door.

As everyone got out of the truck, Stephanie led them to the office where they kept the guns, drugs, and money. When they walked down to the cellar, they were in awe of all the crates that were filled up. They started moving the crates out, but none of them contained money.

"Aye, li'l momma, where the cash at?" Minx asked.

"Shit, hold that thought. Come on, Brittany, I got to show you this," Stephanie said.

Stephanie led Brittany to a room that was located in the back of the cellar. When she unlocked the door, Brittany stepped in, and Stephanie walked to a steel cabinet. She tried each key until she heard the click. As she opened each drawer, Brittany was taken aback. She figured she was looking at $300,000 in each drawer. In the last drawer, there were jewelry containers. Brittany looked at Stephanie, who was cheesing hard.

"Shit, let's get to bagging this loot. We ain't leaving shit behind."

As they were finishing up, Minx walked in. "We been in over ten minutes. Let's get the rest of this stuff so we can head on out."

"Yeah, you right, let's finish this. But there's one more room left," Stephanie said.

"All right, well, point me to it," Minx replied.

Meanwhile, Dana, Jeryca, Deondre, and Pete were at the trap house tearing it up. They found two women in a back room counting the money that they had made.

"Go on and hand that money over, ladies," Deondre said as he pointed his .357 at them.

"Oh, shit! Don't shoot! Here, take it," a prostitute named Cassie yelled.

"See, cooperation goes a long way. Now, you hand your money over also," he said, talking to Brenda.

Brenda bucked immediately. "I'm not giving you a damn dime of my money," Brenda snapped.

"Bitch, hand it over now before I blow your fucking head off," he hissed.

Before anyone could say another word, Jeryca, who had forgotten to use her voice box, came in. "Don't shoot her. That's not why we came here." Before she could finish, Brenda looked at her with a puzzled expression

"Jeryca, is that you?"

Jeryca stood stunned for a second, then glanced over at Deondre, who was cussing and pacing the floor. Dana walked in, followed by Pete, to see what the commotion was all about.

"What's going on?" Dana asked.

"This bitch done came in here talking to me in front of this ho, and she ID'd her. I'm not going to jail behind this simple-ass bitch!" he yelled.

"Well, she just made a mistake, bro. Chill out," Pete said.

"A mistake? We can't afford to make mistakes! Do you know who house we are hitting? These niggas don't play, and I for one ain't going down bad over a mistake," Deondre replied.

Dana took a deep breath and exhaled. "I'm not either." And with those three words, she shot Brenda and Cassie in the head. "We've gotten everything we came for. Let's get out of here," she concluded.

Jeryca staggered out to the garage and opened the back door to the car. She lifted the trunk but said nothing to anyone. She helped them load the money and bags into the car, and before they pulled off, Dana got her confirmation text:

We are leaving the spot now! Successful. See you soon.

She looked at Deondre and smiled. "We're good to go."

They pulled off and headed to Brittany's office. Once they arrived at Brittany's office,

they noticed that Minx and Brittany were standing outside the truck, smiling as they were all
unloading the truck.

"What's up?" Dana asked.

"Girl, I can't believe that this actually went
down without any complications." Brittany
laughed.

Jeryca walked by the two ladies without saying a word and frowning fiercely.

"Well, not everything went according to plan,
but it is what it is," Dana said, shaking her head
at Jeryca.

"Lord, what happened?" Brittany asked.

"Shit, one of her friends recognized her
because she forgot to use the voice disguiser, so
when she asked Jeryca if she was Jeryca, I had to
handle it," Dana explained.

"Handled it how?" Brittany asked.

Deondre, who had walked up, spoke. "She
smoked those bitches!"

"Damn, Dana, I know you must be shook,"
Brittany said.

"Shit, y'all, let's go check on Farrah and take
a load off. I'm kind of tired," Stephanie whined.

Deondre and Minx stayed behind unloading
the truck, and everyone else went inside to get
a drink and rest for a little while. When they
walked in, Farrah was sitting in Dana's office
with a strange look on her face.

"What's wrong, baby girl?" Stephanie asked as she walked into the office with Dana and Jeryca behind her.

"Nothing really. I'm glad that you all made it back safely," Farrah replied.

"Naw, something is wrong. Are you still sour about not going out with us? I told you—"

Before Dana could finish her sentence, a loud bang sounded off in the office, and there was a lot of shouting.

"Get on the floor, muthafucka! Bitch, put that goddamn phone down before I shoot it out your hand. You got to know what this is! It's a fucking robbery! Now, I'm going to keep you company while my guys load up your truck, and we will be on our way. If any of you bitches try anything, I won't hesitate to kill you. Do we have an under-standing?" A man dressed in all black with a face mask stood in the middle of the office screaming.

Everyone followed each of his commands, and they were bound and gagged. The men left, but only after pushing Deondre and Minx into the office as well. The masked men didn't take the time to tie Minx or Deondre up, but they told them that if anyone came out of the office while they were leaving, they would be shot on sight.

***

Austin, Toby's best friend, picked him, Thad, Orlando, and Tim up and took them to his guest-house in Manhattan. Once everyone's nerves were somewhat settled, Thad took a swallow of the gin that Austin had poured him.

"What the fuck happened out there, Orlando? I thought that was a safe location, bro. You assured us that it was."

"Honest, dude, I don't know what happened. I've never had that happen, and I've been moving guns and drugs for years. It had to be an inside job."

"Well, we got to figure out who was responsible for this. I was depending on this play to help me pull off the hustle of the century. I got to straighten my face with Ramon and Sergio. I got a stash put up that I can give them until I can move those guns and weed around. I think I can pull it off, but I got to have my team locked in on grinding hard for the next few weeks," Thad said aloud.

"We can get it done, bro," Toby said.

"Anything we can do, just let me know. I got a couple thousand I can put in on it. I like y'all movement, and I want to get on board," Austin stated.

"Go 'head on with that bullshit. You ain't trying to move with us," Toby said.

"Try me, nigga," Austin replied, looking serious and lighting a blunt.

"Hell, if you serious about it, then we can definitely make that happen," Toby replied.

The guys sat around, and Orlando and Tim decided they needed to see where their crew was. They knew it was safe for them to leave. They walked down to the bus station and caught the bus back to the city.

Thad called Larry, trying to see if he had heard from Chris and Mike, but he got no answer. He figured he would get Brenda to call the precinct to see if they were holding Chris, and find out what everybody's bond was. He dialed Brenda's number and again got no answer.

"Man, what the hell is going on? No one is answering my calls. I'm starting to think that this whole thing was an inside job. Can't trust nobody!"

About an hour later, Thad was laid back on Austin's couch, trying to come up with a logical explanation as to how the police knew about their meeting with Orlando. How was he going to get the money up for Ramon?

Thad's phone started vibrating, and when he looked at it, there was a text message from Brenda's phone that read:

Call back ASAP!

"What now?" Thad sighed. "Yeah?" he said as his call was connected.

Toby sat up as he witnessed several different emotions run across Thad's face. When Thad hung up, he dropped his head and was silent for a minute.

"Fuck, Toby. Man, we got some serious problems. Shit! It's not good at all, bro."

"What's going on now?" Toby asked.

"Man, I just got a call telling me to get to the house, because there were two bodies that needed to be claimed. I'm assuming Brenda is one of them. Fuck," Thad yelled, rubbing his head.

"We need to check to see what's going on with Chris down at the station," Toby announced.

"I will call," Austin replied.

"Thanks, man," Toby said as he got up and began pacing the floor.

Austin called the police station and found out that Chris was under a $450,000 bond. Everyone else's bond was substantially lower.

"We got to get to the bottom of this now!" Thad stormed.

Thad's phone began to ring again, and as he looked at the number, he decided he couldn't talk to them at that moment. How was he going to explain to the Colombian Cartel that he had lost the shipment they sent? He knew, though, in the back of his mind that they already knew about it, and he had no doubt as to who had informed them. He would return their call later. Right now, he needed to go see what was going on back at the house.

"What a fucking day!" he cried.

"What the fuck just happened?" Minx asked angrily.

"I don't know, but it's some grimy shit going on, and I'm 'bout to fucking blow!" Zack yelled as he paced the floor.

"Look, there has got to be an explanation. Why would either of us take the risk of going through with the robbery if we were going to allow someone else to make off with the goods?" Dana said.

"Shit, I can guarantee you this: somebody gonna give up some answers or it's going to be more bloodshed. I didn't go through this shit to come out empty!" Deondre yelled as he started destroying Brittany's office.

Brittany stood up. "I advise you to settle the fuck down! You aren't the only one who lost here. Now, we need to sit down and come up with something, 'cause I can agree that if we don't find out who just hit us up, somebody is going to pay dearly."

Dana agreed, looking around at everyone. "Listen, we gonna get to the bottom of this, 'cause I swear, with all the losses I've taken lately, I don't mind pulling another stunt and killing me a ho. Shit, you called me a stupid THOT once, but baby I'm a THOT with ambition, and my ambition is to get even with Thad and get me some fucking money," she said, looking at Farrah and Stephanie.

Everyone looked around at each other, trying to determine who the traitor could be. Dana didn't trust anyone, but she refused to lie down on it. She was going to get to the bottom of everything and get back the money that was taken from them by any means necessary—even if it meant going on a killing spree. She was taking no prisoners.

to survive. She couldn't understand why they hadn't pulled the plug on the ho yet.

After everyone finally left that fateful Saturday evening after both of the robberies, Dana and Brittany stayed behind at the office, pissed, shocked, and disgusted. Deondre had pitched a hellafied fit, which scared Farrah and Jeryca out of their wits. Zack also stayed behind with Dana and Brittany, but he sat in a different room, making telephone calls to see if he could find out anything. He needed that lick just as bad as everyone else involved. He hadn't put all his efforts into helping plan that robbery and getting his cousins involved for none of them to have anything to show for it. He had a few connects that he was sure could help him. He had heard through the grapevine that Thad was connected with some powerful men, and having similar friends himself, Zack figured he might be able to persuade them to introduce him to the big dogs as well. That's why he and Thad were beefing in the first place. Thad was afraid that Zack could gain control over his territory, and he tried to knock him off before he could make a move on it. Thad had made one grave mistake, though: he didn't kill him. Zack was more determined now than before to get his turn and crush

Thad and Toby, and he was going to use their plugs to do so.

"What's up? How are you guys doing?" Zack asked.

"Man, we still dealing with that bitch-ass Thad and his crew," Tim answered.

"Shit. Orlando still messing with them faggots?" Zack asked.

"Hell yeah, but he's talking about leaving the game, period. You know the police came and questioned him about the bust they made at his warehouse. He told them he didn't know anything about it," Tim replied.

"Hell, he ain't supposed to tell them he know anything. He facing fed time with the amount of weed and the crates of guns they found. I'm surprised he ain't got the hell out of New York by now," Zack said.

"He isn't going anywhere until he can re-up from the hit he took from the bust," Tim explained.

"Well, shit, ask Orlando if he interested in discussing a plan that will rid him of Thad and put a lot of cash in his pocket," Zack proposed.

"I can't promise that he will be interested, but I will see what I can do," Tim responded.

"That's all I ask, my nigga," Zack said before hanging up.

Zack had a few more calls to make to successfully carry out his plan. He wasn't going
to halfway do anything this time. The robbery,
although successfully executed, was planned on
short notice, and the aftermath wasn't thought
out properly. This time, with the right connects,
the right team, and sufficient time to plan everything out, Zack was sure he could take Thad's
money. Zack wanted to take over his territory,
kill his reputation, and then take his life, all at
the same time.

Farrah had been locked in her home since
the robbery. She did what she thought she
had to do to keep her son in her custody. She
knew she had betrayed Dana and them by
telling Larry about the change in plans for the
robbery. If that bitch Debra hadn't squealed
on them in the first place, she wouldn't have
been placed in the situation she currently
found herself in. She didn't know who she
could trust, and she hadn't heard one peep
from Larry since that day.

She constantly thought about how things
could've gone differently, but in the end, she
did what she thought was best. She begged

Larry not to make her do it, but the day that she went to jail, he told her that if she cooperated with his and Debra's plan, he would drop the custody suit. Debra, the fucking bitch Dana brought into the play, betrayed them for a piece of dick.

"Mommy, what can I eat? I'm hungry," Travis said as he ran into the living room.

"Boy, what have I told your behind about running through this house?" Farrah yelled.

"Sorry. What can I eat, Mommy?" he asked again.

"Come on here and let me fix you a peanut butter and jelly sandwich," she said as she stood up and walked into the kitchen.

"Again? I hate peanut butter," Travis whined.

Farrah looked at him with a frustrated stare, which told him to chill out. He didn't say another word, but he bowed his head and sat down at the table, waiting on his sandwich. Seeing him hold his head down made her feel bad. "How 'bout a grilled cheese and fries instead?"

"With turkey?" he asked.

Farrah started laughing. "Boy, you want too much. Yes, you can have turkey."

Just then, her phone began to ring, and it was Dana again. She had called Farrah three times already. Farrah didn't want to talk to anybody.

As she walked past the phone, it started to ring again.

"Damn it!" she yelled as she stomped over to the phone.

"Mommy, you said a bad word!" Travis said in a surprised tone.

Farrah looked at him. "Shut the hell up, boy!"

Travis sighed. "Yes, ma'am," he said in a low whisper.

"Hello, Mom." Farrah answered once she knew it was her mother calling.

"Hey, baby. How are you guys doing? I haven't talked to you in a few days, sweetie. Is everything all right?" her mother inquired.

"Yes, ma'am, we are okay," Farrah replied.

"Can I come over and visit with you for a while? I want to see my grandson," her mother said.

"Mom, you know you can come anytime," Farrah retorted.

"Okay, sweetie, I'm on my way."

After she hung up, she looked over at Travis. "Guess who's coming?"

"Grandma!" Travis shouted.

"Yes, baby. Now, let's fix you something to eat before she gets here," Farrah said. She walked over to Travis, gave him a peck on the forehead, and fixed her son lunch.

***

"Has anybody heard anything from Chris or Keith today?" Thad asked.

Toby shook his head, while Larry sat on the couch in his office, stone-faced. He hadn't heard a single word that Thad had spoken. "Aye, man, I asked you a question," Thad said louder, walking toward Larry.

"Oh . . . Uh . . . Sorry, bro, I was somewhere else," Larry replied.

"I asked has anyone heard from Chris or Keith," Thad yelled.

"I haven't heard from him in a few days," Larry replied.

"A few days? Nigga, you told me yesterday that you spoke to him Tuesday. It's Thursday now, so what's a few days? Man, what the hell is going on with you? Don't give me no lame-ass excuse that it's Travis, 'cause we all know you been dealing with that lawyer chick who's helping you with that. So why all the lies, man? Now, when was the last time you spoke with Chris?" Thad asked angrily.

"I-I d-d-don't remember, really," Larry stuttered.

Just as Thad got ready to stand up again, his phone rang. "Yeah?" he answered.

Thad sat quietly listening to the caller, never once removing his eyes off Larry, who was squirming nervously on the couch.

"All right, but I'm kind of in the middle of something. Can I get back with you later? All right, all right, I'm on it," he said before he hung up.

"Look, nigga, I need to holla at Toby 'bout something, but we will finish this discussion today. Be back here in two hours, and I swear if you aren't back, it's going to be a problem," Thad growled.

"I'll be back. I don't have any reason not to come back," Larry replied.

Larry walked out of Thad's office and stood against the door, listening to what Thad and Toby were saying. "Man, if I find out that nigga had anything to do with us being robbed, I'm going to kill that bastard, and that's on everything!" he heard Thad say.

"Man, you been making everybody suspect. You can't keep doing that," Toby answered.

"Man, I don't give a fuck. That nigga acting way too funny, and he probably know where Keith at, too. They probably both involved. How the hell do we get robbed and busted on the same goddamn day? Man, it's too coincidental. Mark my words: that mutherfucka knows something," Thad replied.

Larry tiptoed away and headed toward his car. "I ain't going out like that. Shit, I bet I don't. Not me," he said aloud to himself.

As he drove off, he called Farrah. When she picked up, he asked her if Travis was there, and when she told him no, he was with his grandma, he hung up.

Dana had grown tired of trying to contact Farrah on the phone, so she asked Zack to let her use his car. She drove to Farrah's house and parked around the corner. She didn't want Farrah to see Zack's car, 'cause she probably wouldn't open the door. Hell, she still might not answer it, but Dana had to try. She needed answers, and the only two who were avoiding her were Farrah and Jeryca.

To her surprise, Farrah opened the door on the second knock. "Y'all came back quick," she said as she opened the door. When she saw it was Dana, her smile immediately turned into a frown.

"Surprised to see me?" Dana asked, as she pushed past Farrah.

"What do you want, Dana?" Farrah asked as she walked quickly to the kitchen.

"Damn, I can't check on my girl? I been calling you for days, and after repeatedly getting your voice mail, I wanted to check on you. Just making sure you're okay," Dana said with a menacing tone, which wasn't hard for Farrah to detect.

Farrah started feeling slightly uncomfortable but forced a smile. "Well, as you can see, I'm good."

"Yeah, I can. You know, Jeryca been MIA also. Have you heard from her?" Dana asked.

"I haven't heard from anyone. Just been spending time with Travis. You know we got that court hearing coming up and all," Farrah explained.

"Yeah, um, you know Debra was at the office, and she told us something kind of disturbing. Sh—" Dana began, but immediately, Farrah cut her off.

"Whatever that bitch said isn't true! It was all her and Larry's idea to rip you off. They used my son against me. You got to believe me," Farrah said, remembering what Deondre had said after Larry left the day of the robbery.

"Say what? I was going to say that Debra told us that Larry was dropping the suit against you, but you telling me that you were partly responsible for us getting hit?" Dana yelled as she advanced on Farrah.

Farrah instantly grabbed a knife from her dish rack. "Don't come any closer! I mean it, Dana."

Dana was far from listening. It was as if she were another person. She grabbed the arm that Farrah held the knife in and they struggled, knocking dishes to the floor. The two women slipped on water that came from a glass that fell on the floor. Dana landed one way, and Farrah another. When Dana looked over, she saw Farrah lying on the floor, struggling to get up with the knife stuck in her arm.

Dana immediately dove on top of her, pulled the knife out, and plunged it into Farrah repeatedly. With each blow, she spoke. "You dirty bitch! You traitor! You going to wish you had never fucked me over!"

As she brought the knife up one final time, she looked down at Farrah's face, and for the first time, she saw the tears running down her face. This was her childhood friend that she was stabbing. Dana dropped her head, raised it back up, and with tears running down her face as well, she stabbed Farrah once more.

"Fuck you! No love lost, bitch!"

Dana wrapped the knife in a towel and walked calmly to Zack's car. No one was out at that moment, but Dana was too discombobulated to even notice. As she pulled off, she wondered how she could explain to Brittany that her "business partner" was responsible for them losing all the money. She just hoped Brittany would handle it as she just did. Dana had become ruthless and more determined to obtain what she wanted: the money

Forty-five minutes later, Larry pulled up to Farrah's house. As he sat in his car, he contemplated his next move. Once he made peace with his decision, he got out of the car and knocked on the door. After the third knock and no answer, Larry pushed the door open and hollered Farrah's name. He didn't get an answer, so he tiptoed through the house, and when he got to the kitchen, he gasped.

"Fuck!" he whispered. He walked over and stood over Farrah, then bent down. "Looks like somebody beat me to it. Don't worry, though. I will take good care of Travis." Larry walked out and got into his car. He exhaled for a minute and pulled off. As he rounded the corner, Farrah's mother pulled up.

"Travis, looks like you just missed your father." She raised the seat up so Travis could get out.

"Grandma, I'm glad Daddy's gone. I want to stay here with you and Mommy."

"Aw, baby, I'm glad you do. Come on, let's take these groceries in so your mother can cook this lasagna."

"Okay, I got to use the bathroom, Grandma."

"Well, go on then." She laughed.

Travis ran to the bathroom, while Farrah's mother walked into the kitchen. "Farrah, I think we got everything we need," Mrs. Walker said. She immediately froze and screamed. "Oh my God! No! No! Baby, get up! Please, God, not my baby! No!" she cried.

At that moment, Travis ran in, and the sight that befell upon his tiny eyes stopped him in his tracks. "Grandma, what's wrong with Mommy?"

As he walked forward, she ran up and grabbed him. He fought against her to get to Farrah, but she successfully removed Travis, who was kicking and screaming, from the house.

She called 911. "Yes, this is Shirley Walker, and I need an ambulance to come immediately!"

"Ma'am, what's the problem?" the operator asked.

"My daughter has been stabbed! Please send help!" she yelled.

"What's the address, ma'am?" the operator asked.

After Shirley gave the operator the information, she was instructed to stay on the phone
until help arrived. They told her not to re-enter
the house, because the assailant could still be
inside.

When the operator said that, Shirley replied,
"The assailant isn't inside. He was leaving when
we pulled up."

The operator asked for the description of the
car that Larry was driving, so she could put an
APB out on it immediately.

Finally, the ambulance and police arrived.
Farrah was pronounced dead at 5:26 p.m.

Larry turned down Holley Avenue when
he heard sirens behind him. He smiled as he
thought about Farrah and how he now only
had three people instead of four to deal with
in order to feel completely free. He wasn't
comfortable knowing that there was someone
around who could finger him to Thad and Toby.
He felt extremely nervous when they informed
him that Austin was the go-to guy until further
notice. That let him know that they didn't trust
him.

Larry looked into his rearview mirror and
noticed the police were on his tail. He slowed

down so they could go around him, but they continued behind him. He then sped up a little bit and turned into a grocery store parking lot to get out of the way, but to his surprise, they followed him.

"What the fuck now?" he whispered to himself.

As the four police cars surrounded his vehicle, Larry didn't move. He kept his hands on the steering wheel, wondering what was going on.

As the officers got out of their cars, they drew their guns. "Driver, get out of the car with your hands up! I repeat, get out of the car with your hands up!"

Larry opened the door and stood up with his hands in the air.

The officer then yelled, "Now, slowly get down on your knees and lie face down! Slowly!"

Larry hesitated for a minute, and then spoke. "Officer, I've done nothing wrong!"

"Get down on your knees! I'm not going to say it again!" the officer commanded.

Larry did as he was told. Three officers rushed toward him and handcuffed him.

"What is this about?" Larry asked.

"Sir, your vehicle was seen leaving the scene of a crime that just happened several blocks from here."

"I had nothing to do with any crime, officer!" Larry cried.

"Sergeant, we got blood on the mat here on the driver's side, and a .38 Special in the glove compartment," another officer yelled.

The sergeant walked over to inspect the car, and then walked over to inspect Larry's shoes. When he saw the blood, he ordered them to be taken off, and he called the Crime Scene Unit.

Larry was read his rights and placed in the back of a police car. He watched as his car was loaded onto the back of a tow truck. He was then taken down to the precinct for booking. He didn't know what to do, but he knew who he had to call. After he was fingerprinted, questioned, and dressed, he was given his one phone call. He dialed Debra's number.

"Hello," she answered after accepting the call.

"Hey, listen. They just arrested me for murder," he whispered.

"Who are they accusing you of killing, baby?" she asked.

"They saying I killed Farrah! I didn't do it, I swear," he cried.

"What's your bond?" she asked.

"I don't have one. What am I going to do?" he asked.

There was a brief silence, and then Debra exhaled sharply. "I don't know what *you're* going to do, but please don't dial this number again."

"That fucking bitch!" Larry yelled after she hung up on him. He knew he was done for.

Chapter Fifteen

Friday morning, as the news about Farrah's death and Larry's arrest filled the street, Thad was dealing with even more stressful issues. He had just received a call from Ramon Silva and Sergio Torres and was informed that his time was nearly up. They were flying up from Venezuela in two months' time, and if they didn't get their money or product, they were going to handle the matter their way. Thad couldn't believe the turn of his luck. He had to figure out some way to get his hands on some extra cash fast, a lot of it, but not so much as to be left totally broke. He had money put aside, and his company was bringing in a large profit; however, it wasn't enough to pay back Sergio and Ramon what he owed them on the shipment they had sent. He also had a few guns and cocaine he could move and make several thousands of dollars on, but he needed more.

He assumed that Orlando wasn't involved with the hit against them, so he was going to continue to use him and his men to move his shit. He really needed Orlando, because Sergio was his connect, and if anything, he could talk to them and possibly get them some extended time.

Ramon and Sergio came from separate parts of South America. Ramon's family originated from Uruguay, and Sergio's from Colombia. Their families met and found a common interest, which brought forth the Bomont Cartel. Formed in 1940, they moved on to build a billion-dollar dynasty. They exported large amounts of cocaine, and huge shipments of guns and marijuana. They supplied the top hitters, located in California, Mexico, Georgia, Michigan, Miami, and Las Vegas. Thad was hoping to add New York to the roster, but he doubted that it would happen now. He just prayed that he and his team lived through the next few months.

"Man, what a fucking month. Nothing seems to be going right. We are several men down, and now this bullshit with Larry. Man, what next?" Thad shouted.

"I know, and for the first time, I don't have any answers. I'm just as confused as you are," Toby admitted.

"Well, I'm down to do whatever. I think we should go on a spree and get as much as we can get," Austin replied.

"Explain yourself, Austin," Toby replied.

"Well, first off, we got enough people to pull a few licks. Who do we all know that got cash long enough to get us to a promising start?" Austin asked, looking at Thad and Toby.

"Who?" Toby asked, looking confused.

"Orlando," Thad answered loudly, proud as a peacock.

"Yeah, but aren't they heavily connected to Sergio?" Toby asked.

"Yeah, but we can hit them, and no one will know it was us. They will assume that it was the guys who hit us. We can do this," Thad replied, feeling a little bit better.

"Well, let's call up our boys and see what's up," Toby said.

"I'm on it now," Austin replied as he began dialing numbers.

"I knew I liked that muthafucka for some reason," Thad said, pointing to Austin.

"Hell yeah! He official. I been told you that," Toby said as he grabbed his cell phone to make a few calls. Thad followed suit and called a few of his contacts.

***

Jeryca was both devastated and terrified over the news of Farrah's death. She couldn't believe that her friend was gone. After hearing about it on television, Jeryca called Farrah's mother. Her sister, Karen, informed her that Shirley wasn't able to talk at that time.

"How is Travis doing?" Jeryca asked.

"Who is this?" Karen asked.

"Oh, I'm sorry. I'm Jeryca."

"Li'l Jeryca from the east side?" Karen asked.

"Yes, ma'am. Me and Farrah been friends for what seemed like forever," Jeryca said.

"Yes, I know. Well, how are the other girls?" Karen asked.

"They're fine," Jeryca stated.

"Maybe you can come over and see if Travis will respond to you. He isn't eating, barely slept a wink last night, and won't talk to anyone," Karen explained.

"Yes, I'd love to come over and visit with Travis, as well as the rest of the family," Jeryca said.

"Okay, well, we will see you when you get here," Karen replied.

Jeryca called Dana to see if she would go with her over to Shirley's house. She needed to be close to her friends. She knew that Stephanie and Dana had issues with her and rightfully so, but she needed to be around them so they could all grieve together.

***

"What? I can't believe that bitch! I brought her ass in and she betrays me for a fucking nigga! I will snap that bitch's neck. Real shit!" Brittany stormed as she paced back and forth in her office after Dana gave her the news. She couldn't believe Debra was partially responsible for them losing the product and money they got from Thad.

"Brit, we got to use our head on this, though. We can't go off all half-cocked. Debra knows where our shit at, and we need her to tell us where it's located. So I say for now, let's play it cool like we don't know shit, and then pounce on that ass and make her tell all, like we did Keith," Dana said menacingly.

"What happened to my sweet little darling?" Brittany said, laughing.

"She no longer exists. I've been pushed and pushed and pushed by my so-called friends and their niggas. I'm on a mission for the money, and I'm taking my respect. I'm an ambitious woman now," Dana said as she held her head back, smiling.

"Aw, sookie sookie now! Look at ya! I'm scared of yo' ass." Brittany laughed.

Just then, Dana's phone rang. "Hello?" It was Jeryca. "Hey, Jeryca. How are you doing?"

"Girl, I'm not taking this too well," Jeryca sniffed.

"Me either," Dana lied.

"Why did that have to happen to Farrah, Dana? Why did Larry do that shit?" Jeryca moaned.

Dana sighed. "I don't know. Listen, I'm going to call Stephanie and see if she wants to go with us. I will pick you up after I get off work. If we didn't have a full schedule, I'd get off now, but we are behind and have several cases that we have to jump on immediately," Dana explained.

"Okay, call me when you're on your way," Jeryca said softly before hanging up.

"All right, girl," Dana said before hanging up.

Brittany looked at Dana and shook her head. "Girl, you know you could've took some time off to go to Ms. Walker's house."

"Yeah, I know, but Brittany, I got something to tell you. I haven't told you everything yet." Dana sighed.

"Oh Lord! Do I need to sit down for this?" Brittany asked.

Dana sat down across from Brittany with her head down, took in a deep breath, and exhaled slowly. When she looked up, she smiled. "I know I can trust you not to say anything, so here goes. When Farrah told me about the situation with her, Larry, and Debra, I snapped. She grabbed a knife; we fought, and she slipped and fell. When I looked over at her, the knife was embedded in her chest," Dana explained.

"What! You know you could've stayed and it would've been self-defense or accidental—" Brittany began.

"Well, the problem with that is, I would've had to explain how she fell repeatedly on the knife in different areas of her body!" Dana laughed.

"Damn, Dana! What the hell? I can't believe I'm sitting here listening to you tell me that you killed your best friend," Brittany exclaimed.

"I don't know, Brit. I just lost it. Once I saw her laying there with the knife in her chest, I grabbed it and went on her." Dana groaned as she slid down a bit in the chair.

"So where is the knife, Dana?" Brittany asked.

"I tossed it," Dana replied.

"I hope you tossed it where it couldn't be found," Brittany said.

"Yes, I hid it very well," Dana answered.

"Well, with Larry and Farrah out of the way, we can focus on Debra," Brittany said.

"Focus on Debra for what?" Debra asked as she walked into the room, smiling.

The two women looked at Debra, shocked that she had almost caught them talking about her.

Brittany stood up. "You just walk into my office without knocking? Really?"

"I saw you two in here and didn't think it would be a problem. But what were you two talking about?" Dana asked again.

"We were just saying that we need to focus on helping you with the caseload you have. We are all behind on our work and need to play catch up," Dana said before Brittany could speak.

Brittany sat down behind her desk and glared at Debra, who was smiling from ear to ear, wearing what appeared to be a new outfit. This burned Brittany up inside, but she couldn't say anything if they hoped to get their money back.

"Shit, I've never seen you with that outfit on. Looks nice on you," Brittany stated without any real emotion.

"Oh, thanks, girl. My boo bought it for me," she said as she twirled around.

"Looks good. But listen, Debra: me and Dana was talking, and I'm trying to help her with this Farrah issue. You know she was killed yesterday," Brittany explained.

"Oh, yeah. Sorry, girl," Debra said, looking at Dana and smiling.

"Thank you," Dana replied.

"I will talk to you in a few. I got to go make a few calls," Debra said as she walked out of the office.

"I can't wait to bash her head in. She—" Brittany started before Dana stopped her.

"Let's discuss it this evening when I come back from visiting Farrah's family. We don't want Debra to know that we know she had a hand in our money getting stolen," Dana said.

Brittany agreed, and they went on about their regular work day. Brittany tried to stay away from Debra as much as she could. When she did go around her, she was cordial and respectful. It pained Brittany to be so nice when she wanted to bash her head in. They had loaded over $500K in merchandise alone on their lick, only for that bitch to steal it from them. Boy, she was ready to snap.

At around twelve o'clock, Brittany told Debra and Dana that she wasn't feeling well and would work from home.

"Okay, sweetie, get you some rest. Hope you feel better soon," Debra replied.

Brittany looked at her for a long minute then stated, "I'm sure what's ailing me will pass. Thank you, love."

"You know I got you," Debra replied.

Dana watched as Brittany bit back her words and smiled.

"See you tomorrow, Dana. Take care, and if you need to talk to me, call me, okay?"

"All right, I will," Dana replied.

Brittany left, and Dana and Debra carried on working for the remainder of the day. At 4:30 p.m., Dana left for the day and headed straight to Jeryca's house. She didn't want to go in due to the incident between her and Jeryca's mother and sister, so she blew her horn. After about three minutes, Jeryca slowly walked out of the house. Her eyes were puffy, and her nose was red.

As she got into the car, she reached over and hugged Dana. "Hey, sis."

"Hey, baby girl. Are you okay?" Dana asked.

"I'm as good as I can be, I guess," Jeryca answered.

"I got to pick up Stephanie, and we will ride on over to Shirley's house," Dana stated.

"Okay, sounds good," Jeryca replied.

As they rode in silence, Dana couldn't help but feel sorry for Jeryca. She looked torn, lost, and afraid. Dana knew that Jeryca and Farrah were close, but Stephanie was closer to Farrah than either of them was.

As she pulled up to Stephanie's house, they saw Stephanie standing on her porch with a female they had never seen. What really shocked them was that this woman was holding Stephanie. It wasn't the type of embrace that a regular friend would give. As they watched the two walk toward the car, Stephanie grabbed the girl's hand, which confirmed Dana's initial thought. This was Stephanie's lover!

Stephanie had told her that she had met someone new and that she liked her. Although this was a shocker for Dana, she couldn't help but smile. Stephanie had a real cutie, and she looked happy again.

"Hey, listen, this is my friend Robin, and I was hoping it would be okay if she rode with us over to Shirley's house," Stephanie said as she approached the car.

"Hey, Robin," both girls replied.

"You know she is more than welcome to ride. Come on, let's go," Dana said.

As they got into the car, Stephanie told Dana and Jeryca how she and Robin met, and how they had been spending a lot of time with one another.

Dana smiled. "Well, I don't care who you are with. I'm just glad you're happy, but you know we got to chat!"

"Oh Lord!" Stephanie laughed. "Yes, I know."

When they pulled up to Shirley's house, there were a lot of cars in the driveway and around the home. They had to park around the corner from Shirley's house, which caused Dana to have a déjà vu moment. She laughed at the irony of the situation.

"What's funny?" Jeryca asked, frowning.

"Nothing, just thinking that we are walking into this house, and for the first time, Farrah isn't going to be there. Man, this is going to be hard," Dana said as she dropped her head. Jeryca rushed over to hug her, and Dana felt a twinge of regret for lying, but to her, it was a necessary evil. She wanted to laugh again at that thought, but she held it in.

Dana walked into Shirley's house and scanned the room. She saw Shirley standing in a corner, talking to some woman she didn't recognize. She saw groups of people talking, and a few were crying.

Dana's gaze froze on a sight that made her heart sink. Over on the couch, curled up in a snug, tight ball, with his head in between his knees, was Travis. Several people approached him, but he simply didn't acknowledge them.

Stephanie and her friend were talking to a few of Farrah's cousins, and Jeryca had made her way to talk with Shirley. Shirley embraced Jeryca and held her for a few seconds, let her go, and then grabbed her again.

Dana decided to make her way over to Travis. When she sat down, she leaned over and said, "Hey, T-man. It's Dana."

He raised his head and began to cry uncontrollably. Instinct made Dana pick him up and hold him. He wrapped his tiny arms around her neck tightly and wept. Everyone stopped what they were doing and looked over at Travis. Shirley began to cry and ran out of the room with Jeryca and Karen on her heels.

Dana's heart went out to both Shirley and Travis. "Hey, li'l man, do you want something to eat or drink? I hear your li'l tummy growling."

"I'm n-n-not h-h-hungry," he sobbed.

"Eat just a little bite for Auntie D," she pleaded.

He finally gave in, but he wasn't going to let her put him down. Dana struggled to hold him up, and as she walked to the kitchen, she overheard Shirley talking and crying at the same time.

"I'm his grandmother, and he hasn't really spoken to me since yesterday. How am I supposed to take care of him on my income? All I get is seven hundred dollars in disability. I'm sickly. I can't raise him alone. What's going to happen to him if I die or become ill? Somebody please tell me!" she cried.

Dana turned around and walked back toward the door.

"Where we going, Auntie D?" Travis asked.

"Auntie D is taking you to Burger King. Would you like that?" she asked.

"Yes, ma'am!" he replied.

"Okay, well, jump down and let Auntie D go and tell your grandma where we are going."

Travis got down, but he stood up against the door with his head down.

Dana told Shirley that she was taking Travis out for a while. Shirley nodded her head with approval. Before Dana could get out the door, Stephanie ran up. "Where you going?"

"I'm taking Travis out for a while," Dana answered.

"We're going to ride with you, okay? All this is too much for me. Dana. It really just hit me that Farrah is really gone." Stephanie began to cry.

"Steph, we got to keep it together. Travis isn't doing good at all, and he doesn't need to see you crying. You can't do that crying if you ride with us," Dana replied harshly.

Robin rubbed Stephanie's shoulders. "Baby, she's right. Look at that little boy over there."

Stephanie sniffed and smiled. "I'm good, y'all. I promise I got this."

"Are you sure? You good, sis?" Dana said softly, rubbing Stephanie's arms.

"Yes, I am. Let's get Travis and go eat. I'm starving!" Stephanie replied, half-smiling.

They left and went to Burger King. Travis ate his food quietly and kept his head on Dana's arm the whole time. He talked to Stephanie about seeing his mother lying on the floor, bleeding.

Dana felt bad hearing Travis describing what he had seen. She had been so angry with Farrah and her betrayal that she had forgotten about the impact it would have on Travis.

She looked at her watch and told Stephanie and Robin that they had to leave. As they gathered their belongings, Travis asked her if he could spend the night with her.

"Baby, I'm sorry. I have to work tomorrow. You know what? Your grandma needs you to be there with her. You got to make sure she eats like you did. Talk to her and make sure she is okay. Can you do that for me?" Dana asked.

Travis sat in silence for a few minutes but finally agreed to stay with his grandma. Dana drove him back in silence. She had to figure out how she could help Shirley and Travis in their time of need.

After she dropped him off, she told Jeryca that they had to go. Jeryca then informed her that she was going to stay the night and help Shirley out for a while. Dana hugged Jeryca and Shirley and then walked over to Travis. She squatted down before him, grasped him gently by the chin, and tilted his head up so that he was looking at her.

"Aye, T-man, remember what I said. Look at me," she said when he looked down. "Remember, you got to be a big boy, okay?"

He nodded his head with tears streaming down his face. Seeing Travis in that much pain ripped through Dana's heart, and she fought back the tears threatening to spill over.

She hugged him tightly and rushed out the door in tears. She wasn't crying from the loss of Farrah, but from Travis's pain.

Chapter Sixteen

"Brittany, are you on board or what?" Zack asked.

"Before I answer that, have you run this by Dana? If she's on board, then I'm on board. You know I'm always ready to make some money, but I want Dana to be a part of this," Brittany replied.

"I'm going to talk to her, but you know Dana will be all for it," Zack said.

"Well, make sure she is, and then we can talk. You know Dana has become hardhearted. I love the new her." Brittany laughed.

"Yeah, me too. I talked to Orlando and Tim this morning, and we had our conference call with their man, Sergio. Brittany, I'm telling you this lick is going to be sweet. If I can pull it off successfully, I'm going to see if we can connect with my people in North Carolina so we can take over the East Coast. These guys that Orlando introduced me to are the real deal,"

Zack whispered after seeing Debra walking by Brittany's office.

Brittany motioned for Debra to come in, trying not to look too conspicuous.

"What's up, boss lady?" Debra said as she bounced into the office with yet another seemingly new outfit on. Brittany noticed it immediately.

"Well, you know our lick went bad the other week, but we have a plan to recoup from it. We need your help on this one. Will you help us once we get everything planned out?" Brittany asked.

"Why do you need me?" Debra asked suspiciously.

"With Farrah's death and all, I don't know if everyone who was previously involved will be available to help," Brittany replied quickly.

Debra thought about it for a few seconds and finally agreed. "Girl, I'm all on it. What do you want me to do?" she asked.

"We haven't gotten everything just right, but when we do, I will get back to you. On a different note, what are you having for lunch today?" Brittany asked.

"I don't know yet. What do you have a taste for?"

"Girl, just let me know where you're going so I can send for something. I'm preparing for this case on Monday, and I probably won't have time to get anything." Brittany sighed, rolling her eyes.

"Okay, I will let you know when I figure out where I'm going," Debra replied.

Debra left Brittany's office, walked over, and knocked on Dana's door. When she walked in, Dana looked up.

"You need something, Debra?"

"When you get time, I need you to look up a case for me," Debra replied.

"Brittany got me on two cases right now, and it's already ten thirty. Get me the case file, and I will see what I can find before twelve. You do remember that we are only working 'til two o'clock since its Saturday?" Dana asked.

"Well, couldn't you work over?" Debra asked, looking confused.

"No, I can't. I am going over to Ms. Walker's house," Dana answered.

"Oh, I forgot about your *friend*," Debra replied, putting an emphasis on the last word.

Dana glared at her and started to respond, but Zack walked in.

"Oh, I didn't know you were in here, Debra," he said as he walked in.

"Yeah, just trying to get a li'l work done," Debra replied before excusing herself from the room.

"I don't know what persuaded you to come in when you did, but boy, I swear I thank you. I was 'bout to go in on that bitch," Dana groaned.

"What the fuck she do?" Zack asked.

Dana sighed. "Just her being in my presence ticks me off. What's up, though?"

"Shit, can you get your girls together tonight?" he asked.

"Hell, I don't know. They so wrapped up in their feelings right now. But what do you want me to get them together for?" Dana asked.

"Come and walk with me to the car, sweet cheeks." He laughed as he grabbed her by the hand.

"Oh Lord, got to be some kind of bullshit that you trying to sweet talk me into," Dana joked as she stood up and walked with Zack out of the office. Dana walked to Brittany's office to inform her that she was going to take a small, ten-minute break.

"Go 'head, lady," Brittany replied.

"It might be fifteen," Zack said, sticking his head in the door.

"Ten minutes, girl," Dana said, quickly dismissing Zack's comment.

Brittany laughed as the pair left her office and the building.

They playfully pushed each other as they walked to the car. He opened the passenger's side door so she could get in. Once they were in the car, Zack looked at her.

"Listen, I got information on a lick that will set us up for the long haul. Shit, I fuck with you, and I need you and your girls on board. Plus, this is still going to get some payback for you with Thad."

"Zack, I don't know if Jeryca and Stephanie would be down with that so soon after Farrah's death. Tell you what: let me talk to them, and I will let you know by four o'clock if they with it," Dana promised.

"All right, I will be waiting for your call. Now, if they aren't wit' it, can I depend on you to work wit' us?" Zack asked as he rubbed her fingers.

"Of course you can. You know I'm down with fucking over Thad, and getting some money is an added bonus. But I got something else for Thad's ass also," she stated.

"That's my girl. Make sure you let Brit know. She said she wasn't in if you weren't," Zack said, smiling.

"That's my muthafuckin' bitch," Dana said, getting out of the car. Once she was out, she bent her head down and looked Zack dead in his eyes.

"Oh, and don't get it twisted; all that hand-rubbing and sweet talk isn't what persuaded me to help a nigga. It's all about that dollar."

As she walked away, Zack watched her until she reached the entrance of the building. He laughed as she turned and waved. He really liked her and couldn't wait to smash her ass, he thought, watching the jiggle of her butt as she walked into the office.

"Man, you ain't talking 'bout shit, nigga. Just pass that blunt and shut the fuck up lying." Thad laughed as he grabbed the blunt from Austin.

"For real, man. Just think about it: how the hell did the Egyptians create all those pyramids? They're aliens. Real talk, yo," Austin replied.

"Don't nobody give Austin any more bud! He done lost it." Thad laughed, choking on the smoke he had just inhaled.

"All right, don't believe me!"

Before Austin could finish, Toby came into the room. "I got Chris on the phone, bro, and you need to hear what he is saying."

Thad could tell by the look on Toby's face that it was important. He grabbed the phone.

"What's up, my nigga?"

"Thad, man, word in here is that Larry was involved with the robbery. They said that Farrah somehow found out, and that's why he killed her," Chris said quickly.

"Man, you are fucking lying. Larry ain't did no shit like that. God damn it," Thad yelled.

"Man, you know the nigga ain't even reached out to me at all. He over in F Block and could've been got at me. I think it's some truth to this shit. The man who gave me the info is solid. You know D-Red?" Chris asked.

"Yeah, man, I know that nigga. Listen, thanks for looking out. You know we got you, my nigga, and we gon' handle this Larry situation. I'm gonna let you holla back at Toby. Keep ya head up, man." Thad sighed, shaking his head.

Thad handed Toby his phone and walked out of the room quietly with his fists balled. Toby knew that his brother was out for blood.

After Toby got off the phone, Austin looked at him. "What's up, Toby?"

"Man, we just found out that Larry fucked us, and he is the reason why we are in our current situation."

While Toby explained to Austin what Chris had just divulged to him, Thad walked in.

Austin looked at Thad. "Let me take care of dude for y'all. I am a part of this now. Trust me to take care of this."

Thad and Toby looked at each other, and Thad sighed. "All right, handle it."

Austin walked out of the room on his phone. Toby flopped down on the couch, and Thad paced the floor. A few minutes later, Toby's phone rang, and Thad looked over at him.

"It's just wifey," Toby said.

"Man, I wish I could get my hands on that fuckin' nigga for real. I knew he was acting suspect. I told you," Thad shouted as he punched the wall.

Toby waited until after Thad finished ranting before he called Tiffany back.

Thad was infuriated, but he was calming down, bit by bit. As he sat down and took slow, deep breaths, he closed his eyes. When he opened them, he called for Luscious, one of his new hoes, to come into the room.

"Yes, sir?" she said as she entered.

Thad looked at Toby and said quietly, "You should excuse yourself."

Toby knew what that meant, and as he was about to shut the door, he heard Thad tell Luscious, "Come over here and give me some head, bitch."

Toby shook his head, disappeared into the dining area, and called his wife.

***

After an hour of pleading her case, Dana finally convinced Jeryca and Stephanie to join her, Brittany, Orlando, and Zack at Brittany's house. Her house was huge and on a large, private lot.

Everyone sat around Brittany's large kitchen table and listened to Orlando and Zack explain every detail of their plan. Dana had told Jeryca and Stephanie that this would be a good move, and it would benefit Shirley and Travis as well as them, which was why Jeryca and Stephanie agreed to help. They knew that it was going to be hard for Shirley to take care of Travis all by herself. Her finances just wouldn't be enough, and to make matters worse, Farrah didn't have any life insurance, which was an extra strain on Shirley. They had to help her out.

After Orlando and Zack finished talking, Brittany began to talk. "All right now, y'all know we got to get our shit back from Debra. Since I brought her in, I will deal with her, but I'm going to need a few hands on deck to assist me."

"Debra?" Stephanie asked.

"Oh, shit! I didn't tell y'all that we found out that Larry and Debra were the ones responsible for the hit on our lick."

"What!" Jeryca yelled and stood up angrily.

"Fuck, I'm in! Just let me know when and where. The how I will leave up to you," Dana said.

"I'm in also. That bitch done fucked up!" Stephanie said.

Jeryca sat back down slowly. "I can't do anything until after Farrah's funeral on Monday."

"Understandable," Zack and Orlando agreed.

Dana, Zack, and Brittany got up and walked into the front room while Jeryca, Stephanie, and Orlando stood talking in the kitchen.

"Listen, you know I had my cousin D-Red spread a rumor that Larry was responsible for hitting Thad. I told him that we needed to get that nigga out the picture as payback for Farrah," Dana whispered.

"Shit, that was good thinking, sis. That way no one will link you to her death, and that's a stress off you," Brittany muttered.

"I know, right? Shit, we need to figure out a day to deal with Debra, and once those two are out the way, I'm in the clear," Dana said, smiling.

The three of them quickly turned around as they heard Orlando clearing his throat. He and Jeryca stood in the doorway, and a few seconds later, Stephanie appeared with a drink in her hand.

Dana immediately smiled but silently prayed that they hadn't heard what they were just talking about.

Stephanie sipped her drink, never taking her eyes off Dana. "Let's go to the club or something. We need to turn up and party like Farrah would expect us to."

Everyone agreed and decided to hit the club. They laughed and danced all night. What shocked Dana was how good Jeryca and Orlando were getting along. They were inseparable. Dana was pleased with how things were coming together.

Chapter Seventeen

Brooklyn Detention Center
Sunday Morning

Larry sat on his bunk, biting his nails. He didn't have anyone he could call to help him in his situation. He knew that Thad and Toby were thinking that he had something to do with the robbery. They would be out to get him if he was released, so he wasn't going to call them. He would've felt somewhat safer where he was if Big Bam wasn't constantly eyeing him and smiling at him. Everyone knew Big Bam was a booty chaser, and he was too damn big for Larry to try to fight. However, he would definitely try him to keep his ass from being penetrated.

Larry looked around his sleeping area. He was in an open dorm. His bunk was located at the far back end of the dorm, against the wall. He figured if he had to, he would sleep with his ass against the wall, which he doubted would stop Big Bam if he wanted to get him.

Big Bam was known in the street and was awaiting trial for a triple homicide that he was caught in the act of doing. He told everyone in the dorm that he knew he was going away for life and wasn't afraid of doing the time. Big Bam was well respected in the dorm, and no one would go against him. He preyed on the weak guys in there, so Larry hoped that Big Bam had heard of him and who he was affiliated with.

Larry's thoughts were interrupted as D-Red approached him and sat on an opposite bunk. "Larry, your boy Chris wanted me to see if you needed anything. He said he don't know why you haven't reached out to him yet."

"Man, I been so twisted up, I don't know shit. But tell Chris I'm good, and thanks."

"You sure, man? You need to reach out to somebody. You can't get by in here alone," D-Red said.

"Man, I'm good. I don't need anything but to be free. I don't deserve to be in here. I didn't do shit," Larry cried out as he dropped his head down into his hands.

D-Red stood up and patted him on the back. "Man, you here. You got to suck it up or you won't make it. I will tell Chris you good for now. Keep your head up."

After D-Red walked away, Larry lifted his head up and thought about what was just said. D-Red was right, but he wasn't ready to reach out to anybody just yet. He was more worried about how he was going to beat his case. He had a son to care for.

At the thought of Travis, Larry began to shake. Travis was now without either parent, and Larry had no clue as to who had him. He was more depressed now than he was before.

Larry stood up and glanced over to where a group of guys were playing cards, and he caught sight of Big Bam, who nodded his head in his direction, smiling.

"Fuck. This nigga gonna be an issue. I feel it," Larry groaned to himself.

Jeryca was meeting Orlando for lunch Sunday afternoon. They had hit it off the previous night, and Orlando had to see what she was about.

"So, what are you going to have, beautiful?" he asked her as they looked over the menu.

"I don't know. Everything on the menu has grabbed my attention, but I guess I will get the crab balls, steak, and fries. Oh, and a salad!" Jeryca said as she placed the menu back on the table.

Orlando was impressed; a beautiful chick who wasn't trying to hide a healthy appetite.

"So, Jeryca, I know I've seen you somewhere before. I just can't pinpoint where," Orlando said once he placed his order and the waitress walked away.

"I don't think so. I would remember you if I did," Jeryca said as she glanced around the restaurant.

"I will figure it out sooner or later, but for now, I want to enjoy your company. Tell me a little bit about yourself." Orlando sat back in the chair, enjoying the view in front of him.

"Well, there isn't a lot to tell," she said. "I've lived in the projects all my life. My father has never been in my life, period. My mother worked hard all her years to take care of us and barely made ends meet. She had several different relationships with men that I didn't like or respect. I never understood how she could deal with a man and he not provide for you. Shit, a man got to bring something to the table besides dick. I have one sister, and I love her to death. We lived a rough life, you know. And I know we deserved more, wearing hand-me-downs from Goodwill and Salvation Army. We barely ate some days, and we never got to enjoy going places, 'cause we couldn't afford it. I don't want to live my life in the projects forever, so I am trying to do all I can to get the fuck out of there."

"So, is that why you are riding with Dana and Zack on this hit?" Orlando asked.

"That's part of the reason, but I want to show Thad that he isn't untouchable. I got plans for him, and this hit is just the beginning," Jeryca explained.

"Uh-huh, I think that's where I know you from," Orlando said, frowning slightly.

"I hope wherever you know me from won't deter you from getting to know me," Jeryca replied, noticing the frown that crept up on Orlando's face.

Orlando looked at her without saying a word for a few seconds. He sat up straight in his chair, but before he could speak, the waitress came up with their food.

"Will there be anything else?" she asked, eyeing Orlando.

"Bitch, if we want anything else, we will let you know with your looking ass!" Jeryca hissed.

The waitress stared at Jeryca for a few seconds, and then turned and walked away.

Orlando smiled and whispered, "I'm very much interested in you, and nothing can deter me from getting to know you. After we eat, what would you like to do next?" Orlando asked, picking up his fork and digging into his food.

"Well, I need to go check on my friend's mother and son before I do anything else. They have been having a hard time since her death," Jeryca explained.

"Yeah, I heard about that, and I am sorry for your loss." Orlando sighed as he grabbed her hand and gave it a slight squeeze.

"Yeah, well, Larry is locked up, and everyone involved in her murder will pay," Jeryca hissed.

"Shit, I can see in your eyes that you mean business. Let's finish eating and get on out of here," Orlando replied, eating more of his food.

Jeryca smiled at the thought of making everyone that she felt had violated her pay. She was going to wait her time and then wreak havoc on several people.

After the pair finished eating, they left the restaurant hand-in-hand, chatting all the way to the car. Orlando opened the door for Jeryca, which was so different from what she was used to. Thad never opened doors for her, nor carried on the type of conversations that she and Orlando had shared. She felt at ease with Orlando and wondered if he could possibly be the one. She knew that only time would tell; however, she couldn't help but feel that he was right for her.

Once they drove up to Shirley's house, Jeryca's smile changed immediately to a small frown.

Orlando noticed it immediately. He got out and walked around to Jeryca's side and opened her door.

"You okay, Ms. Lady?"

"I'm good," she mumbled.

As soon as the pair climbed the stairs, Travis ran to the door and jumped into Jeryca's arms. He buried his head into her chest. A few seconds later, he looked up. "I want my mommy, Auntie Jeryca."

Jeryca stroked his hair and whispered that everything would get better soon.

Orlando was taken aback by the compassion that Jeryca was displaying toward Travis. She was a different person around Farrah's people, especially Travis. He had no doubt that Jeryca would one day make a great mother, which was what he needed.

As he looked around the living room, he noticed several pictures of Jeryca and the three girls. He realized from the smiles and poses that they had been close. As he looked further, he saw pictures of the girls when they were younger.

"Oh, how cute," he whispered as he picked up a picture of the girls standing by a swimming pool, hugging each other.

"They were some awful kids!" Karen said, laughing lightly.

"Really? I wouldn't have guessed that," Orlando said as he placed the picture back down on the table.

"Yes. That Farrah stayed into some mess. But when Travis was born, she slowed down a lot. He was her world, and I don't know what we are going to do with our baby girl gone. You know, her and Jeryca were the closest out the group. They were together all the time. Jeryca has been here since Farrah's death, and Lord knows we appreciate her," Karen said, looking over at Jeryca adoringly.

Orlando was getting to know a part of Jeryca that he absolutely knew she wouldn't have shared with him right away. Jeryca glanced over at him and gave him a partial smile as she followed Shirley into the kitchen.

They spent the remainder of the day with Shirley and Travis, as different people walked in and out. Orlando felt somewhat comfortable being there with Jeryca, and the more he observed her interacting with Farrah's family, the more he realized that her love for Farrah was sincere.

Jeryca sat down next to him after putting Travis to bed. "I'm actually glad you are here, Mr. Orlando."

"I'm glad you let me be here with you, Ms. Lady," Orlando said, smiling.

"I can't believe she is gone, Orlando. This seems like a nightmare," Jeryca said with her head down.

Orlando reached over, grabbed her chin, and lifted her head up. "You know what? I know I just met you and all, but I want you to know I'm here for you."

"I appreciate that," Jeryca said, feeling that he was telling her the truth.

Larry sat with three other guys, playing cards. His head wasn't really in the game because he was thinking of Travis. He loved his son, no matter how he felt about his mother. She was a bitch, and although he had intended to take her life, he didn't do it, and now he was possibly going to spend the rest of his life behind bars.

"Damn, bro. Are you going to go or what?" Steve asked impatiently.

"I wasn't paying attention, man," Larry answered.

"Well, you need to be. I ain't gon' keep babysitting your cards, bro. If you going to play, then keep the fuck up. If you not going to play, get the fuck up. Either or is fine with me," Steve snapped.

Larry sat back, looked at Steve for a second, and then stood up. "Fuck you, nigga. You ain't gonna disrespect me and think I'ma sit down for it. Do you know who the fuck I am?" Larry yelled.

Steve stood up and walked up on Larry. "Yeah, I know who you are: you are a bitch nigga, and I will beat yo' ass for real. Who the fuck do you think you talking to? Huh?" Steve growled.

"Listen, man, I suggest you fall back and get the hell out of my face, 'cause this ain't what you want," Larry replied, pushing Steve back.

As the pair began scuffling around, D-Red ran over. "Y'all need to chill the fuck out before y'all get all of us locked down."

Larry straightened his clothes and walked away without saying a word. He was tired of them suckas trying him. It was war if anybody else stepped to him foul. He didn't have anything to lose, and he didn't care who got locked down afterward. People were going to respect him from that point on.

After the last count time and the lights went down, Larry lay on his bunk with his eyes closed and his arms folded behind his head. He thought about Travis and Debra. He couldn't believe that she had betrayed him as she did. What else should he have expected? She was a THOT like the rest of them.

After about an hour, he dozed off, only to be awakened by someone nudging his bunk.

"Rise and shine, baby. It's time for me to introduce myself," Big Bam whispered while pulling at his boxers.

"Big Bam, g-g-go 'head now. I'm not trying to go there wi—" Larry stammered.

"But he trying to go there with you, nigga," Steve interjected. He was standing at the head of the bunk.

"What the fuck—" Larry began to yell, but Steve clamped his hand over Larry's mouth before he could finish his statement. Another inmate grabbed Larry's feet and held him down firmly. Larry jerked his body around but couldn't break free, no matter what he did.

Big Bam ripped Larry's underwear off and eased onto the bunk with him. "Don't fight it, 'cause it's happening," he whispered.

Larry finally found the strength and twisted at an angle, which caused Steve's hand to slip. Larry immediately bit down on the side of his palm, broke free, and stood up swinging. He hit Steve in the mouth and attempted to hit Big Bam, but he was tackled by another person. As he fell backward, his head hit the side of the steel railing and he lost focus.

When his vision cleared up a bit, he saw D-Red standing to the right of Bam, smiling. "Man, it ain't nothing personal."

Big Bam pulled Larry up by his T-shirt and punched him several times in the face, until he no longer had any strength to struggle. The other two inmates moved back away from Larry and Big Bam and turned around, making sure no one entered the room or attempted to help Larry. Soon after, grunting and harsh moaning filled the dormitory.

Chapter Eighteen

Jeryca, Dana, and Stephanie sat behind the family at Grace Funeral Home. Orlando and Zack accompanied them to the funeral and supported them until it was over.

Dana sat stone-faced as she listened to the sermon. Once they opened the casket for viewing, she refused to walk up there, but Jeryca and Stephanie persuaded her to go. Once she was there, she stood staring down at Farrah with no feeling of regret at all. She couldn't afford to allow herself to feel anything, or she would lose control.

"She looks like she is asleep," Stephanie whispered.

Jeryca began crying uncontrollably. She was talking, but the words were inaudible, and as she stood there, she began falling to the floor. Orlando rushed up, helped her back to her feet, and stayed by her side for the remainder of the funeral.

Farrah's mom had to be taken out by paramedics. She had collapsed after witnessing the funeral coordinators close the lid on her beloved child's casket.

Shirley had decided that Travis wouldn't be allowed to attend his mother's funeral. She felt he was too young to be there. Shirley didn't have the will power or the desire to explain to him why his mother was lying in a casket or why his father hadn't been there. It was all too much for her.

After everyone returned to the family home, Orlando's phone rang. He answered it and began talking, but he never took his eyes from Jeryca's face.

"I need to talk to y'all immediately!" he whispered to Jeryca once he got off the phone.

"What's up?" Jeryca asked, frowning.

"I can't say in here. Just get everybody and come outside," Orlando said as he walked out, taking Zack with him.

Jeryca got Dana and Stephanie, and they walked outside.

"What's going on?" Dana asked as she approached Zack and Orlando.

"Man, dude got killed early this morning," Orlando answered.

"Who got killed?" Stephanie asked.

"Larry! They say he was gang raped and strangled," Orlando replied.

Everyone stood quiet for a minute, before Stephanie broke the silence. "Serve the nigga right! Why the hell should we sit around worrying about that nigga? We need to focus on how we can help Shirley and Travis even more now. Fuck Larry."

Everyone agreed, and Jeryca volunteered to be the one to tell Shirley what they had just learned. By the time that Jeryca walked into the house, the look on Karen and Shirley's faces told her they already knew.

"You heard what happened?" Jeryca asked Shirley.

She nodded her head with a shocked and unhappy expression.

"Why is this happening to them? First, it was Farrah, and now Larry. Travis was sitting here and saw his daddy's picture flash across the screen. He wants to know why his daddy was on TV, and we don't know what to tell him. What is that little boy going to do without his parents? How could this happen?" Karen asked as she held Shirley tight.

Jeryca didn't have an answer for them, but Travis didn't deserve to grow up without either of his parents. Jeryca sat down on the loveseat and bowed her head. She knew that she and the girls held some responsibility for Travis being without his parents. She had to do something to make sure he would be very well taken care of, but what could she do?

"We didn't want him dead just yet! How the hell are we going to find our money with that nigga dead?" Thad shouted after finding out that Austin had set up and executed a hit on Larry.

Austin sat at the bar, sipping his Hennessy with no expression. He had told them he would take care of it, and that's what he did. If they weren't ready for that type of move, they should've told him. He was put in charge to handle Larry, and he did just that.

"Man, fuck that money. We probably weren't ever going to get that shit back with Larry dead or alive, so let's just dead that conversation. Austin did what was necessary," Toby snapped.

"Fuck that money? Did you really just say that shit, man? I can't let shit go that easy. That was our shit that they fucking stole, and I can't imagine letting someone else eat off what we fucking worked for. Fuck that!" Thad yelled.

"Well, ain't much we can do about it now. Farrah and Larry are dead, nigga, so what do you propose we do?" Toby said in an aggravated tone

"What-the-fuck-ever. You mean to tell me that we shouldn't try to get our shit back?" Thad yelled.

"See, nigga, that's why so much bad shit has happened to us. You running around here all hot-headed, not thinking or understanding that there are repercussions for everything that you fucking do. Karma is a bitch, my nigga, and we probably deserved, on some level or another, what has happened. But damn, nigga, we got to use our head logically and make sure we don't get fucked before we get a chance to win. We got to take that loss and re-up how we said we would," Toby explained.

"That don't make no goddamn sense, bro. If karma gon' get us for doing fucked up shit anyway, then why the hell shouldn't we get all we can? Hell, it's damned if we do or don't, and I for one say let's do something," Thad replied.

"Well, since you got all the answers, little brother, then what can we do? I'ma sit here and wait on that answer, Mr. Know-it-all," Toby said harshly.

Toby sat down on a stool next to Austin, who was looking back and forth at the two men.

Neither brother moved him, because whatever was decided, he was good with it. Thad wasn't going to point his finger at him for losing some fucking money they had lost before he came into the picture.

Thad sat down and looked at Toby long and hard before he spoke. "Fine. We will do it your way. It better work, 'cause our asses are on the line. Those Colombians aren't going to wait forever for their fucking money. We owe them a lot more than what we 'bout to get from Orlando. So whatever we do, we got to do it big and fast," Thad said through slightly gritted teeth.

Toby could see that Thad wasn't happy with the end result, but they couldn't waste time chasing invisible money, especially with the Colombians on their asses. If Thad would breathe and think about it, he would see that as well.

"Let's put our heads together and come up with how we will move on Orlando and his boys. Thad, you also need to apologize to Austin for exploding on him like you did. We a team, nigga," Toby said.

"Apologize my ass. Bitch, hit this blunt and let's move forward," Thad replied, passing a fat blunt to Austin.

Austin grinned as he took the blunt, and even though Thad didn't apologize, Austin knew they were good. As he pulled on the blunt and exhaled the smoke, he laughed. "Apology accepted, bro."

Two weeks had passed since Larry was killed, and Dana was getting antsy. She was ready to move forward on their plan to rob and kill Thad. She knew it took time to plan, but she was out for blood, and she wanted Thad's head on a platter. In her opinion, he was the reason that all the bullshit had happened in the past month. Somehow, it was his fault.

However, Zack was adamant about planning the robbery out. He said that nobody was going to lose out this time around, and he meant that. They had held several meetings to discuss the robbery, and it was all falling into place. Zack told her and Stephanie that their Colombian connects were going to be flying to the States soon, and they needed to make sure that everything was dealt with by the time they arrived.

Jeryca had been MIA, choosing to spending most of her time with Travis and Orlando. Orlando was in charge of the lick they were about to do, so Jeryca knew a lot of the shit before

Dana and Stephanie even heard about it. She wasn't sure yet if she was going to participate in the robbery. She felt that enough blood had been shed over irrelevant things.

She wished that she could take back her part in the last robbery, but she knew it was too little too late for that. She felt that Travis and Shirley's well-being depended on her. What really ticked her off was that neither Dana nor Stephanie checked up on Shirley or Travis. Yeah, they called here and there, but they were so wrapped up in their own shit that they hadn't thought much about anybody else.

"Jeryca, sweetie, would you like something to eat?" Shirley asked.

"No, ma'am, I'm fine. Why don't you sit down and relax? Let me get you something to eat."

"Baby, you have been an angel through this ordeal, and I love you for that. You know, you and Farrah used to get into so much shit growing up, I used to think that she would be better off without y'all. But I'm glad she had a friend like you for her short time here," Shirley admitted tenderly.

"Wow, I appreciate you telling me that. I apologize from my heart for being a part of causing so much unnecessary stress on you, Ms. Walker," Jeryca said sadly.

She thought about what Ms. Walker had just said, and in a way, she felt that Farrah would still be alive if she hadn't met them.

"You know, I don't know how I'm going to make it with Travis, but with God on our side, I know we will be just fine. I just pray that you and the other girls stand with us. Travis is going to need someone to talk to. He knows you girls and seems more comfortable around y'all than me. You know if something happens to me, one of you should get him. He doesn't need to be around any stranger," Shirley said as tears fell down her face.

Jeryca stood up, walked over to Shirley, and hugged her. "I will be here for you both, no matter what!"

Jeryca knew that she needed to make one final hit with Dana and Stephanie, but she needed to run a few things past Orlando first. He had shared some hard truths with her, and now she had to divulge some hard truths of her own.

She walked outside, called her mother first to check in, and then dialed Orlando's number.

"What's up, Jeryca baby?" he said as he answered his phone.

"Nothing much. What you up to, boo thang?" she replied, smiling at the face she imagined he was making.

"Girl, you are something else, but I'll be 'boo thang' for you. But I'm just going over a few notes right now. Why? What's up?" he inquired.

"I need to talk to you about something very important. I think you need to hear what I got to say and give me your advice on it. I trust your judgment," she explained.

"I'm all ears, baby," he said.

"Naw, boy. Not on the phone. When can I see you?" she asked.

"You can see me tonight if you wanna, and um, as far as that boy shit, I can show you better than I can tell you that I ain't no boy." He laughed.

"Well, show me then, boo thang. But I stand corrected, Orlando. What time do you think you can come over?" Jeryca asked.

"Um, I can be there around nine o'clock. Where are you at?" he asked.

"I'm at Shirley's, of course. You know I'm not going too far," she replied.

"That's what I like about you, baby J," he responded.

She smiled at the pet name he made for her. "See you later."

"All right. Later," he said softly before hanging up.

Jeryca felt something that she had never felt before with any other guy: contentment and happiness. He made her heart skip, and she smiled whenever she thought about him. To top it off, she could honestly say she was interested in him, not what he had. If he lost it all, she would still be there in his corner.

As that thought raced through her mind, she sighed. "Momma always told me a real man would change my thoughts on how I perceived men, and she was right." She was going to get her some extra money, go back to school, and see where things went with Orlando. It was time for a change, in her opinion. She just hoped that things didn't go haywire during the robbery.

As she walked up to the house, Travis came running out and hugged her. "Is Dana coming over tonight?"

At the sound of Dana's name, Jeryca crunched her nose up for a second. "I honestly don't know," she answered as she led Travis into the house.

Chapter Nineteen

On Wednesday evening, Brittany sat on her couch, talking to Dana on the phone. She was waiting for Debra to come over. She had decided that there was no time like the present to deal with her. She had called Debra immediately after she got home from work. Brittany explained to her that they needed to work on a case so they could be prepared for it when they went to court that following Monday. Debra was reluctant at first, but after a few persuasive words from Brittany, she eventually agreed.

"Is anyone there yet?" Dana asked.

"Yeah, Deondre and Minx are in the back room, girl. What time are you going to get here?" Brittany asked.

"I want to get there after Debra so I can make my grand entrance like the boss diva I am," Dana replied in her gangsta voice.

"Girl, you are crazy for real," Brittany said, laughing.

"You know I'm the top don diva. When I step up in the house, Debra gonna know it's about to go down for real, damn it," Dana growled playfully.

"You too damn much, girl. Just get your ass over here, bitch," Brittany snickered.

"All right. I'm on my way, slut," Dana said before hanging up.

After Brittany got off the phone with Dana, she walked into the kitchen where Deondre and Minx were.

"What time is this chick supposed to get here?" Deondre asked.

"She should be here any minute now. I just hope Zack gets here before she does. Did y'all leave enough space for him to park in the back?" she asked.

"Yeah. If the nigga can drive, he can park back there," Minx replied.

"I'm saying y'all got that damn big-ass U-Haul out there. That's why I asked. I need everyone to be in place and ready to pounce on this bitch as soon as she walks through the door. And Deondre, I'm gonna need you to control yourself and keep your hands to yourself until we get the information we need. If she doesn't cooperate, though, we will get her ass to talk by any means necessary, but we got to keep her conscious and alive. Do we got an understanding?" Brittany asked.

"Yeah, we do, and you remember the same thing, Brit. Considering how much you have talked about killing that bitch, I think you the one who needs to remember that we need her alive," Deondre replied.

Before Brittany could reply, the door knob started turning, which caused Minx to pull his gun. Brittany frowned and raised her hand, telling him to relax. She walked over to the door and opened it quickly.

"Why the hell you playing, nigga?" she asked as she let Zack in.

"Y'all some scary-ass gangstas, huh?" he asked, laughing as he eyed Minx standing back against the wall with his gun by his side.

"Nigga, you were almost shot while you fuckin' joking," Minx replied.

"Well, anyway, I passed ol' girl at the Citgo pumping gas, so we need to get everything in order," Zack said.

Brittany went to her closet, pulled out a long rope, plastic, and handcuffs. Minx pulled out a set of knives and tools. He set them down on the counter and looked them over, piece by piece. He smiled as he placed them back into the case he had brought them in. Brittany couldn't help but notice the sinister look in his eyes, and she shivered with sheer excitement. She wasn't a cougar, but she would be one that night if he was with it.

After ten minutes passed, Brittany's doorbell rang, and she whispered to the guys to be ready once Debra was in the front room.

"Hey, girl, 'bout time your ass got here. Did you bring the files?" Brittany asked.

"Yes, ma'am, I did," Debra said, smiling.

Once she was seated on the couch, Brittany locked the door and turned around. "You want some tea or something?"

"I'd like a shot of gin if you got it," Debra answered.

"Okay, I got you, mami," Brittany said as she walked into the kitchen.

Debra sat on the couch, took out her laptop along with the files, and placed them on the table. She sat back and waited for Brittany to return with her drink. She hoped that the meeting wouldn't take too long, because she had some business to tend to.

When Brittany returned, she had two shot glasses and a small individual bottle of gin. "Here you go, Ms. Lady."

When Debra took the bottle and her shot glass, she saw Deondre, Zack, and Minx coming out of the kitchen. "What's going on?" she asked, immediately looking at Brittany.

"Well, shit, we were hoping you could tell us," Brittany said, grabbing Debra up.

The gin and shot glass fell to the floor, and Minx rushed over, tying Debra's hands behind her back. Debra didn't put up a struggle, nor was she going to try to fight back, because it was four against one, and besides, Deondre was holding a gun on her. She thought this day would come, but after Larry was killed, she figured she was in the clear.

She looked at Brittany for a minute before Minx pulled her into the kitchen, where there was plastic covering the floor and countertops. Debra froze as she suddenly realized she probably was going to die.

"Bitch, move before I punch you in the face," Deondre growled, pushing her forward.

Debra sat down in the chair, afraid to speak as she looked around the room, wondering where Brittany was. Her question was soon answered as Brittany and Dana walked in.

Dana was smiling from ear to ear, "Hey, baby girl. What's going on? Are you wondering what you're doing here, or do you already know?"

Debra shook her head and said nothing.

"If I was you, I'd talk, sweet thang, 'cause your life is on the line," Brittany said.

"I can make her talk. Trust me," Deondre said, holding up a box cutter.

Minx bent down in front of Debra and tied her feet to the chair. After untying her arms, he re-tied them to the chair.

Debra was so lost in her thoughts that she didn't hear what Deondre had said. She wondered how they could've found out that she was involved in the robbery. Larry hadn't told them, and with him dead, there was only one other person who knew where the money, guns, and drugs were located. She knew he hadn't talked. *Or had he*? She couldn't wrap her mind around that. He was the one that got the ball rolling from the beginning.

Debra was shocked back into reality after Brittany slapped her across the face. "Bitch, I know you heard me, damn it! Answer the question: where is our muthafuckin' money?"

"I don't know what you are talking about!" Debra groaned, reeling from the stinging slap of her face.

"You a lie, bitch. Man, Brit, let me handle this," Deondre said, walking over to Debra with the box cutter.

Brittany looked at Debra long and hard, and the look on her face told her that she was easily going to cooperate. She turned to Deondre and nodded her head. She took a couple steps back as he moved forward. With one swift motion of his arm, he cut Debra across her face. She cried out as the pain ripped through her face.

"Debra, you need to tell us where our shit is, or I'm going to leave Deondre in here with you for a few minutes, and you don't want that. We already know that you had something to do with the robbery, so just tell us where the shit is. You didn't participate in it, so why the fuck do you think you should benefit in it? Waltzing around the office, flaunting your new clothes, paid for by the fucking money we took. Bitch, start talking!" Brittany yelled, getting more agitated by the minute.

Brittany looked at Deondre, giving him the go ahead to slice into Debra more. She then told Dana to go with her to the front room. Before they made it out of the kitchen, Debra choked out, "Brit, wait! I will tell you where it's at. Just please, don't let him kill me."

"Well, shit, you need to start talking. Why the hell would you make this harder on yourself than it needs to be?" Zack asked.

Debra ignored Zack and kept her very tear-ful eyes on Brittany. "Everything is being kept at this warehouse on North Eleventh Street. We placed it there after the robbery. Larry and Neo sold a few bags of cocaine and weed, but they couldn't find a buyer for the guns, so the major-ity of the guns are still there. I swear I didn't plan on going through with this, but I guess greed and jealousy set in. I been yo' girl all these years, and you placed your trust in these bitches instead of me."

"Debra, that's a lame-ass excuse for betraying us. You did it for a piece of dick. There's more to this, and you're going to tell me what the fuck it is," Brittany replied.

"Fuck that shit. Just off this bitch and let's gather everybody and go get this loot," Dana hissed.

"I'm with Dana. Let me cut this bitch throat and be done with her," Deondre cut in.

"No. I need to know the real facts. Just shut the fuck up, you two, and let me do this how I see fit," Brittany replied, agitated.

Dana stepped back, shaking her head. She walked over to Zack and leaned against him, watching Brittany grill Debra.

"Do you see how they want to kill your ass? And I'm the only person keeping them from doing it! Tell me the truth, Debra, the whole truth, or I will let them at your ass right now," Brittany commanded.

Debra dropped her head, and tears fell from her eyes. "When I first met Larry, he was referred to me by my best friend of ten years. He told me that my services were needed on a possible custody case. He explained that they would pay me top dollar to represent Larry if the case went to court, and if I won the case, my pay would triple. I agreed, and then I met Larry. He started complimenting me from the beginning. When I told my friend, he suggested that I get to know him and try to persuade him to leave the game. I thought that they were looking out for Larry, so I agreed," Debra explained.

"Okay, and then?" Brittany asked.

"Well, the night you called me, Larry overheard a portion of the conversation we had. It was the day you said you didn't need me to join you all in the robbery, and because I was angry, I told Larry what you guys were planning. He came up with the idea that we should keep quiet and let you all do what you had to do, and if you were successful, then we would hit y'all afterward."

"Okay, so who is the guy that referred you to Larry, Debra?" Brittany asked.

"He ain't got nothing to do with this, though, Brit. I swear to you, this was all me and Larry's idea," Debra cried.

"Naw, ho, this just doesn't sound right to me. Answer Brit's question, and also tell us how this nigga fits into all this," Minx interjected.

Debra sat quiet for a few minutes, until Dana walked over, grabbed her hair, and snatched her head back. "Listen, we don't have time to be playing with yo' ass, damn it. Answer the fucking question."

Before anyone could stop her, Dana punched Debra in the face, which caused her eye to swell instantly. She screamed out in agony. Zack ran over and pulled Dana back. Brittany was yelling for Dana to leave the kitchen, but Dana refused to go.

"What's his name, Debra? Can't you see that this is getting way out of control?" Brittany growled as she rolled her eyes at Dana.

"It's Thad's right-hand man, Chris. Chris is ready to get out of the game himself. When he learned that you all were planning to do this robbery, he convinced me to roll with it as well, but to report everything back to him. But when he got locked up, it ruined our plans.

"Once he found out that Larry had been arrested for Farrah's murder, Chris felt it was best to intervene a bit and make sure Larry didn't make it out of jail. Chris wanted access to the money, drugs, and guns once he was able to make bond and was finally released from jail. He said that Thad and Toby were really out for themselves, and Larry was a dirtbag for how he played his son's love for him against his mother. So he had no regrets.

"Chris paid a moving company to move everything from where Larry had it to an abandoned warehouse that I purchased for him, and that's where everything is now," Debra further explained.

"Damn, it's some real shady-ass people around this bitch. Can't trust nobody," Minx said, shaking his head.

"Yeah, I'd say that's some real slimeball-ass shit. But hey, this trick was all in it, and that's why she needs to die right now," Dana responded.

"No, wait. We need to get the information and the keys to the location. Zack, once we get the keys to the building, you, Minx, and Deondre will go check it out, and we will stay here with Ms. Debra. Once you call me confirming that our shit is there, we will let Debra go," Brittany said as she laid out her orders.

"Let her go? Did you say let her go?" Dana asked angrily.

"Yes, I did, and I won't explain my reasons why," Brittany answered, annoyed.

"You mean to tell me after all I've fucking done to insure we don't get caught up, you're willing to let her go? This makes no sense. I did some fucking shit that I never thought I'd have to do—" Dana started, but was cut off immediately.

"Listen, Zack, get her the hell out of here until she calms the hell down," Brittany said, motioning to Zack.

"Zack ain't got to get nobody. I will go into the front room, but you got to explain the logic in letting this bitch go," Dana yelled before walking out of the kitchen.

After Brittany finished up in the kitchen and got the information that they needed about the warehouse, she walked into the living room and got a set of keys out of Debra's purse.

Dana didn't look at Brittany or speak a word to her. Brittany knew that Dana was pissed, but she really didn't care at that point. After she gave the keys to Minx, the guys left and headed over to the warehouse. Brittany taped Debra's mouth and walked into the front room. She sat down next to Dana.

"Listen, I have chosen to keep Debra alive for a while. I don't think it's wise to kill her now. It's too much going on, and it will draw unwanted attention and heat our way. You got to trust me, Dana."

Dana tried to understand the logic that Brittany was trying to point out, but she just wasn't comfortable with Debra being left alive. She knew that the two women were friends way before she came into the picture. After experiencing major betrayal from Farrah and the rest of the girls, people she once viewed as her ride or die bitches, she wasn't sure if she could trust anyone, especially someone she had only known for two years.

Dana shook her head and looked at Brittany with tears in her eyes. "Brit, I hope you aren't trying to cross me out, 'cause I don't think I could bear losing another friend. I look at you as my big sis. You have taught me so much and been there for me in times no one else was, so I just hope you are genuinely thinking of our best interests here."

"Dana, I got you. You should know that you can trust me after everything we have endured lately. Don't start doubting me now. That bitch is as good as dead, but we got to do this shit right. We can't have dead bodies popping up on us back-to-back. Let shit cool down, then we can follow through with getting rid of her and anyone else we deem to be against us," Brittany replied.

Dana sighed. "I don't want to doubt you, but I know you two have been friends for a good while, and I just don't need any more bullshit-ass friends turning on me," Dana explained.

"Just trust me, Dana. I got you. And Debra killed our friendship when she turned on us for a fucking man," Brittany replied.

"I understand, and I trust you, sis. We good," Dana said, smiling and hugging Brittany, but in Dana's mind, it was now her against the world.

Thirty minutes later, Brittany's cell phone rang. "Yeah?" she said as she answered it.

"Everything that she said was here is here. What next?" Zack replied.

"We will leave it until we figure out a place to store it. But we can't leave it there for too long, 'cause Debra isn't the only person with the information on that location," Brittany responded.

"I may have a great spot, but let me check with my man," Zack said.

"When you going to get at him?" Brittany asked.

"As soon as I get off the phone with you," Zack replied.

"All right then. Do what you do," Brittany said before hanging up.

"Are we good to go?" Dana asked.

"Hell yeah, baby girl." Brittany laughed.

Chapter Twenty

Stephanie and Robin spent a lot of time together over the course of two months. They had grown closer than ever, but Stephanie still didn't feel comfortable telling Robin about all the things she had done in the past or planned on doing with Dana and Brittany. Whenever the group decided to meet to discuss the robbery, Stephanie would tell Robin that she either was going to or had been to Shirley's house to check on the family, or just spend time with Travis.

"Bae, when you go to work, I'm going to see Dana. She wants to have lunch today. She told me to tell you hello also," Stephanie said as she stood in the mirror pinning her hair up.

"That's what's up. Steph, you know for a white girl, you got a fat booty. I love watching it when you walk. It jiggles, and Lord, when I touch it, my clit stand straight up," Robin said, laughing, walking up behind Stephanie and wrapping her arms around her waist.

"Girl, you are a mess. But I'm glad my ass can bring you and your clit so much joy. Now stop that. You're going to be late, damn it!" Stephanie squealed when Robin started kissing her on her neck.

"I'll be late for a li'l bit of that juicy ass," she replied as she began rubbing on Stephanie's breasts.

"Well, while I'd love to oblige you, my baby, I got to go. But I promise we will pick up where we are leaving off tonight," Stephanie moaned.

Robin sighed but agreed that they could wait. She loved Stephanie and was extremely attracted to her. She had never been with a white woman and never imagined in her wildest dreams that she could feel the way she did about Stephanie.

"All right, babe. What time do you think you will be back here?" Robin asked.

"I honestly can't say, but it won't be late, I promise," Stephanie answered. The two kissed for a few minutes then Robin left.

Stephanie was dropped off at Dana's apartment to meet with everyone and discuss more details of their next lick. They had found out a week earlier that they were holding Debra hostage until everything was completed. They didn't want her to squeal on them to Chris and Thad.

When she walked into Dana's apartment, Jeryca was already there with Orlando. Stephanie hadn't dealt with Jeryca much since the day she saw her fucking Chris. Jeryca noticed the difference in Stephanie, and she wasn't going to leave Dana's house without getting to the bottom of it.

Stephanie spoke to everyone and sat next to Brittany on the couch. They had already moved all the dope, guns, and drugs to one of Orlando's warehouses located on the south side of Brooklyn.

"All right, we will execute this robbery in about two weeks. Friday will be the perfect time. We have studied the layout of the building, and we know Thad and Toby's movements, thanks to Minx and Deondre scoping them out. So if everyone is ready for this, say aye. If you aren't, or if you have any misunderstandings about what will occur, please speak up now," Zack demanded.

Everyone signaled they understood and were ready to move forward.

Jeryca stood up and asked Stephanie if she could speak with her outside, and Stephanie agreed. Dana watched the two walk outside, and she prayed that they didn't get loud or start fighting.

Brittany gave Dana a sideways glance and smiled. She was also aware of why there had been animosity between the two women. She walked to the window and peeped out.

Dana started laughing. "Get the hell away from the window, nosy."

"Shit, I want to see what's going to happen." Brittany laughed.

Orlando cleared his throat so that the two women would at least respect the fact that others were in the room listening to them. He didn't want them to speak on what was going on outside, because to him it wasn't any of their business. Brittany and Dana snickered as they walked toward the den with all the guys in tow.

Stephanie stood on the porch, waiting on Jeryca to speak. After a few moments of awkward silence, Stephanie spoke. "Well, what do you want to talk about?"

"I want to know why you have been so cold to me lately. I haven't done anything to you, period. The whole time we were dealing with Farrah's death, you never once reached out to Shirley, or me, for that matter. You were barely talking to me at the funeral, and I want to know what's going on," Jeryca cried.

Stephanie looked down at her feet then back at Jeryca's face. How dare she stand before her, trying to look all innocent? She was a ho, and Stephanie was going to give her an earful of what she thought about her. "Jeryca, I know that you would like to stand here like you haven't done anything, but bitch, you got to know that I know you fucked Chris while we were together. You were my girl, and you go and fuck my man. How dare you feel the need to question me about anything? You are trifling, and you don't deserve to have a friend like me. I would never have fucked Thad knowing that you were with him."

"What are you talking about? I never fucked Chris," Jeryca denied quickly.

"Bitch, yes you did! I saw you with my own two eyes. I flattened his tires while y'all sat parked at the abandoned apartments. You are a liar if you say it wasn't you. Matter of fact, say you didn't fuck him, and I will punch you in your fucking mouth," Stephanie said as she stepped forward.

Jeryca was speechless. She didn't realize that Stephanie had seen them. No wonder she was treating her like a stranger. But how could she still be angry with her about a loser like Chris, especially after everything they had been through lately? Hell, if she hadn't slept with Chris, Stephanie would probably still be with him, instead of the new love she had.

"Stephanie, I know I hurt you, but if it wasn't for me, you wouldn't be with Robin now. In a way, I did you a favor," Jeryca said, smiling.

"Did me a favor? Bitch, you destroyed our friendship. I don't give a fuck about Chris. I just couldn't believe that you would do that shit to me. You were like my sister, and now you are standing in front of me, talking 'bout you doing me a favor. Bitch, fuck you."

At that moment, Stephanie slapped Jeryca and pushed her to the ground. She dove on top of her and began beating Jeryca furiously.

Dana and Brittany ran out, along with Orlando and Zack. They lifted a still-swinging Stephanie off Jeryca, who was curled up on the ground, covering her head.

"Stephanie, what the fuck!" Dana yelled. "With everything going on, we don't need the cops being called over here. Damn, you got to be smarter than that. Damn, y'all need to go before the cops are called."

"Why are you yelling at me? You know what this bitch did. Then she sitting out here, talking 'bout she did me a favor. Fucking ho-ass trick.

Yeah, I said it. You slept with all those niggas, sucked dick for money for Thad's ass, and then slept with my man for what? A nut? Bitch, you ain't shit," Stephanie screamed.

Jeryca immediately looked at Orlando, who was looking at her as if he saw a ghost. She assumed that he was disgusted from what he'd just heard, and she walked quickly up the road, trying to avoid any more embarrassment. She had gotten her ass beat by a white girl, and then the bitch exposed her for being a whore.

My day couldn't get any worse, she thought.

A few seconds later, Orlando drove up on her and told her to get in the car. Jeryca hesitated for a second, until Orlando spoke.

"Please get in. I want to talk to you. I don't care about none of what was said back there. We all have a past that we aren't proud of. As long as you protected yourself when you were out there, you good."

Jeryca smiled and walked slowly to his car. Once she was inside, she put her seatbelt on, and he looked at her.

"I have something I need to get off my chest also."

"What's that?" Jeryca asked.

"Not here. We need to go to my house and talk," Orlando said as he drove up the road toward the highway.

Jeryca was silent most of the way to Orlando's house. She didn't know what he had to say, but it couldn't be good. He looked too serious. They made small talk here and there until they reached their destination.

Orlando got out and walked around to open Jeryca's door. Once she was out, he grabbed her hand gently and guided her into his house. Once they were inside, he asked her if she wanted a drink.

"Yes, I just want some tea, if you don't mind," she said quietly.

"Tea it is. I think I want something a bit stronger." He laughed.

He disappeared into the kitchen, and Jeryca leaned back on the couch. Usually, she would be at ease because she loved being at Orlando's house, but after the events that had just occurred, she was a bit uncomfortable.

When he returned, he handed her a bottle of Brisk tea and a glass of ice, while he popped opened a bottle of Ciroc.

After he took a sip, he sat down next to Jeryca and cleared his throat. "First, I want to say that I didn't realize this until a few minutes ago. I hope you won't hold what I'm about to say against me, but remember when we first went out and I asked you if we had met before?"

"Yes, I remember that," Jeryca replied.

"Well, now I remember where it was. One night about four months ago, I was at Thad's . . . business location, and he introduced me to his top girl." Orlando sipped his drink before going on. "It was you," he whispered.

Jeryca sat still, waiting for the punch line, but when none followed, she frowned up and shook her head. "Why wouldn't you tell me this before? How is it you are just now realizing this?" she asked angrily.

"The night I was with you, I had been drinking heavily. I don't remember a lot about that night, but I kept trying to picture where I knew you from. When ol' girl blurted out that you tricked for Thad, that's when it dawned on me. I hope you know that I really like you, and I want to see if this can go further, but if you don't want to after finding this out, I will respect your wishes. But just know that I think we can become so much more," he explained.

Jeryca sat quietly for a minute. She didn't know what to say, but she liked Orlando a lot.

She didn't want to lose him behind past mistakes and if he was willing to overlook her wrongs, then she could overlook his revelation.

"Jeryca, please don't sit there quiet like that. Say something. Tell me what you want to do," he pleaded.

Jeryca looked at him and smiled. "I'm here for the long haul."

"That's what I'm talking 'bout."

The two embraced one another and spent the rest of the evening together.

Dana had grilled Stephanie for over an hour about how she handled Jeryca. Stephanie was angered by the fact that Dana seemed to be sticking up for Jeryca, knowing she was in the wrong.

"Dana, if that bitch had slept with your man, you'd be livid too. Then she standing out there, talking 'bout she did me a favor. I fucking snapped. What else could I have done?"

"Dana, you know that she was right for reacting how she did. Jeryca was asking for it," Brittany said.

"Exactly! She deserved every fucking punch she got," Stephanie replied.

"Hell, for a white girl, you got some hands on you." Deondre laughed.

"I learned from the best. My besties had them hands, especially Farrah. I remember when we were younger, Farrah was the main one in the bunch who stayed fucking a bitch or nigga up." Stephanie laughed.

At the mention of Farrah's name, the whole atmosphere seemed to change briefly.

Dana was the first person to speak up. "Well, you still should've held your composure. That was unacceptable in my book."

Stephanie looked at Dana long and hard. She couldn't believe that Dana was still coming down on her about that fight. It had happened, and it couldn't be changed. Even if she could change it, she wouldn't.

She decided to ask Minx if he would take her to CVS where Robin worked. She wasn't going to sit around listening to Saint Dana run the fight into the ground. Dana got on Stephanie's nerves, trying to be righteous, especially now when she had been the shadiest of them all lately.

Minx agreed to take Stephanie to CVS, and when she was walking out the door, she said her goodbyes to everyone except Dana. She was livid with her for coming down on her so hard.

When they pulled out of the driveway, Brittany looked at Dana and said, "You know you were wrong for that."

Dana looked at her and shrugged her shoulders. "Fuck her and Jeryca. I'm done with both of them after this lick. Shit, I don't forget shit. How the fuck I'm wrong?"

Brittany started laughing and softly pushed Dana, who was also laughing. "Gotta love ya hateful ass."

Stephanie walked into CVS and waited for Robin to clock out. Robin knew immediately that something was wrong. As soon as she clocked out and they were at her car, she asked Stephanie, "Bae, what happened to you?"

"Shit, got into a little scuffle with Jeryca, but I'm good," she answered.

"Are you sure?" Robin inquired.

"I'm positive, baby," Stephanie replied.

"Come and let me suck on those lips, mama," Robin said playfully.

"You ain't got to ask me twice," Stephanie said as she walked toward Robin.

After they locked lips, Robin leaned back against the car. "What do you want for dinner?"

Stephanie looked in her eyes. "You on a platter is good enough for me."

"Umm, sounds like a plan to me," Robin replied as she unlocked the doors to her car. They got in and pulled off with Stephanie feeling totally complete and hell-bent on getting Jeryca again, and getting even with Dana somehow.

Chapter Twenty-one

Wednesday morning, Detective Rone was sitting behind his desk when Detective Harris popped his head in. "Aye, did you catch that game last night?"

"Heck yeah, and I was heated. The Patriots shouldn't have won that game, man," Rone complained.

"Whatever. I should've bet your ass. They were going to win no matter what. They're just that good." Harris laughed.

"Man, whatever. Those bastards are known for cheating, and they are starting the season off doing what they do best, I guess," Rone said as he leaned back in his chair.

"Whatever. You're just hating on my team. Everybody knows they're the best!" Detective Harris stated.

Just then, Rone's phone began to ring. "Detective Rone speaking," he replied.

"Detective Rone, I have some information I think you would be interested in having," the caller said.

"Oh yeah? Well, first tell me who this is?" he asked, signaling at Detective Harris to remain where he was.

"I will tell you who I am at a later date, but right now, I think you need to put your focus on trying to find Debra Fuller before she winds up dead like Farrah and Brenda. The first person I'd contact is Dana Crisp. I know you know her," the caller replied.

"How—?" Before he could finish his reply, the caller hung up.

Detective Rone looked at his partner and told him what was just said.

"Man, looks like we may need to contact Dana Crisp," he said.

"Yeah, but first we need to do some research on Ms. Fuller to see if she is indeed missing. Remember what happened last time we were told that Dana Crisp was involved in a missing person's case," Harris replied.

"I'm going to run a background check and see if I can pull up any information on her. I want you to pull out Farrah Walker's case. Her name was mentioned as well. Something is fishy here," Rone said as he started typing away on his keyboard.

"Farrah Walker's case is closed. Her murderer was killed in jail, remember? Why should we reopen that case?" Harris asked.

"Just oblige me please, sir," Rone said without taking his eyes off the computer screen.

"Yessuh, boss." Harris laughed, mimicking how black folks used to answer their masters back in the days of slavery. He even added a dance to go with it.

Rone looked at him and shook his head, laughing. "Get out of here, Harris."

The two men busied themselves with their tasks. At about 4:30 p.m., Rone had found Debra's information and was shocked to discover that she was once listed on Larry Bigelow's visitation list. She also worked for the law firm that Dana Crisp worked for.

He decided that he was going to follow up with the missing persons tip and see what he could find. He was going to start with Dana and pay her a visit at her job. If Debra wasn't there, he was going to investigate further. He knew Dana, and couldn't handle having her life in his hands while he slept on the case. From the moment he met her, he was in awe of her, but he couldn't let his infatuation get in the middle of his case. Besides, Dana didn't even know he existed.

After Detective Rone locked up his office, he headed toward Detective Harris's office. "I'm 'bout to call it a day, but tomorrow we are going to pay an unofficial visit to Holmes, Howell, and Fuller law firm. If anything is amiss, we will start a missing persons case file on Debra Fuller."

"All right, I'm with you on that," Detective Harris said as he stood up and stretched. He was ready to call it quits for the day also.

"Let's go get a few drinks," Detective Harris suggested.

"Deal. We can catch the highlights of that botched-up game from last night." Rone laughed.

"That game was on point and you know it. You are such a hater, man," Harris joked.

The two walked out of the precinct and headed off to the sports bar, where they chilled for about two hours. The following morning, they drove to the law firm where Dana worked, and when they walked through the door, Rhonda, Brittany's receptionist, greeted them.

"May I help you, gentlemen?"

Detectives Rone and Harris displayed their badges. "We are here to see Debra Fuller, please," Harris said, showing no emotion.

"Ms. Fuller isn't in at the moment. May I assist you, or would you prefer one of the other attorneys?" she asked.

"No. Has Ms. Fuller been in today at all?" Harris continued his questioning.

"Sir, I don't feel comfortable answering your questions. I'm just the receptionist. Maybe you'd like to speak with Ms. Howell," she replied.

Just then, Dana walked out of her office, carrying a few files. When she saw Detectives Harris and Rone, she stopped dead in her footsteps.

"Don't tell me Jeryca is missing again. You can't find your pet rabbit? What the fuck do you want now?" she asked angrily.

"Well, actually, Ms. Crisp, we aren't here for you. We are looking for Debra Fuller. Is she coming in today?" Detective Harris asked.

Dana looked at both men, apologized for her outburst, and attempted to walk past them.

"Ms. Crisp, do you happen to know where we can find Ms. Fuller? We need to speak to her about an urgent matter," Detective Rone said as he stood blocking her way. He admired her beauty, but he couldn't let that stop him from effectively pursuing his case.

"No. I don't know where she is at the moment, but I will have her contact you as soon as she gets in," Dana replied.

"Please make sure you do. It is important that we speak with her," Detective Harris replied.

Brittany walked out at that moment. "Hello, I'm Brittany Howell. May I help you with anything?"

"We are looking for Debra Fuller. Do you know where we might be able to find her?" Detective Rone asked.

"Well, I think she is out with a client. Let me check our log," Brittany answered, never once looking nervous. "Yes, you see here, she signed out for the morning. She may be back in later today. If you like, you can leave me your card and I will tell her to contact y'all."

Detective Rone handed Brittany and Dana his card. "Whichever one of you sees her first, please have her contact us."

"Will do, Detective," Dana said, smiling sweetly.

After the detectives left, Brittany asked Dana to come into her office. Once Dana walked in and closed the door, Brittany looked at her.

"What the hell was that all about?"

"Hell if I know, but we need to figure something out, Brit," Dana whispered.

"It ain't but one thing we can do at this point in time," Brittany replied.

"And that is?" Dana asked.

"Have Debra call them," she answered.

Dana sighed and rubbed her head. "Brit, you think that's a good idea?"

"Hell, it's the only idea. I told you we didn't need to kill her right away. These bastards just proved my point," Brittany said as she watched the two officers outside her window.

"What do you think, Rone?" Detective Harris asked.

"I don't know, but when we talk to Debra, and I'm sure we will, I'm going to request that we meet with her. If they don't produce her, then I'm going to start my own investigation. Something just doesn't sit right with me on this case," Detective Rone replied.

"I know what you mean, but we can't make Debra meet with us, even if she isn't being held against her will. We got to have a valid reason and evidence that she is being held against her will before we file a missing persons report," Detective Harris reminded Rone.

"Let me worry 'bout that when it's time," Detective Rone replied before getting in the car to go back to the station. He took one more look at the office and saw Brittany and Dana peeking out the window. "It's something up with those two. I'm going to get to the bottom of it if it kills me."

***

After the two detectives pulled off, Dana looked at Brittany and said, "Damn, Brit, why do think they are looking for Debra?"

"Shit, I don't know, but do you see now? It was a good thing we didn't kill her," Brittany replied.

"Yeah, you right. Well, you need to get her to call them tonight. We don't need any extra shit getting in our way," Dana said.

"Yeah, I'm going to get on that as soon as we leave," Brittany said as she walked back into her office.

As Dana walked into her office and shut the door, it dawned on her that Brittany could've set that whole scene up for her benefit. She knew that she was upset that she didn't kill Debra, and now all of a sudden, these cops show up wanting to question her.

What the hell is Brittany up to? Dana was starting to doubt if Brittany was as loyal as she first thought. She decided that from that point on, she was going to have to keep a close eye on her.

Zack and Orlando were sitting in Orlando's factory, playing cards. They were waiting on a package from Ramon and Sergio to arrive.

"Orlando, you and Jeryca have been spending a lot of time together. It's getting kind of serious between you two, huh?" Zack asked as he drew a card from the deck.

"Yeah, I like her. She has been very honest with me about a lot of things, and the more I get to know her, the more I like her. What's going on with you and Dana?" Orlando asked.

"Man, she is a hard one. I mean, she is cool, don't get me wrong, but she won't let me into her personal space. I know she trusts me, and I think she is feeling me, but I'm not sure. I can't—naw, I won't—keep waiting for her to come around," Zack replied.

"I feel you on that. Man, I need to find me another warehouse where I can start this clothing distribution company. You know, since the raid at my other spot, the cops padlocked my shit and have seized it. They can't finger me as being part of the drug bust, but the shit was mine and in my name, so they assume I know something about the deal. Yesterday, the courts sent me a letter saying they have taken possession of it. I have two weeks to come forward and talk to them or they will sell it, but you know what? They can have that shit for real. Hell, I got this building here and another one across town.

I'm good for now, but man, I spent close to nine hundred thousand for that fucking warehouse," Orlando said.

Just then, Orlando's phone began to ring. "Hello?" he answered.

"Orlando, this is Brittany. How are things going there?" she asked.

"Things are good. No problems at all from our little visitor," he said as he looked toward the back room.

"Listen, I need you to go back there and tell her that she needs to call a Detective Rone from her cell phone and talk to him. Make sure it's on speaker phone and you scare the hell out of her before she talks to them, so that she knows she will die if she says the wrong thing," Brittany explained.

"Detective Rone? What the hell does he want from her?" Orlando asked.

Zack had laid his cards down on the table and was eyeing Orlando questionably.

"I don't know what he wants, but we are about to find out. Wait about an hour and then have her call him," Brittany replied.

Brittany gave Orlando Detective Rone's phone number, and after they hung up, Orlando told Zack what was going on.

Zack shook his head and looked at Orlando. "I don't know why she don't off the bitch, cement her body, and then toss it in the ocean. It would work well for all of us."

"Man, let them women do it their way for now. If things get any more out of hand, we will just have to back out. We got bigger plans, and nothing can interfere with that. Sergio and Ramon will fuck with us on whatever we need them to," Orlando said as he walked to the office.

Orlando pulled out Debra's purse from his locked desk drawer and grabbed her phone. He opened it up and saved the number that Brittany had just given him in her phone. He put the phone in his pocket and walked to the back room, where they were holding Debra. He unlocked the door after he motioned for Zack to join him. The two men walked into the room and turned on the lights. Debra squinted as her eyes focused on Orlando and Zack.

"Listen, in about an hour, I'm going to come in here and bring you your phone. There's a detective who wants to talk to you. I'm going to warn you right now: if you say anything that I think isn't right, I'm going to kill you. I don't care what Brittany said. You will die today. Do you understand that?" Orlando asked.

Debra nodded her head, acknowledging that she heard what they said. They were men of their word, and she knew that. She wasn't going to give them any reason to hurt her, although she figured they were going to kill her anyway.

"I think we should kill you anyway, so trust I don't have a problem getting Deondre over here to do the job. Play with us if you want to," Zack said, looking in her eyes so that she could see he was serious.

Orlando turned and walked out of the room with Zack on his heels. Zack turned the lights out, then closed and locked the door.

"I think we got our point across, don't you?" Zack asked Orlando.

Orlando laughed and walked back into the main area of the factory. "Come on and let me finish whooping that ass in Casino."

"Whatever. Let's put some real money on it then." Zack laughed.

Chapter Twenty-two

Thursday afternoon, Thad sent one of his new recruits, Michelle, to bond Chris out of jail. His bond had been dropped, and they needed him in on the hit they were planning against Orlando and a few other people. Chris had no idea that they were coming for him, so when the deputy called out his name, he was asleep on his bunk. His bunkmate, D-Red, nudged him.

"Aye, man, they're calling your name."

"Yeah!" Chris yelled, wondering what they wanted.

"Pack your stuff. You just made bond," the deputy replied.

"I just made what?" he asked, making sure he had heard them correctly.

"Do you want to go home or not?" the deputy yelled back.

"Shit, I'm on my way," Chris yelled.

Chris packed up all his belongings that he needed to take and gave D-Red his toiletries and all the food he had just bought from the jail store.

"Aye, man, hold it down out there," D-Red said as he gave Chris a hug.

"All right, you take care of yourself in here, boy. I'ma put a few bucks on your books every Friday, man. You just stay safe," Chris replied.

As he headed out the door, he paused. "All y'all keep yo' head up."

Chris walked down to be processed out, and once everything was completed, he headed out the door. He looked around, but he didn't see anyone he recognized. He sat on the bench outside the jail, wondering who the hell had bailed him out. Seconds later, a beautiful blond woman approached him. She looked like she was in her early thirties. Her eyes were blue with brown specks; her nose was small with a cute tip and freckles around it. She was short with a slightly heavy build, but he thought she was gorgeous.

"Are you Chris?" she asked him.

"Yes, I am, and who are you?" he asked curiously.

"I'm Michelle. Thad sent me to get you. They want you to meet them at Toby's house now. I will drop you off, and they will take you wherever you have to go afterwards," she explained.

"All right, let's go. Do you have a phone? Mine is dead, and I need to call Thad or Toby to let them know I'm out," Chris said. He wanted to confirm what Michelle said before he got into the car to go anywhere with her.

She handed Chris her cell phone, and he called Thad.

"What's up, bro?" Chris said once Thad answered the phone.

"What's up, nigga? I see Powder got you," Thad laughed.

"Who?" Chris said, looking at Michelle.

"Powder. That's my newest goon. She is taking Keith's place. But she good people, man. So, she will drop you off over here, and I will take you to your car when we finish up," Thad replied.

"Finish what?" Chris asked.

"Man, don't worry about all that. Just get your ass on over here. I know you ready to turn up and get you some pussy, nigga. We got to discuss business first, then party later. You wit' that?" Thad responded.

"Hell yeah, I am. We on the way, bro," Chris said before hanging up.

"We good to go now?" Michelle asked.

"Yeah we are, *Powder*," Chris replied, putting an emphasis on her nickname.

She eyed him before unlocking her car. "I see you gonna be trouble."

"All good trouble, though." He laughed.

"Shit, I hear you." She smiled.

"Damn, you are a beautiful woman," he blurted out.

She smiled and pulled out of the parking lot, headed over to Toby's house. Once they pulled up, Chris saw four different vehicles in the driveway. Two he knew, but he couldn't for the life of him figure out who the other two belonged to. He got out of the car, and as he walked toward the door, Michelle pulled off.

As he got closer, he could hear everybody inside talking. They were laughing and talking loud. He stood there, dreading that he had to see them. He didn't feel the connection to them any longer, and he felt that they only got him out because they needed him to help on the next lick they had planned. He needed to get that money, though, which was why he was going to allow them to use him.

Chris knocked on the door, and Tiffany opened it. "Look at what we got here!" She hugged him, and Thad rushed over and gave him a hug too.

"What's up, baby boy?" Thad asked.

"Shit, just happy to see these streets again, bro," Chris answered.

"Do you want a drink or something?" Tiffany asked.

"All I need is a blunt and information." Chris laughed.

"Come on in the front room. Toby and Austin are there as well," Thad said.

Once everyone welcomed Chris home, they sat down and laid out the plans for their hit against Orlando. Once everything was settled, Chris asked them if they had heard from Keith.

"We ain't heard shit from that nigga yet. Wherever he at, he need to stay, 'cause I'm gonna blow his fucking head off. I know he was in that bullshit with Larry, and that's probably who got our shit," Thad replied.

"I don't think Keith would've done that. He ain't got it in him," Chris said.

"I don't put anything past anybody. He's suspect until he surface and prove he didn't do it," Thad replied.

"What's on the agenda for tonight?" Chris asked, changing the subject.

"I'm gonna do whatever you want to do. This is your night," Toby said.

Tiffany stood in the doorway, looking at Toby. She loved the money that he brought into the house, but she hated the fact that she was left alone all the time. He never explained where he was going or why. They didn't have any kids, but she hoped that one day he would want to retire from the game and start a family.

She looked at Toby and motioned for him to come into the other room. He stood up and followed her into the kitchen, while Chris walked outside with the phone to his ear.

"Toby, I was hoping we could spend some time together alone tonight. Do you have to go?" Tiffany asked.

"My man just got home, and we got to show him a good time. Baby, I won't be out late, okay?" Toby replied, kissing her on the forehead and returning to where Thad and Orlando were sitting.

"Chris still outside on the phone?" he asked.

"Hell yeah, probably trying to beg Stephanie for some ass." Thad laughed.

"Probably is." Toby laughed also.

Thad turned his attention to one of the strippers that wouldn't leave him alone. He looked at Toby and smiled. "Bitch gon' make me stick my dick in her mouth before I leave from here." He laughed.

"Boy, your ass gon' catch something for real. I keep trying to warn your ass, but you won't pay your big brother no mind," Toby said, shaking his head.

It had started raining, and it was coming down pretty hard. Stephanie was lying next to

Robin and was relaxed. She felt at ease whenever she was with her. She figured Jeryca was right about one thing she'd said the other day: she had done her a huge favor by sleeping with Chris and removing him from her life. It didn't change the fact that she never wanted to deal with her again, but she was happy.

"Bae, what you gonna cook tonight?" Stephanie asked.

"Shit, I figured you would cook," Robin replied.

"I can. What would you like?" Stephanie asked.

"I want seafood, baby," Robin replied.

"I ain't cooking no seafood." Stephanie laughed.

"I guess that means we will go out for dinner then," Robin replied.

"I don't want to go out. It's raining, and I want to stay here, lying next to you," Stephanie whined.

"Yeah, but I want seafood, baby," Robin replied.

"Here you go!" Stephanie said as she placed Robin's hand between her thighs.

Just then, her cell phone rang, and when she picked it up, she saw that it was Chris. "What the fuck is he calling me for?" Stephanie murmured aloud.

"Who?" Robin asked.

"That muthafuckin' Chris," Stephanie replied.

"Let me answer it, bae," Robin said, reaching for the phone.

Stephanie handed Robin the phone.

"Hello?" Robin answered.

"Can I speak with Stephanie?" Chris asked.

"Stephanie isn't available at the moment. May I ask who's calling?" Robin asked, winking and smiling at Stephanie.

"Who is this?" Chris asked, getting annoyed.

"I'm Stephanie's girlfriend, and again, who is this?" Robin asked.

There was a brief silence on the other end, then a low laugh. "Stephanie don't have a girl-friend. I'd put my life on that. So who the hell is this?" Chris asked.

"All I can say is die, nigga, 'cause right at this moment, Stephanie is playing in my pussy, and I'm loving it. Say hey, baby," Robin said as she put the phone close to Stephanie's mouth.

"Hello?" Stephanie answered.

"Stephanie, what the fuck is going on? This bitch saying you her chick, and I know that's a lie," Chris growled.

"Well, Chris, she is telling the truth. She is my baby," Stephanie answered, never taking her eyes off Robin.

"I need some pussy, Stephanie. I just got home, and I am in need," Chris replied.

"Didn't you just hear what was said? I am with someone now, and I wouldn't disrespect her like that. Shit, I wouldn't disrespect myself like that," Stephanie responded.

"Shit, she can come too. All of us can play." Chris laughed.

Stephanie grabbed the phone from Robin and hung up. She didn't want to hear any more of his disrespectful, lame-ass comments.

A few seconds later, Stephanie's phone rang again, and she saw that it was Chris calling back.

"Girl, turn that bitch off. Let's get dressed and go get something to eat," Stephanie said as Robin picked it up, getting ready to answer it.

"Girl, I will cuss that bastard out. He had his chance with you and he blew it. I got you now, and he can get over it," Robin hissed.

"Look at my bae, all protective and shit," Stephanie said, smiling.

"I'm so serious. You are taken now, and I'm not losing you." Robin started singing "Forever My Lady" by Jodeci.

Chris stood on the porch and watched the rainfall. He was angry, yet amused by how Stephanie had just played him. He always got what he wanted, and he could get Stephanie back if he wanted her. He was going to wait and see how things played out concerning her.

He scrolled through his contacts and found Debra's number, but when he called, it went straight to voice mail. He was getting worried now and wondered what the hell was going on with her. He had called her several times in the last week, and each time, it went to voice mail. He was going to find out what was going on with his friend as soon as he could get away from Thad and them.

"Aye, man, you just gonna stand out here in the rain? Come on in and let's blow a li'l kush and then hit the Oasis," Austin said as he stood in the doorway.

"I'm coming. What y'all niggas got to eat? You know I been starving down there in county," Chris said, laughing.

"I think Tiff made some chicken and broccoli Alfredo and some hot wings. You should see if it's finished, 'cause I'm hungry my damn self," Austin admitted.

"I will get Toby to ask her, 'cause you know Tiffany will cuss yo' ass out quick." Chris laughed.

"Hell yeah. She will go from zero to a hundred quick," Austin replied.

"Who will?" Toby asked.

"We were talking 'bout Tiffany and how she'll cuss a person out without thinking twice. So we figured we would get you to go and see if the food is done," Chris replied.

"Y'all trying to get me cussed out, huh?" Toby asked.

"Shit, bro, better you than us. Besides, we at yo' crib," Austin said as he walked into the front room and sat down next to Thad.

"Thad, man, are you hungry too?" he asked, looking at him and smiling.

"Hell yeah, I got the munchies for real. Here, twist this blunt. I'ma go and see what's ready, and then we can head to the Oasis," Thad said as he stood up and walked past Toby.

"Good luck." Toby laughed.

Chris laughed along with them and sat back as he inhaled the smoke from the blunt. It felt good to be free, and he needed to get high after experiencing everything he had in the past few months. A few seconds later, they heard Tiffany cussing and saw Thad walking quickly back in the room.

"Got him!" Toby laughed.

Chapter Twenty-three

Friday morning, Dana went to work and walked into Brittany's office. "Have you talked to Orlando or Zack today?"

"Yeah, they called me about thirty minutes ago, checking in as usual. Why? What's up?" Brittany asked.

"Girl, I guess I'm just paranoid about the whole Debra situation," Dana answered.

"You still on that? I told you I would handle the situation, but we don't need any unnecessary attention drawn to us. First of all, we are running a law firm that is well established, and I don't need any unwanted or unnecessary scrutiny from the law. You know just like I do that a lot of things I do ain't one hundred percent legit, so feel how you want to feel, but I'm not going to move recklessly because you want me to," Brittany snapped.

"You know what, Brittany? I never thought you would show a shady side. Now, where was all that talk when things got out of control with Farrah? You were praising me for that, but when it's your turn to fix shit, you find every excuse why you can't! Tell me why that is," Dana said angrily.

"I don't have to explain shit. I just said what I had to say, Dana, and if you can't comprehend the truth, that isn't my fault. Just like it isn't my fault that you been running around town half damn cocked. Yeah, I praised you for doing what you been doing, but girl, you can't keep trying to do things to jeopardize what we got going on," Brittany said, getting agitated.

"Whatever, Brittany. I think I'm going to leave early today. I'm suddenly feeling sick," Dana replied.

Brittany looked at Dana long and hard, and without batting an eye, she said, "Suck it up. There's work that needs to be done. Get out your fucking feelings and complete those files that are on your desk. Our clients don't pay us big money to get sick out the blue and put they shit to the side. If that's a problem, Dana, I can find someone else to do your work for you permanently. It's nothing personal, but I have a business to run, *little girl*."

Dana felt like she wanted to cry. Brittany had never spoken to her in that tone, and she was deeply affected by that. Dana shook her head. "I got it."

"Good. Now, please trust me a little bit, Dana. I know what I'm doing," Brittany said. Dana walked out of Brittany's office and didn't say a word.

Brittany stared at the door for a few seconds after Dana left. "Baby girl might become a problem," she muttered to herself. Brittany picked up the phone and called the one person she assumed could talk to Dana.

Dana sat at her desk, angry and hurt. She felt that betrayal was all around her. She needed to get away and quick. She needed the money from the robbery they pulled on Thad, and then she was going to bounce. She had decided to tell Zack and Brittany that she was out of the next robbery. She felt that she couldn't trust them and wasn't going to set herself up for failure.

She sighed and pulled a file from her drawer to begin doing an analysis on the case. After fifteen minutes, her phone rang.

"Holmes, Howell, and Fuller Associates."

"Hey, it's Zack. What's up, Dana?" he asked.

"Hey, Zack. How are you doing?" Dana asked, frowning. She didn't know why he was calling her on the office phone rather than her cell.

"Shit, nothing. I just talked to Brit and was wondering if we could meet somewhere later and talk," he replied.

Dana laughed and shook her head. "Wow, you too? This is too much for me."

"Hold up. It ain't no 'you too.' First of all, I just wanted to check to make sure you are good, so you can kill the attitude," Zack retorted.

"You know what? First of all," Dana mimicked, "you have never called my office phone, so that makes you suspect in my book, and second of all, don't ever speak to me in that damn tone. Y'all got shit twisted."

Zack laughed. "I'm not even going to respond, Dana. Can we meet or not?" he asked again.

"Maybe tomorrow. I'm busy tonight," Dana answered. She wasn't busy, but she wasn't going to meet him anywhere. She had to gather her thoughts and find a way to win without any of them.

"All right, Dana. Look, I don't know what's going on with you, but please chill out with the extra drama," Zack said.

"I hear you. I got to go," Dana said and hung up.

Dana was heated. She wanted to cuss Brittany out for calling Zack, but she refrained from doing it. She worked on her case file until noon and decided to call Stephanie. She needed a night out.

She hadn't talked to her since they had words about Stephanie and Jeryca fighting. They talked for an hour and decided that they would meet at the Oasis to get a few drinks.

Stephanie asked Robin to join them, and she happily agreed. Stephanie and Robin decided to go out to dinner before they met Dana at the club. They talked and discussed things they each wanted to do before they died.

"Bae, I want to go to Hawaii. I want to put on a grass skirt and dance barefoot in the sand," Robin said, staring off into space.

Stephanie could see how important it was to Robin to go to Hawaii from the look in her eyes when she talked about it. "I'm going to make it happen for you, Robin. If I don't do anything else, I'm taking you to Hawaii," Stephanie said.

Robin smiled at Stephanie and took a sip of her wine. "Babe, I believe you. Are you ready to go to the Oasis?"

"You don't believe me, but I'm serious. We are going to go and soon," Stephanie said as she stood up and laid a tip on the table.

Robin knew that Stephanie was serious, but she didn't want her to feel as if she had to do it. After they paid the bill, they left and headed to the Oasis. When they got there, Dana hadn't arrived, so they grabbed a table and ordered a few drinks. Stephanie was enjoying herself, until her eyes landed on Chris.

"Shit, what the hell is he doing here?" she whispered to herself. He was smiling at her, and Robin didn't miss the look exchanged between them.

"Bae, who is that?" Robin asked, already knowing the answer.

Stephanie looked at her and muttered, "That's Chris."

"Well, I will say you got great taste in men as well as women." Robin laughed as she leaned over and kissed Stephanie.

A few minutes later, Chris was making his way to Stephanie's table. "How are you doing, Stephanie?" he asked.

"I'm good, Chris. How are you?" she replied.

"I'm good. You still looking good, Stephanie," he said, smiling.

"This is my baby, Robin. Robin, this is my ex, Chris," Stephanie replied, ignoring Chris's last comment.

"How are you? Damn, you are a sexy li'l thang also. I'd love to buy you two ladies a drink," Chris drawled.

"Thank you, and yes, you can buy us a drink," Robin answered before Stephanie could refuse.

"All right, what do you want?" Chris asked.

"I want a Tom Collins," Robin said, smiling.

"I don't want anything, thanks," Stephanie replied.

"Come on, Steph. Don't be like that. I'm just trying to be a nice guy," Chris said.

"I'm good, Chris. I got a drink right here," Stephanie replied.

"All right. Maybe later," he said as he walked to the bar to get Robin's drink.

Stephanie looked at Robin and grabbed her hand roughly. "Bae, you can't play with a man like Chris. I see it in your face, all the flirting and shit. Don't do that."

"It's harmless, Steph." Robin laughed, using the nickname Chris used for her.

"To you it's harmless, but to him, it's something else. Please just listen to me on this," Stephanie said.

When Chris returned, Thad and Toby accompanied him. "Hey, lady, long time no see," Thad said.

"Yeah, it's been a while. How is the family?" Stephanie asked. She wasn't feeling the whole situation at all. She didn't want to see them. She knew that they were after the people who robbed them, and she didn't want to set off the wrong vibe.

"Everyone is good. Sorry to hear about Farrah. We been meaning to go by Shirley's house to check on Travis, but for some reason we just haven't made it," Toby said, smiling at Robin.

Stephanie noticed the look and immediately introduced her. "This is my girlfriend, Robin. Robin, this is Thad and Toby."

Everyone spoke and talked for a few minutes longer, before they were interrupted by Dana.

"Well, ain't this cozy."

"Hey, come on and have a seat," Stephanie said quickly.

Dana sat down and looked at Thad long and hard, without cracking one smile. She didn't speak to any of the guys at the table, period. Chris excused himself, along with Thad and Toby, but not before Thad broke the silence between him and Dana.

"Dana, you're looking gorgeous as ever. By the way, have you heard from Keith lately? He seems to have disappeared with some things that belong to me."

"I haven't heard from Keith in a while. Enjoy your night, fellas," Dana replied before turning her attention to Robin. "How are you doing, Ms. Robin?"

Once the men were gone, Dana looked at Stephanie. "What the fuck did they want?"

"Shit, Chris came over first, and before we knew it, we were surrounded by their asses," Stephanie answered.

"Well, anyway, I'ma go get me a drink. I'll be right back, okay?" Dana replied as she stood up and walked to the bar.

When she returned, she sat down, and the ladies talked about several things. They were enjoying the atmosphere in the Oasis. They had drunk several drinks, so one girl after the other had to take a bathroom break. When Robin stood up for the third time and excused herself from the table to go to the restroom, Chris, who had been checking out the ladies' table all night, followed her to the bathroom door. He blocked her entrance and smiled.

"Stephanie got her a fine-ass chick."

"She sure does, and I got me a fine-ass female as well, and I plan on keeping her," Robin stated flatly.

"Listen, I'm not trying to stop what y'all got going on, but I need to talk with Steph, one-on-one. Do you think that will be possible?" he asked.

Robin laughed. "When pigs fly," she answered.

"Shit, I can make that happen, baby girl," he replied.

"Listen, I got to go in here and piss and get back to my baby. So unless there is anything else you want, move," Robin demanded.

"All right, all right, don't get so defensive. Look, here is my number. Call me and let's chat about it," Chris said as he wrote his number down on a napkin and placed it in her pocket.

Robin rolled her eyes and pushed past him into the restroom. After she finished, she stood looking in the mirror and then at the number Chris handed her. She didn't know why she wasn't throwing it away, because she knew deep down that she was playing with fire.

She returned to the table, and the ladies danced and enjoyed the rest of their night without any further interruptions from Chris or his crew.

Saturday morning, Stephanie lay in bed, thinking about Chris. She couldn't believe that he had cornered her in the bathroom at the Oasis last night and attempted to fondle her and kiss her. She fought him off and walked quickly back to the table where Dana and Robin were waiting. She didn't tell Robin what had happened, but she wanted to. The kiss that Chris planted on her left her lips—both sets—tingling. She loved Robin, but she ached for Chris.

She shook her head as if trying to shake the thought of Chris from her head. He was bad for her, and she knew it. She couldn't do that to Robin. She was in love with someone who loved her back for her.

"Hey, bae, I'm 'bout to head on to work, okay? I love you," Robin said as she leaned down to give Stephanie a kiss.

Stephanie grabbed Robin's face to prolong the kiss. "You got to go now? I know you got a few minutes to spare."

"Bae, I got twenty minutes to get to work, so no, I don't have spare time. I'll see you tonight." Robin laughed as she walked out the door.

"Oh, well. I got to do something. I'm horny," she said quietly. As she searched the drawer, she pulled out her vibrator, put lubrication on it, and laid back. She climaxed twice with Chris on her mind.

Robin arrived at work and started counting out medication. She was amazed by how Chris and Stephanie were acting last night. At first, she had an issue with him calling her, but for some reason, she found herself sexually attracted to him. Although she wasn't going to give Stephanie up to him, she was definitely game to share her with him. She wanted a three-some, and if he could fuck as good as he looked, it could be a regular occurrence.She figured she would run that idea by Stephanie when she clocked out for lunch.

The morning seemed to creep by, and she couldn't wait to call Stephanie. Once she clocked out, she called Stephanie and got no answer. She tried a second time, and still no answer. She pulled the number out from her wallet and dialed Chris up.

"Yeah, who is this?" he asked.

"This is Robin. You haven't by any chance seen Stephanie?" she asked, holding her breath, hoping he would say no.

"Maybe I have, maybe I haven't. You can come see for yourself if you like," he moaned.

"Where are you at?" she asked.

Robin knew that Stephanie wasn't there, but for some reason, she had to go see to be sure. Chris gave her the hotel's address and room number, and they ended the call.

For the rest of the afternoon, Robin worked hard to push away the thought of her, Chris, and Stephanie getting together. When 5:00 p.m. came, she rushed out to her car and dialed Stephanie's number.

"Hello," Stephanie answered.

"I have been calling you all day, boo. What's going on? Where you been?" Robin asked.

"I went to see my cousin, and we kicked it for a while. I called you back, but I guess you were back on the clock. What do you want me to cook for dinner?" Stephanie asked.

"Oh, um, bae, I'm going to be a little late tonight. We got to do med pull and got a new shipment coming in," Robin lied.

"All right, I got to deal with it, I guess," Stephanie said sadly.

"You know I'ma make it up to you," Robin stated.

"I know you will. I love you," Stephanie said.

"I love you too. I'm going to call you back later, okay," Robin replied.

After she hung up, she drove to the Ramada Inn and Suites and went to the room that Chris told her he was in. She knocked about three times and finally, Chris opened the door.

He looked shocked at first, then he smiled. "I didn't think you were coming."

"Well, I just want to make sure my girl not here," she replied.

"Come on in and see for yourself," Chris said as he moved to allow her to enter. As he closed the door, he smiled. He knew that she knew

Stephanie wasn't there. It was kind of bittersweet. "So take a look around and see if your girlfriend is here." Chris laughed.

Robin turned around, looked Chris in the eyes, and said provocatively, "You and I both know that I know Stephanie isn't here, so let's stop playing. You see, I refuse to lose my bae to you, but after seeing the chemistry you two have, I know it's something there. I think we can all form some sort of relationship, so I'm here to see what you're working with."

"Is that right? Well, we can definitely do that," Chris replied as he walked toward Robin. He grabbed her by her waist and walked her backwards toward the bed. When he laid her on the bed, he undressed her and then himself, and smiled once he saw the look on her face. She looked frightened, which made him laugh aloud. "This is going to be fun."

An hour later, Robin walked out of his hotel room, fully satisfied and content. She understood now why Stephanie was fucked up about him. Once she arrived home and walked into her apartment, Stephanie was sitting on the couch, waiting on her.

"Did you work hard, bae?" she asked.

"Yes. I'm tired, so I'm going to take a shower and we can eat dinner, okay?" Robin said, walking toward the bathroom.

"I didn't cook dinner yet, but let me ask you a question before you get in the shower," Stephanie said.

"Go 'head, bae," Robin said, kicking off her shoes.

"If you were at work, why, when I called down there, did they say you were already gone for the day?" Stephanie asked.

Robin looked at her for a minute then replied, "We did inventory at the main pharmacy, Stephanie. Why are you questioning me about being at work when you know that's all I do?"

"Bae, I was just heated, 'cause they told me you weren't there, and you told me you were working overtime. I'm not accusing you of anything," Stephanie explained.

"You know you got me, girl, and I'm not going anywhere. I'd be a fool to let you go," Robin said, looking Stephanie in the face.

Stephanie could see that Robin was sincere about what she was saying. She smiled. "I know, bae."

Robin prepared her water and got into the shower. As she washed her still-pulsating clit, she couldn't help but smile. She had done a very bad thing, but Chris felt so damn good. She couldn't wait to see him again.